Dear Sylvia,

Happy reading!

Love,

Kimberly Knight

STRIKE OF THE GOLDEN EAGLE

BY

KIMBERLY KNIGHT

This is a work of fiction. Names, characters, places, incidents are either a product of the author's imagination or are used fictitiously, and any resemblance to actual persons, living or dead, business establishments, events, or locales is entirely coincidental.

"Strike of the Golden Eagle," by Kimberly Knight.
ISBN 978-1-60264-038-2. (soft); 978-1-60264-040-5 (hard).

Library of Congress Control Number on file with Publisher.

Published 2007 by Virtualbookworm.com Publishing Inc., P.O. Box 9949, College Station, TX 77842, US.

Manufactured in the United States of America.

ACKNOWLEDGMENTS

My thanks to Mario, Debbie, Melinda, Michelle, Sherri, Joanne and Norm for critiquing, editing, and offering astute advise of the early drafts of this book.

Dedicated to my husband, Mario,
for his patience, caring, understanding
and love.

Love doesn't make the world go 'round.
Love is what makes the ride worthwhile.

Franklin P. Jones

PROLOGUE
ONE WEEK AGO

MANHATTAN WAS QUIET. SOON THE ENTIRE island would be alive...except Emil Niculaie. Tamara waited for two hours for him to exit the building. She shivered, her body covered with goose bumps. Her legs cramped as she crouched in the squat position below the stairs of the apartment building, her nerves raw. For the past two weeks Niculaie had been coming down the steps and heading for the subway at four in the morning. It was possible to set a clock by him, but not this morning. Even though Tamara felt ice could be chipped from her body parts, perspiration dripped into her eyes. Gently placing the rifle on the ground, she wiped her forehead with her palm. The sound of the hinges on the door alerted her to immediate attention. It was Emil. Looks were often deceiving. He didn't look like a cold blooded assassin. But, usually none of them did...just the average businessman off to do a normal day of killing. She grabbed the rifle and aimed the scope at the entrance. Her finger twitched on the trigger, but her aim was steady. The rifle fired with lethal precision, hitting Emil directly between the eyes. He dropped with a thud, dead before he hit the ground.

CHAPTER ONE
PRESENT DAY

THE CLOCK SAT ON THE NIGHT STAND WITH ITS piercing voice slicing the air. Tamara silenced it with a quick stroke of her hand. When she awakened at six, daybreak had cast a magical blush across the sky as the sun ascended from the horizon. Tamara stretched her arms and squeezed her eyes shut, yearning for Sunday. Her sheepdog mix, Toby, snuggled in his bed beside her, mirroring Tamara's stretching. The lick of Toby's wet tongue on her hand forced her to sit up. Donning a pair of slippers and trudging into the bathroom, she splashed cold water on her face and squinted in the mirror. The face in the mirror peered back with a look of disgust.

Tamara Mantz, get a grip. You have work to do. It's not Sunday, and you can't sleep in.

She stepped into the shower and let the hot

water pulse over her body, filling the room with steam. She turned around, allowing the jets to massage her back. Remembering the time, she turned off the water and quickly stepped out of the shower stall. After partially dressing, she dashed to the kitchen, emptied a carton of yogurt into the blender, added a banana, a little ice, and turned it on. Without another thought, she slipped a white cashmere sweater over her head between gulps. Crooning, “Toby, be a good boy,” she grabbed her purse, jacket and shoes. Closing and locking the door, Tamara left her comfortable Seacliff Beach home in her silver BMW heading toward Innovative Insights Corporation where she was the CEO. She applied her eye makeup whenever she was forced to stop at a signal, so that by the time she had reached her San Jose office at eight, she was able to step through the door the image of a professional businesswoman.

She looked stunning in a teal jacket and skirt by Calvin Klein, teal pumps, and her favorite white cashmere sweater. Her smooth chocolate brown hair hung loose about her shoulders. The golden highlights made a striking contrast. She wanted to look especially good this morning for a meeting she had scheduled with three press moguls from Taiwan. Having missed her usual stop at Starbucks for a mocha, she was feeling the need for a quick boost. The fragrance of coffee beans enticed her, and she was drawn to the bland company brew in the machine sitting on the counter. She poured herself a cup and grimaced as it slid down her throat.

Lance, her right hand man, who always had a skillful ear for knowing when she was getting coffee, popped his head out of his office and said, “Hey, Tamara, what’s going on?”

She turned, looking at Lance. “What do you mean?”

“Your office is full of big wigs. I think they’ve been waiting for you for quite awhile.”

“Terrific...just what I need this morning. Well, let’s go find out.”

As Tamara opened the door to her office, she was met by all five members of the Board of Directors. With them all present, the large office, with floor to ceiling windows, appeared smaller than usual. George, the Chairman of the Board, was seated at Tamara’s large mahogany desk. When she entered the room, two Board members were looking at paper work, and two were standing by the window on the far side of the room, talking.

George was tall, blond, large shouldered, maybe thirty, and extremely ambitious, having moved up in the company to his present position very quickly. There was no denying that he was good at his job, but the problem was that he knew it.

"What'd I miss? Was there a meeting scheduled I was unaware of?" Tamara questioned, straightening her shoulders.

George jumped up and moved from behind the desk. "Good morning, Tamara, how lovely you look today. No, no meeting scheduled, but take a seat. We have something to discuss with you." He turned to Lance and dismissed him with a wave of his hand.

Tamara looked around, sensing the tension in the room, and chose to remain standing. "Yes, how can I help you?"

George rubbed his hands together, his eyes focused on the Board members. "Well, there's no good way to put this. We have to let you go, Tamara."

Sucking in a breath, she asked, "You're saying I'm fired? But–"

"If you want to put it that way, yes," George stated. "The Board has agreed to a company buy out, and I'm afraid that part of the agreement includes terminating you." All five of the Board members avoided eye contact with Tamara.

She walked slowly and deliberately up to George, staring directly into his eyes. "Why would they want me out? I surpassed all projections for sales for the quarter. It–it doesn't make any sense. I've–"

George put a hand on her shoulder, interrupting her. “We appreciate what you’ve accomplished for the company, Tamara, but this is the way it is. You’ll have a nice severance package waiting for you, and we may even be able to find a place for you in one of our departments, if that would be acceptable to you.”

Tamara shook her head and drew back. “You’re not giving me any reasons?"

“I don’t know the reasons, Tamara.” George shrugged, looking directly at her. “I’m just the messenger. If you want answers, talk to the Chairman of Arrowmac, Inc.” The Board members nodded in approval.

“How could all of you let them do this to me? Doesn’t my loyalty and hard work count for anything?” Tamara stared into the faces of each Board member. “Well, doesn’t it? They can’t take over if you don’t let them. Why do we need a merger?”

All the Board members, with the exception of George, showed their discomfort. George seemed to be enjoying his new position. His growing confidence was evident. One Board member’s eyes were glued to the floor, one was looking down and fiddling with some papers in his lap, and another was fidgeting in his seat with his foot wagging up and down, staring at the ceiling. She didn’t know what the fourth one was doing. He seemed to be staring off in space.

"This is a business decision; it's nothing personal," George continued with a dramatic flair to his voice. "It puts our company in a better position to gain a larger percentage in the world market. It's a complete restructure of focus. The CEO taking over your position is a relative of the Chairman of the Board, and I understand he's a master at addressing growth opportunities and market needs, as well as providing for a smooth transfer so that the merger won't disrupt services to our present clients."

She nodded without smiling, acknowledging that their minds were already made up. "When do you want me out?" Tamara glared.

"Take as long as you need today," George said, smiling.

Tamara considered the situation and said coldly, her eyes narrowing in irritation, "I'd like you all to leave my office now." She gave them a look that would melt an iceberg. The directors looked at each other, picked up their papers and walked out.

Tamara sat at her desk, shaking her head and mumbling out loud under her breath.

I can't believe it. What a bunch of bullshit. Who needs them. Not me, that's for sure. I don't need anyone. And they want me gone today!

Tamara stared at the wall clock as it ticked

the numbers away.

There was a soft knock on her door, and Lance stuck his head in. “Need an ear? I couldn’t help but hear all the loud voices. You all right?”

“Oh sure. I’m great. Just my ego is shot to hell. I thought I was indispensable. Loyalty and hard work don’t mean a damn thing to these puppets.”

“So, you’re fired?” Lance asked, sitting down in a chair next to her.

“Oh, no, I’m ‘let go’ as they term it. Yes, I’m fired, canned, discharged, whatever you want to call it.” Tamara slammed her fist on the desk. “I should have known. You can’t trust your own mother. I learned that at a young age. Damn! Those jerks!” she hissed through her teeth.

“It’s hard to believe. You’ve done so much for the company,” Lance said. “People’s lives don’t mean shit to these corporate heads. I’d like to see someone squash them like the rats they are. Did they tell you who’s taking your place?”

“Yeah, there’s been a merger. It’s some relative of the Chairman of the Board.”

“I wonder what they’ll do with me. You won’t be the only one to go. That’s for sure.” Lance shook his head back and forth.

Tamara shrugged out of her teal jacket and flung it over the chair. Then, she pulled a box out of the closet and started tossing some things in it.

She stopped, saying, “The one thing I know is you can’t trust any of them. Just watch your back, and take care of number one.”

“Can I help you with anything?” Lance asked.

Tamara took a few deep breaths. “No, thank you. I’ll just pack up a few things, and I’ll be out of here. Thanks anyway.”

“It was good working with you, Tamara. I wish you a lot of luck. This shouldn’t have happened to you. What are you going to do?” Lance asked as he opened the door to leave.

“Oh, don’t worry about me. I’m sure I can find something with one of our competitors.”

“I’m sure you will. You’ll be successful, whatever you choose to do. See you later. Don’t be a stranger.” Lance pulled the door shut.

Just let them stew in their own juices when the Taiwanese press arrives. I’ll be long gone. Tamara gathered up the rest of her belongings and left the building without a glance back.

As she was lost in thought, it was fortunate her BMW knew the way home. Pulling into the driveway, she turned off the ignition, put her head back against the seat and shut her eyes, but only for a moment. She got out of the car and slammed the door, leaving everything in it. Toby ran to the door to greet her. No matter where he was, he always seemed to recognize the sound of her engine and made it to the front door before she came in.

Tamara's home wasn't particularly large, but it had a great room with a fireplace and a deck jutting out over the ocean, an open kitchen with granite counter tops and an island in the center, plus a large bathroom with white Italian tile on the walls and floor. French doors on the side of the living room led to a small pool and hot tub surrounded by large rocks for privacy. Upstairs, were three bedrooms, one of which she had turned into an office. The master bedroom had floor to ceiling windows overlooking the ocean, opening to a beautiful teak deck. Once inside, she welcomed the safety of her comfortable nest.

She ripped off her clothes, ran down the stairs, threw open the French doors and dove in the pool. The cool water surrounded her, giving her a feeling of renewal and peace. She floated for a while and then did laps. After about thirty minutes of vigorous laps, Tamara emerged from the pool refreshed and ready to take on whatever or whoever came her way. Her usual relaxation was to go running, but she decided on a swim for a change. She took a quick shower, put on a robe and made her way to the kitchen. After dumping some cereal in a bowl and pouring milk into it, she wandered over to the couch. Pulling one leg under her, she picked up her book and had just settled back to relax when the ring of the phone broke her reverie.

A familiar voice on the other end informed her that her orders were ready.

Oh great...just when I was getting comfortable. Having two careers really throws me sometimes.

She quickly threw a few things in a bag, called the boy next door to feed Toby and drove her BMW to the post office. She picked up the package with her instructions inside and continued on to the airport. Tamara arrived at La Guardia Airport approximately eight hours later, grabbed a couple of hours of sleep in the airport lobby, and arrived at the Conference Center in Manhattan, by taxi, at 8:00 a.m. She checked in at the lobby desk, leaving her bag with the clerk, and walked directly to the conference room. The speaker was walking up to the podium as Tamara looked for an empty seat. The noisy room suddenly grew silent, and a deep voice commenced a speech on the development of the infrastructure of the tropical lowlands of Eastern Bolivia. His thick dark hair matched his trim beard and mustache. His piercing brown eyes, accentuated by dark eyebrows, carefully scrutinized the audience. When the speech ended, Tamara followed the speaker as he walked out of the auditorium. When she caught up with him, he turned and smiled expectantly at the beautiful woman who seemed so friendly.

The next day when Tamara was back home, she picked up the newspaper. An article on the first page read that a suspected member of the drug cartel dropped dead from unknown causes after giving a speech at a conference in New York.

Isn't that interesting! And he was giving a speech about trying to help his people. How hypocritical is that? Well, that's another one down.

Tamara awakened early Sunday morning and sat bolt upright in bed, remembering with dread that this was the day her grandmother had summoned her for dinner. There weren't many things that bothered her, but this was one of them. She didn't know how she had done such a good job of forgetting, or maybe not really forgetting, only pushing it to the far corners of her mind. She had to be there by 2:00 p.m.

Her grandmother must have something she wanted from her, or she wouldn't have been so insistent. Pulling the covers over her head, she turned over and attempted to go back to sleep. Toby jumped on the bed and snuggled in next to her. Toby was a mutt, most likely a cross between an Old English sheep dog and Aussie shepherd. Tamara had found him wandering the beach, covered with tar. It had taken her several washes to get him clean. She had placed an ad in the paper, hoping to find his owner, but with no response, Toby had found a new home.

After tossing and turning for a half hour or so, she finally gave up and slowly climbed out of bed, placing her feet on the cold hardwood floor. *Where'd my slippers go?* She groped around and pulled them out from under the bed.

Okay, Grandmother, you win. You've ruined my day again. Maybe I should announce to your dinner guests that your precious granddaughter, who you raised to be just like you, got canned.

The thought of her grandmother's reaction made her giggle. *Oh, Tamara, now you're being mean. That's something Grandmother would do.*

Later in the afternoon, Tamara pushed the button on the gate of her grandmother's home in Los Altos Hills and announced her arrival. When the gate opened on command, she drove around the large circular driveway, parked in front of the door, and took a deep breath before getting out of the car. It had been ten years since she had been gone from this life, but it all came back with a rush every time she approached the mansion. Her grandmother never stopped reminding her how fortunate she was that she had taken her in when her mother abandoned her.

The door was answered by Gracie, who had lived with Tamara's grandmother for almost twenty years. Gracie was her grandmother's assistant, but she actually ran the house. She was the cook, butler, driver, secretary and all around errand runner. How she had put up with her grandmother all of these years, Tamara could never figure out. Gracie probably looked older than her years. Tamara thought she was maybe only in her fifties, but she had gray hair, and her face was deeply lined. It was surprising that she had lost her youthful figure, because the pace Grandmother always had her moving should have kept her thin as a rail.

"Who's at the door, Gracie?" Grandmother called from upstairs.

"It's me, Grandmother, Tamara."

"I'll be right down. Wait in the study, Tamara."

Gracie gave Tamara a quick hug and said, "You look tired. Have you been working too hard?"

"Oh, Gracie, don't worry about me. I'm fine...really." Tamara squeezed Gracie's hand and gave her a smile. "You're the one who should be tired. You work really hard, and you're not getting any younger, you know. Grandmother keeps you hopping."

"Now, don't turn this around, young lady. I know tired when I see it. I want–" Gracie was interrupted in mid-sentence by Tamara's grandmother, approaching them from the stairs.

"I thought I told you I'd meet you in the study. You don't listen any better than you did when you were a child," Grandmother said, taking Tamara's arm and leading her into the study. "That will be all, Gracie. I'll call you if we need anything." She waved her other arm in the air in dismissal.

Tamara's grandmother always made her feel as if she were a child again. She wondered what it would take to make her grandmother say something nice to her. She looked at her stern unapproachable face and said, "Grandmother, why did you ask me to come over?"

Her grandmother stopped and turned her head, arching her eyebrow and looked directly in her eyes, "Do I need a reason to ask my granddaughter to visit?"

Tamara knew better than to carry it any farther. She shrugged her shoulders and kept her mouth shut. Her eyes turned to the many books that lined the shelves.

I wonder how many Grandmother reads, or are the books there only for show?

"Actually, for once you were right. I heard from your mother, and I thought you should know," Grandmother said, continuing walking.

Tamara spun around and stared at her grandmother. "You mean after all these years, my mother suddenly appears out of nowhere? What's going on?"

"She's sick, Tamara, and she needs us." Grandmother sat down on the leather sofa in the study. "Now, sit here beside me." She patted the seat.

Tamara did as Grandmother said and took a seat next to her. She frowned and crossed her legs. "She's sick, so now we're supposed to go to her with open arms? I cried for her for years, waiting for her to come back to me. She never did. Every time I heard a car driving up or saw a woman with bleached blond hair, I thought it was my mother, but it never was. Now, she's sick and she wants me?" Tamara shook her head. "What's wrong with her?"

"She has cancer, and it doesn't sound good. She really wants to see you." Her eyes revealed her love for her wayward daughter.

"Where is she?" Tamara asked, letting out a sigh.

"She's in Seattle at a cancer treatment center. She's all alone and has no one. She said her boyfriend left her after she got sick and lost her hair. I've already seen her, Tamara. I'm asking you to please go to her." She leveled her gaze directly into Tamara's eyes.

"I'll do as you wish, Grandmother, because I owe you. You took me in when my mother deserted me. I don't like it, but I'll do it for you." Tamara folded her arms across her midriff in resignation.

"Thank you, Dear. Now let's go have dinner," Grandmother said, a slight smile on her lips.

Well, at least there's no company for dinner. Grandmother's always trying to set me up with some friend's rich son or grandson...but this news is worse.

Tamara's head was spinning when she returned home.

Why would my mother want to see me? She hasn't cared all of these years. Does she want forgiveness because she thinks she's dying? Does she want money? Does she want someone to care for her? Well, I have things to do before I go running up to Seattle to see her. I plan to take care of myself first, since I'm the only one who does take care of me. My mother certainly never has.

The next morning, Tamara called Excel Media, Inc. and made an appointment to see Frederick Mason. She arrived early, dressed in her nicest Armani suit with a lavender blouse and pumps to match. Even the women's heads turned when Tamara walked by. She greeted the receptionist, who sat behind the desk in the large attractive reception area. "Hi Sally. How's it going today?" Tamara leaned over, smelling the bouquet of apricot roses and purple iris adorning Sally's desk. "What beautiful flowers. They smell so good."

Sally looked up from her work. "Oh, Tamara, how good to see you. Yes, I'm really enjoying the flowers. Do you have an appointment?"

"Yes, I do. I'm here to see Frederick Mason."

"Let me buzz him for you. Have a seat for a minute," Sally said, motioning to the chair and pressing the intercom button at the same time.

Sally stood up and motioned Tamara to go on in.

Frederick stood in the doorway, the admiration clearly showing on his face. "Well, you're a sight for sore eyes, Tamara. Come on in and have a seat. I was really happy to get your call. Does this mean you're considering our offer?" Frederick beamed.

"Well, actually, Frederick, I'm not only considering it, I'm here to offer my services to your corporation. I must tell you though that Innovative Insights is being taken over, and I'm out on my ear. I was grateful that you had offered a position to me, and I'm here to see if you still want me."

Frederick led Tamara to a seat and then sat down at his desk, leaning back in his chair. "Of course we still want you. It's our gain and their loss. You're the best. It's too bad it had to happen this way, but we'll take you however we can get you."

"Good. I plan to slaughter the competition," Tamara said, looking out the window with her eyes riveted on the Innovative Insights building.

Chapter Two

THE FIRST SNOW OF THE WINTER WAS GENTLY falling on the asphalt. Christopher York sat in Dunkin' Donuts, savoring a cup of coffee, while gazing out the window. The aroma of coffee beans permeated the room. It seemed to him that the snow made the Boston landscape appear clean and pure, much like a world without terrorists. It was his favorite time of year. Christopher had come from Harvard where he was scouting out new recruits. He picked up the newspaper and turned to the business section. A picture of a woman popped out at him, a picture of Tamara Mantz. He scanned the article and discovered that Tamara had been let go when Innovative Insights was bought out by Arrowmac, Inc. He raised his eyebrows. He didn't believe she was well known enough to have made the papers, and she hadn't called him to let him know what happened. He frowned, deciding a call was in order.

Tamara was a student at MIT in Cambridge, Massachusetts the first time Christopher saw her. The woody scent of fall was in the air. He noticed her first with her long dark hair blowing in the crisp autumn breeze. The highlights in her hair matched the carpet of yellow, brown and golden leaves on the ground. Later, he discovered that she met all the qualifications for his selective undercover unit...A loner with no close family ties; highly intelligent; technology and science majors; fluent in several languages, with the added benefit of being at the top of her class. He watched her several times on the women's pistol team and saw she was proving to be an outstanding marksman, actually the best on the team. She measured up to all the requirements for the covert unit of highly trained operatives. But, even with all the right qualifications, it was never a given that any subject had what was necessary to be an assassin. Tamara Mantz did.

The mirrored building reflected ribbons of color as Tamara walked through the doors of Excel Media, Inc. She stepped into the spacious reception area and saw Sally busy at her desk. Men and women crisscrossed the lobby intent on their labors. She observed that the place was teaming with life. Walking past the office with the large gold plated letters reading Frederick Mason, she came to one with a more modest name plate, walked in, and took a seat behind the desk. She pulled open the drawers, looking for a spot to leave her purse. Tamara surveyed the room and noticed that someone had already left several files on her desk. Frederick Mason poked his head through the door, "Morning Tamara. You have a few minutes?"

Tamara rose and smoothed her skirt, motioning for him to take a seat. "Of course, Frederick. Come on in. For you, I have all the time in the world...well, almost," she said, laughing.

They had known each other for several years, having met in San Francisco at a convention. Ever since, he had tried to persuade her to leave Innovative Insights and come to his company. She had liked him right from the start. He wasn't a particularly good looking man, but had a dynamic quality about him. He was probably close to fifty, and his thinning brown hair had already receded from his forehead. Tamara wondered why he called himself Frederick instead of Fred or Freddy. Freddy didn't really fit him, but Frederick seemed so formal. Maybe someday she'd ask him.

"We need to send someone to Philadelphia to speak at a conference. Would you be able to go on short notice?"

"Certainly. What would I be speaking about?" Tamara asked.

"What I mean by short notice is leaving tomorrow afternoon. You'd be speaking the following day, so it would leave you only today to get ready. Your topic will be "*Expanding Your Horizons,*" with the emphasis on the latest developments in our company. We'd have to get you up to speed real quick."

"Whoa, you're not kidding when you say short notice. That's fine, I guess. I can do it." Tamara thought to herself that it was no big deal to be ready to take off at any time. She was used to that. In fact, having only a day to prepare was easy for her. She spoke at many conferences; that wasn't a problem, but she needed a good understanding of Excel Media's current offerings. She was well aware that they were always on the cutting edge of new technology.

Frederick Mason told her he and Ted Kaufman would meet her in the conference room in a half hour. Strange as it seemed to ask Tamara to speak when she was just beginning with the company, Frederick knew her as an outstanding speaker, one who could "motivate the dead."

It started to rain as Tamara's taxi pulled up at the hotel. The plane ride was uneventful. In fact, she actually had a short nap on the plane, unusual for her. Tamara quickly paid the driver, pulled out her umbrella, and made a dash for the door to the lobby. After checking in, Tamara reviewed her notes, turned off the TV and placed the remote on the night stand. Even with the nap, she was tired. She shut off the light and went to sleep.

The alarm startled Tamara. She usually awakened before it went off. The water pulsing from the shower head quickly woke her. She rinsed off the soap and stepped out of the shower ready to tackle the challenges of the day. Tamara looked at the clock, gathered up her briefcase and papers, and grabbed her purse. It seemed there was never enough time. She told herself it was a good thing the conference was at her hotel.

She entered the filled-to-capacity main conference room and took a seat on the stage. It grew noisier and more crowded by the minute. Latecomers stood against the back wall. Glancing over the audience as the chairperson spoke, she locked eyes with a man in the front row. She couldn't seem to draw her gaze away. He looked at her as if he could see the real Tamara Mantz. It wasn't possible. She didn't even know him. She forced herself to focus on the Chairperson.

"And now, it's my great pleasure to introduce

our speaker for today, Ms. Tamara Mantz."

Tamara walked to the microphone, smiled at the audience, and began speaking as a seascape flashed on the screen. "History books tell us that people once thought the earth was flat, and when they got to the edge of the horizon, they would simply fall off. We now know better. But, what are we doing to expand our horizons? We, at Excel Media, Inc. are making major breakthroughs in communications technology, which I'm excited to share with you now."

This was the thing about speaking that Tamara loved. Seeing the audience eagerly awaiting her next words, she felt excitement...a definite high. After the speech was over and all questions answered, Tamara received a standing ovation. She felt like bowing. What was she? No more than an actress on the stage. But, she didn't bow. She simply smiled and thanked the audience, making her way off stage. Suddenly, she remembered the man in the front row. She looked and was disappointed when she didn't see him. Picking up her things, she walked to the exit door. Someone held it open for her. Tamara looked into the eyes that had already bewitched her once.

"That was a great speech," he said with a grin.

Catching her breath, she said, "Why, thank you."

"They talk about selling the Brooklyn Bridge.

You could sell that and then some." He flashed a wide smile.

Tamara laughed. "You flatter me too much."

"Why don't we go in the lounge. I'll buy you a drink," he suggested. He took her arm and led her into the bar.

He didn't even think I might refuse. I don't know this man. Well, it wouldn't be the first time...and he is gorgeous.

Tamara could never afford to get truly involved with a man, or with anyone. So, it made sense to have casual affairs. She didn't like to call them one night stands, even if that was what they were. She finally found her tongue and spoke, "I don't even know your name." She tossed her hair over her shoulder and laughed.

Oh, I don't believe it. I'm acting like a school girl.

Her new acquaintance found an empty table and pulled out the chair for Tamara. "I'm sorry, I feel like I know you. My name's Grant, Grant Larson. I'm not usually so forward. I know it doesn't seem that way, but it's true...Honest. Where are you from, Tamara? I know Excel Media has a few offices around the country. I think the main one's in the Bay Area. Is that where you live?"

"That's right, I live at Seacliff Beach in California. How about you?"

"Well, I'm a Californian too, from a little farther south, but it's still California...Santa Barbara," Grant said.

The cocktail waitress interrupted their conversation. "Hello, my name's Sally. Can I get you two a drink?"

"Hi Sally." Grant turned to Tamara and asked what she'd like.

"I think I'll have a chocolate martini," she said, her hands folded beneath her chin.

"Make mine a regular with two olives please," Grant said.

After the cocktail waitress walked away, Tamara asked, "What do you do, Grant? What brought you to the convention?"

"I work for Rochester, Bergman and Fellows, Inc., and one of my jobs is keeping up with all the latest developments of our competitors. You know how this field is. Everything's changing daily."

"I know what you mean." Tamara nodded her head in agreement. Her tongue licked the chocolate covered rim of the glass before she sucked an ice cube into her mouth.

After a couple of martinis, Grant asked, "Are you staying here? I mean in this hotel?"

"Yes, thank heavens. I would've been late this morning otherwise. I couldn't seem to get my act together, but that's nothing new. I always have trouble with time...not enough of it," Tamara said.

"I have those days. I'm staying here too." Grant signaled the cocktail waitress for the bill. "How about coming up to my room for a nightcap?"

"Okay, I'd like that," Tamara responded, putting her glass down.

Grant hadn't noticed how tall Tamara was until she stood next to him. It wasn't often that a woman was taller than he at five feet eleven. He thought she must be at least six feet.

He observed her tall, lean and muscular body. It looked like all muscle, not an ounce of fat. She seemed in better shape than he was...one spectacular woman! He tried not to think about her beautiful breasts, but they were sticking right out there like two majestic mountain peaks. He'd have to be dead not to notice them. But, that mane of hair, that was really her crowning glory...such a deep chocolate color with fascinating golden streaks.

Tamara interrupted Grant's thoughts by asking, "How long are you staying at the convention, Grant?" She took his arm as they left the bar. She thought he was one gorgeous man, sort of like a rainbow you wish wouldn't disappear.

"I was planning on seeing some of the exhibits tomorrow and flying out in the evening. What about you?"

“I don’t know for sure. I may leave in the morning. It depends.”

Grant wondered what it depended on, but decided not to push it. He hoped it depended on him. They reached Grant’s room, and he opened the door to his luxury suite.

“Well, this is nice, much better than my room. Glad we came to yours.” Tamara laughed.

Grant laughed back. “I have my company trained well.” He opened the mini bar and said, “I see some Grand Marnier, Kahlua and Chardonnay. What’ll it be?”

“Oh, I’ll have some Grand Marnier on the rocks please.”

“Sounds good. Think I’ll join you.” Grant pulled the Grand Marnier out of the cabinet and poured a generous shot in each glass. He extracted some ice from the ice bucket, which was waiting for their use.

Tamara sat down on the couch. Grant handed her a drink, walked over and flipped on some music before sitting down next to her. The sounds of Jen Houston singing *Penchant for Pleasure* filled the air. Tamara rattled the ice in her glass and then took a sip and settled back into the cushions. She looked deeply into Grant’s eyes and felt a warm comfortable feeling wash over her. The longer she gazed, she felt that comfortable feeling changing into stirrings of desire. Realizing they had held eye contact for what must have been a very long time, she would have broken the stare in embarrassment, had their lips not come together. She couldn't believe what was happening. She felt a tingling sensation running from her chest to the tip of her toes.

What is this man doing to me? And all this just from a kiss?

Tamara pulled back and looked at Grant. "Hey, you've had a little experience with kissing. I'll have to watch out for you. This could get you everywhere."

"I don't want everywhere. I just can't get enough of your lips," he murmured, tugging gently at her bottom lip before they surrendered to a deep passionate kiss. He was like an expensive box of chocolates. She couldn't get her fill.

When Tamara awakened in the morning, she silently slipped out of bed. She pulled on her clothes and glanced back at the handsome man fast asleep in the bed, his beautiful sky blue eyes now closed. She would like to have run her fingers through his wavy sandy blond hair, but there was no time. She hadn't meant to spend the night, but it happened. Her eyes absorbed every feature as if taking an imprint. She loved looking at Grant, but she needed to escape before he woke. She left his room and took the elevator three floors down to hers. Quickly packing her overnight bag, she left the hotel and headed for the airport.

Tamara reached the ticket counter at 7:00 a.m. She asked about the next flight for Seattle and was told there was a plane leaving in an hour and a half. She purchased her ticket, bought a book and a cup of coffee, and headed to the waiting area. She found it difficult to read; her thoughts kept returning to Grant. She knew very little about him. She didn't need to. She felt as if she had known him forever. This wasn't the norm. One night stands were standard for Tamara. She planned to never get involved.

In Seattle, Tamara caught a taxi and went directly to the treatment center. She asked at the reception desk what room Robin Mantz was in. The smell of sickness permeated the building. Tamara stood in the doorway staring at the frail woman with the sunken cheeks lying in the bed. Brown stubble intermingled with gray had replaced the long bleached blond hair. Even with the gaudy hair, her mother had been pretty. She wondered where that woman had gone. The name on the chart read Robin Mantz, but the woman on the bed bore no resemblance to her mother. Tamara walked closer, staring down at this stranger and stood next to the bed. The woman stirred and slowly opened her eyes.

"Tamara?" she asked, barely audible.

Tamara gazed into her eyes and saw a small glimpse of what was once her mother.

"Yes, it's me. I'm here," she whispered.

"I wanted to see you, but I was afraid to hope you'd come," her mother said, looking up at Tamara with hopeful eyes.

"What do you want, Mother?" Tamara folded her arms in front of her.

Robin Mantz cleared her throat and took a sip of water. "I just wanted you to know that I'm sorry I was such a shitty mother. You deserved better than me. I should have never had a kid."

"But you did. You had me," Tamara's stomach tightened, and she walked over and looked out the slats of the blinds on the window.

"I wasn't cut out to be a mother. You were better off with your grandmother. She gave you everything."

Tamara turned toward her mother. "Oh yeah, everything, but what I needed most, a mother."

"I didn't know what to do with a kid. I was young, and I–Oh, God, I wasn't even sure who the father was," Tamara's mother pleaded, struggling to speak. She was out of breath. "I'm sick, Tamara, and I need you to forgive me. Can't you see? Don't you understand?"

Tamara silently regarded the woman begging

for forgiveness and felt no emotion. She believed she should have felt something...anger, pity, anything, but she didn't. She felt numb.

Tamara moved away from the window and stood next to her mother. "I forgive you, if that's what you want," Tamara said. "I'm sorry you're sick."

"I guess I deserve it. I wasn't a very good person." Tears welled up in her eyes.

Tamara looked at her mother and said, "No one deserves cancer."

"I'm dying, Tamara. They keep doing things to me, but I know they aren't doing any good."

Tamara handed her a Kleenex, and Robin dabbed at her eyes. Tamara didn't know what to say and stood silent. After a full minute she said, "At least you're being taken good care of. The place is clean."

"I was too young, Tamara. I couldn't be tied down with a kid. I needed a life." She turned her head away.

"But what about me? You left me and never came back. I always looked for you. Every time I saw a woman with blond hair, I thought it was you coming for me. But you never did. I was so scared the day you left. Some neighbors called Grandmother when I gave up waiting for you to come home. How did you know she'd take me? You took off and left me all alone?"

"My mother always knew what to do. I knew you'd have a better life with her."

"Grandmother never had time for me. She was like you. She gave me everything but herself. Gracie was my salvation." She knew she shouldn't have spoken the words, but it was too late to take them back.

"Gracie? Gracie was the housekeeper," her mother said.

"Gracie was the closest thing I had to a mother. She was there for me when Grandmother would let her be."

Her mother looked up at her and spoke, changing the subject, "You're really a beautiful young woman. I was pretty once. I hope you have a better life than I had." She attempted to reach up and touch Tamara's face, but her hand dropped back down.

"So, you have no idea who my father is?" Tamara asked.

"Not really. I was sleeping around with a lot of men at that period of my life, probably just rebelling against any authority. You know how your Grandmother was. She knew how to pitch the commands."

A nurse entered the room and said, "It's time for a shot, Robin. Do you need one?"

Tamara's mother turned to the nurse and said flatly, "I'm always in need of one, but I'd rather wait until my daughter leaves. They make me go to sleep."

"Go ahead and take it," Tamara said, glancing at her watch. "I have to leave shortly anyway. I need to fly back to San Jose today. I have to work tomorrow."

"I love looking at you. It makes me think of when I was young. Enjoy your life, Tamara. It goes by so quickly." This time her hand made it to Tamara's hand, and she patted it shakily.

"Goodbye, Mom." Tamara leaned down and kissed her on the cheek and walked out the door without looking back.

Chapter Three

TAMARA BOARDED THE PLANE, FOUND HER SEAT, and sat back to relax. It felt good to have some closure with her mother. She probably shouldn't have said some of the things she did, but she couldn't help it. She'd been holding it inside for so long. It felt good to finally express her feelings, although she didn't know if her mother really heard her. It didn't matter. It felt good to say it. She was glad she went.

Her thoughts turned to Grant. *Why am I even thinking about him? None of the other men ever meant anything to me. It feels different with him for some reason. Probably only a physical attraction. Well, it doesn't matter. I'm never going to see him again, so why can't I stop thinking about him?*

Meanwhile, Grant was having some thoughts of his own. When he awakened in the morning, he stretched his arm out and found the bed was empty. He called Tamara's name, but she didn't answer. Grant jumped out of bed, pulled on his robe and went to the bathroom. He knocked gently, hoping to hear her voice answer. No response. He pulled the door open and found the bathroom empty. He couldn't understand why she left. Why didn't she wake him up? Soon confusion turned to anger.

She could at least have told me she was leaving. Didn't she like me? Was I totally inadequate? I thought it went great. I really thought I'd found someone special. Maybe there's an explanation. An emergency came up, and she didn't have time to leave a note. What was I...just a one night stand? I don't think so. I think it meant something.

He shook his head and went in to shower.

Tamara pulled into the driveway of her Seacliff Beach home, perched high on a bluff, overlooking the ocean. Entering the living room, she was startled by the voice of Christopher York.

"Hello Tamara, sorry if I frightened you." He

was slouched in a chair in the corner of the room.

"Oh no, I just left my skin back at the door...no problem." Tamara stopped and took a breath. "What's wrong with you anyway? What are you doing in my house? Couldn't you come to the front door and knock like any civilized person?" Tamara set her bag down next to the door. "So much for a watch dog. You're a big help, Toby." Toby, wagging his tail, sat next to Christopher.

"If you remember, I'm not any civilized person. You didn't call me when you lost your job." Christopher rubbed Toby's back. "What can I say. He loves me."

She shook her head, ignoring his remark about Toby. "I didn't. I'm sorry. I took care of it. I have another one that works just fine," Tamara said, shrugging her shoulders. She took off her jacket and set it on the couch along with her purse.

"No need to get cocky with me, Tamara. You know we need to be kept informed. We set up the cover up for you in the first place."

"Nevertheless, it's handled."

"Okay, I'm waiting," Christopher said, folding his hands behind his head and leaning back.

Tamara walked to the couch and sat down before speaking. "The new job is with Excel Media, Inc., a competitor of Innovative Insights.

They've been after me for some time to come with them." She let him digest the information.

"I know who they are. When were you planning on telling us?" Christopher asked, leaning forward.

Tamara crossed her legs. "All right. I'm sorry. I should have called you right away. I would have, but something came up and I had to fly to Seattle."

"I heard about your mother. I'm sorry." He stared intently at Tamara. "But, if there's a next time, we have to be the first one you think of."

"I promise, Christopher," Tamara said, looking directly into his eyes.

Christopher walked over to the couch, sitting down next to Tamara. "Now, changing the subject, I need to talk to you about your next assignment. Our sources have located Abdul Alhmad, so you can see how important this next job is."

"My God, we've been trying to find him for...I don't know how many years. They really know where he is for sure?" Tamara asked.

"Yes, but we'll have to move quickly."

"Okay. Fill me in. What do I need to know?"

"This guy has diplomatic immunity. He's a master of disguise. We were lucky. We found him by accident when we were looking at someone else. We've never had a voice print. No one could get a picture, but we did have a sketch of him by one of his teachers as a kid of around fifteen. We put a composite together aging him to what he would probably look like today. While checking on another suspect, we ran his voice print and had several hits of Abdul's voice on the disk, but we didn't know at that time who it was. Checking back through unsolved terrorist acts, we discovered the same voice print on several of them. Further investigation revealed the voice was that of a diplomat from Oman. There were similarities of the aged picture to what he looks like today under his present identity. From a six month accumulation of evidence, we have proof of his involvement in over twelve unsolved terrorist crimes worldwide. With his immunity factor, he needs to be eliminated. He goes by the name of Armon Hadad."

"My God, Christopher, he's been terrorizing the world, working under the guise of a diplomat." Tamara shook her head.

"What makes this even more dangerous, is that you need to get information from the subject before you kill him. It's been leaked that he's the mastermind behind an assassination plot on our president. This is a really dangerous one, Tamara. It's enormously risky. You don't have to take it. You've been one of our best operatives on extremely dangerous and sensitive missions, and we know this is going to take the best. But, if you don't want to take it, we understand. It could be a suicide mission. Just let me know your answer in twenty four hours."

She raised her eyes and looked at him, taking it all in. "Christopher, you know better than to put a challenge to me. Of course, I'll do it. I'm expendable. If something happens to me, who's going to care except me?"

He took both of her hands in his. "That's probably what makes you so good. You don't have fear, but sometimes you need it, Tamara. In this case a little fear might be a good thing."

"Don't confuse fear with caution, Christopher. I use a great deal of caution."

"I can't impress on you enough, Tamara. This guy isn't your usual hit. He's the mastermind behind some of the worst terrorist attacks around the world." Christopher looked at his watch. "Okay then, I'll leave it in your capable hands." He gave her a wink and opened the door, but Tamara stopped him.

"What about Emil Niculaie? Wasn't he one of the worst Romanian assassins of all time? I nailed him, didn't I?"

Christopher looked at her and smiled. "What can I say? I warned you."

Tamara was changing her clothes after a lunch hour run when she heard a knock on her office door.

"Just a minute. I'm coming," she called, pulling a top over her head on the way to the door. She opened it and stopped dead in her tracks, looking into Grant's eyes. Fumbling for words, she managed to ask, "What are you doing here?"

He closed the distance between them. "I had to see you, Tamara. I needed some kind of closure other than you sneaking out on me," Grant vented.

Tamara winced, turned, and walked toward her desk. Grant reached and grabbed her shoulders. "Please don't turn away from me, Tamara," Grant said gently. "Was I only a one night stand to you? It was much more than that for me, and I thought it was for you too. Was I wrong?" He looked intently into her eyes.

Tamara stood perfectly still, mesmerized by his voice and eyes. Attempting to pull herself together, she responded, "I can't talk here. Can you come to my house after work and we'll talk?" She knew she needed time to think without Grant's distracting presence. She couldn't help but notice the snug fit of his jeans and his handsome brown leather jacket. She shuffled through some papers on her desk.

"You know I will," Grant said.

Tamara wrote down directions and said, "I'm sorry, but I have a meeting and have to go. See you later." She left the office, leaving him standing alone and feeling frustrated.

Grant thought their meeting had been short and sweet; he still knew absolutely nothing. It was his own damn fault for being stupid enough to come there. *He* walked out of the office and closed the door.

Tamara couldn't believe how shaken she was seeing him. *What's wrong with me? I've got to be crazy giving Grant my home address. Why didn't I meet him some place else? I can't get this involved with anyone.*

She didn't know what she was going to tell him. Should she lie, tell him he was only a one night stand to her, or should she be honest and admit her deepest feelings... feelings for him that were unknown to her, and actually scared her? Tamara pulled herself together and attempted to concentrate on business.

She didn't know how she made it through the meeting, but finally it was over, and she was away from the office, heading for Seacliff Beach. Tamara couldn't seem to still her racing heart as she drove over the mountain. Bumper to bumper traffic kept her at a snail's pace. At last, she pulled up the hillside into her driveway, cutting the engine. She hoped there'd be time for a shower before Grant arrived. Hearing the doorbell, Tamara reached for a towel. She quickly dried herself and threw on a robe, calling, "I'll be there in a minute." She ran down the stairs with her hair flying in the breeze.

Sliding the chain lock free and opening the door, she said, "I'm sorry. I went running at noon and needed a quick shower." Not only was he standing there in that damn sexy jacket and jeans, but he had dark aviator sunglasses on. Why did he have to look so damn handsome?

"I guess I should have given you more time, but I couldn't wait any longer," Grant said, his eyes appraising her in the white terry cloth robe, with her hair hanging in ringlets, dripping onto the robe. Then he noticed Toby. "Who's your friend?"

"This is Toby, my best friend. We've been through a lot together. Come in to the living room, Grant. I'll run upstairs and pull something on," Tamara said, walking forward.

Grant pulled his eyes away from her and leaned down to pat Toby. "What a spectacular view you have! I have a home overlooking the ocean too, but I'm not right on top of it like you are. This is wonderful."

"Thank you. I really enjoy it. I look forward to the peacefulness of it after a hectic day in Silicon Valley. There's something soothing about the ocean." She looked at Grant, making eye contact, and quickly turned away. "Make yourself comfortable. I'll be right back."

"I'm not going anywhere," Grant said as he took off his jacket and laid it across the back of a chair.

Tamara ran upstairs to change. Flustered, she couldn't decide what to wear. Just the sight of Grant made her tingle.

What's wrong with me? I'm acting like a school girl again. Just put anything on...but I want to look good. Well, that sounds like I care what he thinks. That's because I do. Why?

She slipped on a pair of jeans and a sleeveless sea green tank top, brushed out her damp hair and applied some lip gloss. Taking one last critical look at herself in the mirror, she opened the door. She saw Grant remove his sunglasses and put them in his shirt pocket as he watched her coming down the stairs, admiration reflecting in his eyes.

Tamara sat on the couch, and this time she couldn't seem to pull her eyes away from Grant.

He returned her gaze. "Are you ready to answer my question?" he asked, moving next to her.

"I will," she said, jumping to her feet, "but would you like a drink first?"

"No, thank you, I need to hear your answer now, Tamara." Grant took her hand in his and pulled her back down next to him.

Tamara felt a chill run down her body. She looked into Grant's eyes and said, "I planned for you to be a one night stand. I thought you were, but I was wrong. You were something more. I haven't been able to get you out of my mind. Grant, I've never had a close relationship with anyone in my life, even my own mother. She deserted me. My grandmother raised me, but she didn't really want me. I was a burden to her. I guess you could say...yes, you could say I'm very much a loner. I don't know if I'm even capable of having a relationship with someone. You're a nice guy. I don't want to hurt you. You'd be a lot better off walking away now."

"Tamara, I lost my wife three years ago. She died. I haven't looked at a woman since then until you. There had to be a reason you came into my life. I felt the first stirrings of life when I met you. I couldn't believe it. It felt so right. When I woke up that next morning and you were gone, I was devastated. You brought me to life again, and then you were gone...poof, like you never existed. But you did exist, and I was alive again. I had to find you."

"I don't know. I can't think straight when I'm around you. I don't even know myself, and that scares me. I'm thirty years old, and I've never been in love." Tamara covered her face with her hands. "Now, I'm embarrassed."

"We can take it slow, Tamara...whatever makes you feel best. I just know that I don't want to lose you now that I've found you." Grant leaned down and kissed her gently on the lips. He pulled back and looked at her. "I won't pressure you, Tamara. I want to get to know you better. Why don't we go someplace and get something to eat."

"No, I have some steaks in the freezer, and we can make a salad, if that's okay with you."

"Sure, whatever you'd like. Want me to barbecue the steaks?" Grant asked.

"Sounds good to me. I'll show you where the barbecue is."

"I'd just as soon stay here and relax than go out. Hope you don't mind," Tamara said.

"Of course not. Why would I mind. That's great," Grant agreed.

After popping the steaks in the microwave to thaw, they walked out on the deck, which jutted out over the rocky cliffs. They heard the waves crashing on the rocks and sand below, with their rhythmic melody continually repeating itself, endlessly rolling in and out. The smell of the salty air permeated the atmosphere.

"I bet you spend most of your free time watching the waves break against the rocks from here. I know I would," Grant said.

"I do, but not as much as I'd like. It's very

calming for me. I never get tired of it. I'll go make a salad while you put the steaks on, okay?"

"Sure, I think the coals are about ready. How do you like your steak?"

"Medium rare, please."

"You've got it."

Tamara placed the salad on the table and uncorked a bottle of Merlot. She considered lighting candles, but thought better of it. She might be making the scene too romantic. After all, this was supposed to be a getting to know you dinner. "How're the steaks coming?"

"Be right in. I'm putting them on a plate now," Grant answered.

Tamara walked over and opened the sliding glass door for him.

"They smell great," Tamara said as Grant set the plate on the table. They sat down, and Tamara poured each of them a glass of wine. She spread a napkin across her lap. "I hope you like Merlot. I've kind of gotten hooked on it lately."

"Merlot's great, and I particularly like BV. Good choice," Grant said. He picked up his glass and swirled it, took a deep sniff and held his glass up for a toast. "May we have many moments like this." He took a sip and placed his glass back on the table. "Umm, good. So, tell me about yourself, Tamara. You have any siblings?"

"Not that I know of. I told you, my mom

deserted me. Actually, I just saw her. She's dying of cancer. I never knew my dad, and my mom claims she doesn't have any idea who he was. Mom was Russian. In fact, my grandfather was born in Russia. I don't know about my dad. My grandmother lives in Los Altos Hills with Gracie, her companion, housekeeper, all around whatever. Gracie's actually the person who helped me survive childhood. Grandmother bought me everything I needed. I mean I had every kind of toy you could imagine, but she never had time for me. No, she was busy with her bridge club, all her charity functions, whatever. If I wanted to talk to someone other than my doll, I went to Gracie. Oh, Grandmother kept me busy with lessons in everything...ballet, piano, languages, social graces, you name it. She wanted to be sure I didn't bring any friends over after school to disturb her. Anyway, enough about me. What about you? What's your family like?"

"Well, my childhood was pretty different from your childhood. My mom and dad have been married for thirty-six years, and I'm the oldest of three kids. I'm thirty-five. I have a sister, Kathleen, who's around thirty, I think. She teaches first grade and still isn't married. She's been going with this jerk for three years. I guess I shouldn't call him a jerk, but, damn, I wish she'd dump him. He's afraid of commitment and probably won't ever marry her. I guess I think she's just wasting time on him. Then, I have a kid brother, Barry, who's in college and just turned twenty. You'll like him. Anyway, I come from a close knit Irish family. They're all friendly and outgoing, and all live in the Santa Barbara area."

"You're so lucky."

"I know I am. Let's see, what else? I was named after my grandfather on my mother's side who died before I was born. His name was Grant, and he was actually English. I told you I was married and lost my wife three years ago. Her name was Malika. She was killed by a car bomb explosion, and they still don't have any explanation for it. She was an airline stewardess and was on her way to a flight to the East Coast when it happened." Grant shook his head.

"How terrible for you. Did you have any children?" Tamara asked.

"No, we were married for four years and were just starting to talk about trying to start a family."

"I'm sorry."

"It was really hard for a long time. I couldn't believe it really happened. I kept thinking I'd see her walking through the door with her bag in hand...that she was just gone on a flight, but then reality finally hit. We only get one chance at life, Tamara, and we have to keep going. I think I'm finally ready to begin living again."

"I'm hardly the best person for you to get involved with, Grant. I don't have that settled a life. You've been hurt enough. I don't think you need me in your life to mess it up. You don't know anything about me. I'm no good for you."

"Let me be the judge of that, Tamara."

"I'm only trying to warn you," Tamara said. "So what do you do with your spare time? Do you have any hobbies?"

"Yeah, I do. I'm into bird watching. I find them fascinating creatures. And I do a lot of kayaking, mainly in the ocean along the coast. How about you? What do you do for relaxation?" Grant asked.

"Well, I'm a runner. Running makes me feel really good." She cleared her throat and took a sip of water. "I love to swim, and I read whenever I get a chance."

"You look athletic. You're probably in better shape than I am. How about we take a walk down on the beach. Is there a way to get down there from here?"

"There's a path we can take, but I have to warn you, it's hell to pay getting back up. I do it all the time, so I'm used to it."

"I think I can handle it," Grant said, standing up and extending his hand to Tamara to help her up. Grant grabbed his jacket, and Tamara pulled on a sweater. They walked down the path with a flashlight marking their way. The night was dark, with the moon slipping in and out behind clouds. The waves enticed them with their magnetic sound reverberating on the rocks and sand below. They reached the bottom and walked the beach for a while. They stopped, sat down and took off their shoes, allowing the waves to splash over their feet. Tamara felt the dampness as she dug her toes into the sand.

"I wanted to show you the cement ship. See it out there?"

"Oh, yeah," Grant said. "I didn't realize that's what it was."

"Seacliff Beach is part of Aptos and is home to the cement ship, the S.S. Palo Alto." Tamara extended her arm and pointed. "Here it is in all its glory. It was built way back during WW1 when metal shortages gave them good reason to attempt something like that. The war ended before the ship got to ever see service. It ended up being towed to this spot, and for a little while became a casino and monster party boat. Over a period of time, heavy storms caused the ship to crack and break across the center. So, now it lays in pieces on the floor of Monterey Bay. For a long time, fishermen loved to fish off its hull, and now it's home to hundreds of birds."

"That's really interesting. I'd like to know

more about it," Grant said.

Tamara responded, "There's a visitor's center we can go to sometime if you want."

"I'd like that." They got up and continued walking the beach.

At last, they collapsed on the dry sand and sat in silence, watching the ocean roll in and out. Grant put his arm around Tamara and drew her to him. Tamara couldn't believe how good it felt having someone to share the beauty of the moment with her. She had never felt so comfortable and safe. She snuggled up to Grant, leaning her head against his shoulders. Her eyes closed, and soon she was fast asleep. Grant couldn't keep his eyes away from Tamara's tranquil face. He loved looking at her sleeping in his arms. Carefully, he slipped his jacket off and placed it over her, thinking how fortunate he was that she had come into his life.

Looking down at Tamara as she awakened, Grant's eyes reflected the magnificent colors of the sun breaking the horizon.

"We slept here all night?" she asked incredulously. "I can't believe it. I remember feeling content and safe. I'm sorry. You must have been really uncomfortable. I have your jacket. Weren't you freezing?"

"No, not with you in my arms."

Tamara reached out and put her hand over

his. Suddenly, she jumped to her feet, brushing off the sand. “Oh, no! I have to be at work for an important meeting early this morning. I completely forgot. We’d better head back.”

“Sure, let’s get going. I have to fly back home today, but I’ll be back soon. Actually, I’d like you to come to Santa Barbara so you can meet my family.” Grant got to his feet.

“You sure you want to do that? Isn’t it a bit soon? We hardly know each other,” Tamara insisted.

Grant raked his fingers through his hair as if trying to comb it. “I know everything I need to know. That’s good enough for me.”

Tamara smiled at Grant and thought to herself that he didn’t know anything.

CHAPTER FOUR

BEFORE LEAVING FOR THE EMBASSY, ABDUL relaxed on the balcony of his secluded resort hotel room in Oman, sipping tea. He liked being back in the capital city of Muscat. He enjoyed the near silence, with only the sounds of the ocean calming him. Abdul had been born in Oman, but raised in Boston and attended Harvard University. His parents belonged to a small cell of terrorist supporters who were very clear in their hatred for America. Abdul was indoctrinated and allowed to participate at a very young age. At eight he transferred money between cells on his bike and gradually increased his responsibilities, blossoming into a full fledged terrorist and mastermind of numerous unsolved terrorist acts throughout the world. Abdul became a master at disguises and coverups as well as a top munitions expert schooled in making and disarming explosives. At present, he was a special assistant to the U.S. Ambassador to Oman, a perfect guise, enabling him to infiltrate and access the areas necessary for his plans. His position brought him to the states a couple of times a year and to many other places around the globe. He had dual citizenship and kept an apartment in Boston, but found it more convenient to stay at a hotel while in Oman.

Abdul pulled on his jacket, locked the door, and made his way to the embassy, never suspecting he was under twenty-four hour surveillance.

Meanwhile, Tamara walked into the meeting with Frederick Mason, armed with a world trade publication which Christopher York had sent her. "Frederick, I'd like you to read this article. It's something I think we should jump on."

Frederick put down his pencil and motioned for Tamara to take a seat. "Well, that's really interesting. The technology management arm in Oman is taking bids on a system upgrade and are willing to spend a mint to do it." Frederick leaned back in the swivel chair and studied the article.

"They want it to be world class, even though I've heard they're already top notch. I like that they're inviting bids from several companies," Tamara said. "I'd love to make a presentation to them and take our best engineer along with me. What do you think?"

Frederick sat up straight. "Sounds good to me. We want to show them what technology can do for them from an economic perspective. Take Hani Alradi. He speaks Arabic and is familiar with their customs. I think he could be of real help to you. He's a master at finding out what their vision is."

"Good, I think I met him. About my age, dark hair, dark eyes, sort of a serious look?"

"Sounds like you've met him. I think you'd work well together. He's an excellent engineer and has a very dry sense of humor. Anyway, I think the two of you should get together and plan your attack. Hit the air as soon as possible. He looked at his watch. I'll call and make the arrangements." Frederick walked out of the room.

Tamara thought back to when she was first approached by Christopher York on the MIT campus, eleven years ago at the end of her junior year. It hardly seemed possible that all those years had slipped by. She had been a loner even then and spent most of her spare time reading, studying, or practicing target shooting. Excelling in class was important to her, and she felt that most of the social activities associated with college life were frivolous. She didn't have time, nor want to make time for that sort of thing. She was flattered when an older man of fortyish had sought her out because of her academic achievements. Christopher met with her many times over the next year. She looked forward to his visits, thinking of him as her friend. She knew he was a recruiter, but didn't really know what he was recruiting for, only that his candidates had to have high scholastic standing. He seemed to have a knack for turning the conversation to her whenever she broached the subject.

It was at the end of her senior year that Christopher told her about his special black operations unit.

"What does 'black' mean?" she had asked.

"It's a secret unit that isn't legal and not recognized by the government, but is contracted out and financed through the defense budget. Black ops tend to have a bad name because to some people they're thought of as ruthless, but our unit does the things that are necessary to keep America safe. Only two high placed government officials even know about the unit. And, I really think you're a perfect candidate for our operation. You've got what we need...high intelligence, lack of family ties and the ability to speak several languages. It takes months of searching for the right person because we'll be investing a great deal of time and energy in your training."

Tamara listened, immobile. "I guess I don't really understand what you're asking."

"You'd be trained to eliminate enemies of our government by different means, who for one reason or another, we are unable to bring to trial. It's much like being in the army. Our unit serves the country by eliminating its enemies."

"Kill? You mean I would be an assassin?" Tamara looked at Christopher in disbelief.

"If that's what you want to call it, but remember, you're doing it for the good of our country, helping to make America safe. We're talking about terrorists and drug traffickers who kill women and children...people who think they're above the law. Maybe I misjudged you. Maybe this is something you couldn't handle." Christopher paused and looked closely at Tamara. "It's a unique and exciting career, Tamara...a challenge. You must love this country. The rewards are great. Just to let you know, you'd be making more than the President. Besides the money, you have the knowledge that you're making a difference. There's an intensive training program plus specialized instruction, all with pay, and we set you up with a cover job in the line of work of your choosing. You'd be in it for life, Tamara, so it's a big commitment. It's not something you just walk away from. Think hard. I'll get back to you in a few days for your answer."

She was sitting in the shade of an old oak tree when Christopher turned and waved as he walked away. Tamara stood watching, not moving. She felt as if she'd awakened from a dream, but it wasn't a dream. It was real. Christopher was real, and what he'd told her was real.

He's asking me to be an assassin for the government. Why me? Why does he think I'd be perfect for the job? Why not choose a man? No, I suppose they need women too. I don't get it. Well, maybe I do. He knows I have no close family ties. I'm at the top of my class, foreign affairs major, and speak several languages fluently. I guess I do fit the bill. But, how can he know I have what it takes to be a killer? He must have seen something...maybe my detachment and distrust for the human race...maybe because I depend only on myself. And I can't stand terrorists thinking they can get away with killing innocent people. God, I just read about a bombing in Iraq where innocent women and children were blown away. Maybe I am a good candidate. I have no one, nothing to lose. It would sort of be like being in the army. I'd be serving my country by getting rid of mass killers and protecting American interests. What's he mean, "I'd be in it for life?" I know it's dangerous. Yes, I could get killed, but, life's a risk anyway. When I think about it, Christopher did ask me leading questions in the past. No wonder he wanted to know my thoughts on what should be done with people like Hitler and Saddam Hussein. Now that I think of it, he came up with lots of situations and asked, "So what would you do?" Yeah, he found out a lot of my thoughts, but he couldn't know if I could actually kill someone. I know I'm physically capable, but what about emotionally? Well, maybe, if they were bad enough. I don't know.

Early in the afternoon Tamara and Hani arrived at the Grand Hyatt, located on the sandy beach of Shatti Al Qurm in the heart of the diplomatic and government district of Muscat. Oman was fascinating to her. As she neared the coastal region, groves of date palms came into view.

Tired from the flight, they unpacked, had a light dinner, and went over their presentation. Tamara walked to the window and gazed at the beautiful azure waters of the Gulf of Oman. In Muscat, she didn't get the artificial feel which typifies much of the region. It seemed quiet and slow paced, without the hustle and bustle so noticeable in many cities.

Hani's face displayed a shadowy growth of stubble, and his dark hair was messed. Frederick had told Tamara that Hani was thirty-five, an MIT graduate, and had been in the top one percent of his class. He had a doctorate in computer science in addition to his engineering degree. He was highly sought after by numerous companies, but Excel Media had tied him up for the next five years with a very lucrative contract. His father and mother, born in the Middle East, were both professors, one at Harvard, one at Cambridge. With grandparents and other family in Oman, they often made visits to their homeland for Hani to become familiar with his roots.

Hani had noticed Tamara the moment she walked into Excel Media, finding her extremely attractive. The fact that he was married didn't curb his gaze.

Tamara looked at Hani and said, "I'm totally beat. What do you say we pack it in?"

"Good idea. We can wrap this up pretty quickly in the morning. What time do we meet with Management and see their system? We can't really finish the presentation until we see what they have anyway," Hani said, gathering up some papers and placing them in his brief case.

"We're meeting them at 11:00 a.m., and you're

right. Right now we're only making an educated guess as to their needs. But, that's okay, we're pretty well prepared for whatever. See you in the morning." Tamara slapped the folder closed and left the room. Tamara had no intention of going right to bed. She had work to do. She immediately called the contact Christopher had given her on one of the several disposable cell phones which was provided. She and Hani were invited to an embassy cocktail party the following night for technical representatives to get together with government officials. Her contact informed her Abdul would be in attendance.

Grant returned to LAX in time to pick up his Ford Explorer. He climbed into the front seat and started the engine, threw his things into the back seat, and wheeled his car out of the parking garage. After the drive up to Santa Barbara, he had barely enough time to clean up before going in to work. His mom had called and invited him to dinner that evening, telling him his sister and brother would both be there too.

I guess you don't always appreciate your family until you talk to people who aren't fortunate enough to have loving parents and siblings they actually care about, and who care about them. You take them for granted. But, Tamara really has no one...no mom to kiss away the hurts, or dad to teach her to throw a ball or bring her little unexpected gifts. Sure, I fought with my sister some and tried to get my little brother to quit tagging along with me, but now I'm sure glad I have them. And my grandparents were great. I still miss my Nana. Her arthritis was so bad. I remember her hardly able to get out of bed most of the time I was growing up. I was glad she lived with us though. I loved listening to her stories of the old days. Thank God Dad's parents are still going strong. My Nan and Papa are the greatest. I remember the little treats Nan left me in her bread box. She always knew I'd be by after school.

As Grant drove into his driveway, he wondered how Tamara would like his house. He had a different view of the ocean with his home being set back in the hills. He could still see the ocean, but not the close up view with the roar of the waves breaking on the rocks and sand. His home was a Spanish style ranch house spread out on a couple of acres. The land had actually been owned by the family for years and had been a wedding present from his parents when he married Malika. He pushed open the car door and got out and opened the wooden gates to his property before entering. At that moment, he felt lonelier than he had in a long time and wished that he had Tamara with him. He knew it wasn't possible, but he wished it anyway. When he called her from the airport, she told him about the Oman assignment and that she wouldn't be back for a couple of weeks. Two weeks seemed like an eternity to him.

Oh well, better stop feeling sorry for myself. I'm lucky I met her. I almost didn't go to that conference.

He showered before driving to work in Thousand Oaks. Then later, he'd go to his mom and dad's for dinner. He drove the Explorer through the gate, got out and pulled the gate closed. He often thought about getting an electric gate installed, but since it wasn't really there for security, he continued to get out to open and close it manually.

Lance heard through the grapevine that Tamara had gotten a job at Excel Media. He made up his mind to call and congratulate her on a good choice. To his disappointment, her answering machine came on. "Hey, Tamara, it's Lance. Heard you got a job at Excel Media. That's great. They're lucky to have you. I thought you'd like to know, I got the ax one week after you. Not to worry though. I've got some good leads. Talk to you soon. Call me." Lance set the phone in its cradle and leaned back in the stuffed chair, stretching his legs out in front of him and talked out loud to himself, "Who the hell wants to work for that piss ant company anyway. At least I had a little warning. Poor Tamara got blindsided."

Good old George had called him in to give him the good news shortly after the takeover. It seemed that he was expendable along with several others.

After breakfast, Hani and Tamara met with the telecommunications officials and engineers. They spent the day going over the technology management arm's present system and finding out what their needs were. After the goodbyes, Tamara and Hani both felt comfortable that they were ready to put together a good presentation to convince management that their company would be the best choice to make them a world leader in this ever-changing industry.

Tamara turned to Hani when they arrived back at their hotel and said, "I forgot to tell you. We're invited to a U. S. Embassy cocktail party at seven tonight. We'll get to meet with some of the government officials. It should be kind of fun. It'll be a good chance to network a little. Don't forget, you'll be my escort. Hope you don't mind." Tamara laughed, putting down her briefcase, while she fumbled in her purse for the room key.

"I'd be happy to escort you. I'll be by to pick you up around quarter to seven, if that's okay with you," Hani responded.

"Great. See you then," Tamara said, closing the door to her room.

Hani waited until he heard the lock click on.

Tamara stood in front of the mirror, trying to make up her mind what to wear. She didn't want to be overdressed, but on the other hand, not underdressed either. It was a good thing she only had a few outfits with her because she tried on everything in her suitcase. She decided on a three quarter length sleeveless black dress with a scoop neck which showed off her well rounded figure nicely. She applied fresh makeup and brushed her hair. After putting on gold spiral earrings and a necklace with a sapphire suspended by a gold chain, she appraised herself in the mirror and decided she was ready to go. She looked at the clock and discovered it was already seven o'clock. Hani hadn't arrived to pick her up. The phone rang. Tamara quickly picked it up. "Hani, is that you?"

"Yes, I'm sorry. You better go without me. I'll

be there later. I just had a disturbing phone call. It'll take me a while to get ready. Sorry." Hani hung up without giving Tamara the opportunity to respond. She stood looking at the phone for a minute, wondering what disturbing news Hani had gotten. She called for a taxi and went downstairs to wait.

Tamara saw the stretch of beach front approaching. With the Bay of Oman in the foreground and the Hagar Mountains behind, the U.S. Embassy presented a dramatic sight. Tamara drove through the double walled perimeter and walked into Reception. She was escorted to a large room already brimming with people. After scouring the room, looking for a familiar face, she accepted a glass of wine from the tray of a circulating waiter. She felt a presence behind her. Turning around, she stared into the face of a man so close she could feel his breath. She drew back and quickly appraised him. He was in his mid forties with dark hair, olive skin, dark brown eyes, framed by heavy brows, a trim mustache and beard.

"Sorry, did I startle you? You looked as if you were looking for someone. Can I be of assistance?" the man asked politely.

Tamara smiled slightly and said, "No, thank you," and started to move away.

"Wait, please, can't I get you an appetizer?

But first, let me introduce myself. I'm Armon Hadad."

Tamara immediately recognized the name and wondered why she didn't recognize him from the picture she was shown. "Why thank you. I'd love an appetizer," Tamara replied. She couldn't believe her good fortune, actually meeting Abdul Alhmad without any effort. He carried himself well and had a diplomatic demeanor about him. She should have expected that.

"May I ask your name?" Armon asked.

"Of course, I'm sorry. I'm Tamara Mantz. I'm here from the United States, representing Excel Media."

"I thought you sounded as if you were from the United States. I'm the U.S. Embassy Ambassador's assistant. Now that we're properly introduced, let's go have an appetizer." They made small talk, walking over to the appetizer table. After their plates were prepared, Armon led Tamara out to a courtyard where they sat down on a corner bench.

"I have to admit, Tamara, you were an elegant sight standing in the foyer tonight in your lovely dress, your hair flowing softly about your shoulders. I couldn't resist coming over to meet you."

Tamara balanced the plate on her lap and turned to Armon. As she started to speak, Hani appeared in the courtyard. "I've been looking everywhere for you, Tamara. I'm sorry I'm late."

Armon stood and extended his hand to Hani. "I'm Armon Hadad. And you are–?"

"Hani Alradi. I was supposed to be Tamara's escort tonight, but I'm afraid I'm not doing a very good job of it. It looks as if you've been well taken care of though, Tamara." Hani took Tamara's hand, pulling her to her feet and said, "Shall we go do a little networking?"

She turned to Armon, holding his gaze for a long moment. "Thanks for rescuing me. I enjoyed talking with you. Perhaps I'll see more of you during my stay in Oman."

Armon quickly stood, his eyes locked on Tamara's. "I'll be calling you. What hotel are you at?"

"I'm at the Grand Hyatt. I'll look forward to your call."

Hani led Tamara back inside. Tamara could feel the tension, but didn't know why Hani was upset. Hani reached and took two glasses of wine from the tray, handing one to Tamara. "Now, let's get to work."

Tamara placed her hand on Hani's arm. "How're you doing? You seem upset. Was it the phone call, or have I done something to upset you?"

"No, Tamara, it wasn't you. I came in here

upset and was taking it out on you, I guess. I had a very upsetting phone call. I'll tell you about it later," Hani said, placing his hand on her arm and leading her over to a group of people engrossed in conversation.

After leaving the cocktail party, they rounded the bend in the hallway on their way to their rooms when Tamara asked, "You've been deep in thought all evening, Hani. What happened with your phone call?"

Hani looked at Tamara, pausing a minute, as if deciding whether or not to say something.

"Would you like to come in for a while?" Tamara asked.

"Maybe for just a minute."

Hani walked in and sat down next to a small table. He turned to Tamara and said, "In my culture it would be considered invading another's privacy to ask a question like you did, but I understand that it's different in the U.S., and who's to say which way is better. I thought my marriage was going well. My wife called me tonight and told me she was leaving me. She didn't even have the decency to wait until I got home to tell me to my face. She didn't tell me why, and I didn't ask." Hani stared at his hands.

"Oh Hani, I'm so sorry. I shouldn't have asked, but you seemed upset. I was worried about you," Tamara said, reaching over and patting his hand.

"My parents won't understand this because in my culture women may divorce their husbands, but only if they have been missing for more than a year or jailed for several years. I've tried to be a good husband, but I guess I wasn't what my wife wanted."

"Is your wife from America?"

"Yes, she was born in America, but her parents are from the Middle East. Rona is what I'd call a liberated woman. She's always fighting for some cause or other. But, I love that about her. She's full of life and joy. Actually, her name means 'my joy.' Hani stared off in space. "Why would she leave me?" Suddenly realizing he wasn't alone, he stood and said, "I must leave now. Excuse me for bothering you with my problems."

Tamara placed her hand on Hani's shoulder. "You're not bothering me. We work together, Hani, and I feel like we're becoming friends, and friends tell each other their problems. Go get some sleep now, and I'll see you in the morning."

Immediately after Hani left her room, the phone rang. She picked it up and heard a man's voice with a subtle accent on the other end of the line, "Is this Tamara?"

"Yes, this is she."

"Hello, Tamara. This is Armon. I apologize for calling so late, but I'd love to see you again, and I didn't want to wait until tomorrow. I was afraid I'd miss you. Would you like to join me for dinner tomorrow evening?"

"Why, yes, I'd love to, Armon."

"Wonderful. Shall we say 8:00 p.m.?"

"That'd be fine."

"I'll pick you up at your hotel then."

"Good, I'll meet you in the lobby."

Chapter Five

GRANT WHEELED UP IN FRONT OF HIS MOM'S Spanish style home in an old residential neighborhood in Santa Barbara. His sister, Kathleen, heard the door open and ran to greet him.

"Hi, Big Brother. I beat you. You always say I'm the late one in the family so I was determined to get here before you." Kathleen grabbed Grant and gave him a hug.

"Good for you...major accomplishment," Grant retorted, wetting his finger and placing it on her forehead. "Gold star for you."

Her eyebrows furrowed. "Well, it's not easy, you know, with all the meetings and papers I have to grade."

"I know you work hard. Teachers earn their meager pay. You wouldn't catch me in your shoes, even with all your holidays and vacations."

"You just love to get me all riled up, don't you. If I didn't know what you were doing, I'd be really mad and fall into your trap."

"Okay, you got me. How's that boyfriend of yours? Is he here with you?" Grant asked casually.

"No, Sam had to work late tonight. That's another touchy subject. I know you don't like Sam, but he's a really good guy."

"I didn't say I didn't like Sam. I don't like the way he treats you. He takes you for granted. You deserve a guy who knows how wonderful you are. You know, what a great catch you are." Grant stepped over to Kathleen and put his arms around her. "I guess I'm just being overprotective of my baby sister. You're the only sister I have, and I don't want you hurt."

Kathleen looked up at Grant and hugged him. "You don't have to worry about me. I keep hoping Sam will make a commitment, but he's had some pretty bad experiences with women, and I'm getting the backlash from that."

"Well, he needs to get over it." Grant swung around and headed for the kitchen. "Guess I'd better go and say hello to the folks."

Suddenly, Barry charged in from the kitchen with a ball in one hand and a chicken leg in the other. "Hey Bro, how 'bout shootin' some hoops?" Enticing odors from the kitchen permeated the room.

"Why not? I need the exercise. But, I need to say hello to Mom and Dad first. I'll meet you out there in a few," Grant said. He loved having some one-on-one time with his little brother who wasn't such a kid anymore.

He continued into the kitchen. "Hi, Mom. What's for dinner? The smell is killing me. It really smells good," Grant said, strolling over to his mom and giving her a hug. He reached past her to pick up the lid on the pot, but she playfully slapped his hand.

"You've always been underfoot in the kitchen. You're the only one of my three kids who actually likes to cook. "It's chicken and dumplings," she said, stirring the mixture.

"I have to cook if I want to eat, Mom. I'm just lucky I like it." He reached in the refrigerator and took out a beer, twisting off the cap. "Where's Pop?"

"I think he's out in the garage tinkering on something. What've you been doing? I haven't talked to you all week."

Grant pulled out a stool and propped his elbows on the counter. "Well, I have some good news. I've met a woman I like a lot. Her name's Tamara."

His mom stopped stirring the dumplings and looked up at him, smiling broadly. "Oh, that's wonderful, Grant. Who is she? Tell me all about her."

"She's wonderful, Mom. She's smart and pretty, and she's really nice. She lives up near Santa Cruz, but I met her at a conference where she was one of the speakers."

"When do we get to meet her?"

"Soon, I hope. She's out of country right now. But, after she's back, I plan to bring her down to meet the family."

"Great, it's about time you start living a little. You've been a workaholic ever since Malika died," his mom said, wagging a finger at him.

"I'm gonna go check on Dad," Grant said, heading for the garage. He poked his head out the kitchen door and spotted his dad by the work bench. "Hi Pop. What're you up to?" He walked over and gave his dad a hug.

His dad laid the toaster down on the bench and hugged his son. "Well, hello there, son. I'm up to no good. Want to join me?"

"How's retirement going?"

"I don't know. I looked forward to it for so many years, but now that it's here, it seems really strange. I keep thinking I need to be down at the station. I go around the house looking for things to do. I guess I need a hobby. Oh, Harry stopped by yesterday to see what I was up to."

"That's good. Did he make Detective yet?" Grant asked.

"Yeah, actually he made it last month."

"Good for him. You know, Dad, you've worked hard all your life. It's about time you had time to do the things you never had time to do when you were on the force. How about those Dodgers! Did you catch the game yesterday?" Grant asked.

"Sure did. I won a bet with Harry." His dad picked the toaster up and studied it. "There's not too much more to fix around the house. I think I have everything working."

Grant laughed. "Speaking of games, I better get back out to Barry. I promised to shoot a few hoops with him. See you shortly at dinner." Grant walked out the door.

Grant found Barry already shooting hoops in front of the garage. "I finally made it. Sorry, but I got tied up. How're ya doin'?" Grant grabbed the ball and threw it at the hoop, sinking it.

"Well, I could totally use some advice. I met this girl, but it's weird. First, I think she kind of likes me, and then next thing I know she's like shining me. I don't know if she's playing hard to get, or if I've done something wrong."

"So, tell me what happened," Grant said, dribbling the ball.

"Oh, I don't know. I asked her to the movies Friday night. She told me she thought that was fine. Then she saw me the next day and told me that she like checked her calendar and she was sorry, but she was busy on Friday. Could we make it another time. I said okay and walked away." Barry threw the ball and missed.

"I don't know what to tell you, Barry. It could be she really did have something else she had to do, especially since she asked to make it another time. Then again, she could have been trying to get out of it, but I don't think so. I'm no help. I'm just as in the dark with women as you are. They're a different species," Grant said, shaking his head.

"No kidding. Well, thanks for trying." Barry stole the ball from Grant and made a great bank shot as they heard their mom calling that dinner was ready.

"Guess we better head in. I'm starving," Grant said. "Maybe we can play after dinner."

When dinner was over, Grant's dad started singing "My Wild Irish Rose," and the entire family joined in. After a while, they moved over to the piano. As his dad played, they all gathered around and continued singing until they exhausted their Irish repertoire and switched to more modern songs. Barry was good about keeping them up to date on the latest hits.

Finally, Mom said, "I think we'd better clean up, or we'll be up all night." Kathleen and Barry carried the plates into the kitchen while Grant went to the sink and scraped them off before placing them in the dishwasher. Grant's mom and dad took the left over food and prepared it for the refrigerator. Within a short time, with all hands helping, the kitchen was in order.

"Great meal, Mom," Grant said. "I didn't realize it was so late. Guess I'd better head out. I've got work tomorrow. Sorry we didn't get to play more, Barry. Next time." He grabbed his jacket and walked toward the car. He stopped and called, "Hey, Barry, you want to go bird watching with me Saturday? You have time?"

"Yeah, totally. Actually, it's a good weekend for me. I'm light on homework for a change." Barry wasn't sure what Grant found so exciting in bird watching, but he was willing to find out. He loved doing things with his big brother and was glad he had asked him.

Very early on Saturday morning Grant arrived at the family home to pick up Barry.

"Hey, this is an awful time to be up on a Saturday morning. How 'bout we stop at Starbucks and pick up some coffee?" Barry asked, yawning.

"I brought a whole thermos full. Help yourself," Grant said, pointing to the back seat. "It may not be Starbucks, but it'll serve the same purpose."

"Good, I need it. I was out totally late last night."

"Oh yeah? Doin' what?" Grant asked as he turned his head and backed out of the driveway.

"You know that girl I told you about, Sally? Well, she came up to me and told me she like made a mistake...that she could go out with me Friday night. I said great, when I should have said I already made other plans. Oh well, anyway, I took her to the movies last night." Barry pushed his seat back and stretched his legs out in front of him.

"So, what were you doing to get home so late?" Grant asked.

"Oh, she wanted to go clubbin' afterward. I took her to a few places, and we danced and had a few drinks. She's already twenty-one, so I felt sort of stupid. One of the places wouldn't serve me," Barry said, pouring the coffee into a paper cup and taking a big swallow.

"Yeah, I remember those days. I don't get carded much anymore. In fact, I'm happy when I do," Grant said. "By the way, we're driving to Ventura Harbor and taking a boat over to Santa Cruz Island. They load up at eight o'clock."

"Sounds like fun. How far is Santa Cruz Island from the mainland?" Barry asked.

"About fifteen miles, I think. It's the largest

island in the chain that makes up the Channel Islands National Park. I think it's about twenty two miles long. So, how'd you like the girl? What's her name...Sally?" Grant asked.

"Yeah, I liked her. She's hot, but I can't figure her out," Barry said.

"Don't try. You'll get it all wrong anyway. This is the voice of experience talking."

A low bank of clouds settled close to the water as they boarded the boat. They grabbed a sweet roll and settled back on the deck to enjoy the trip.

"You better put some sunscreen on your face, Barry. You can still get burned on an overcast day," Grant said, handing the tube to Barry. "Better to be safe than sorry. We don't need any for the rest of our body yet until we take our jackets off." Grant ducked his head against the cold morning wind. "It's chilly out here."

Barry shivered. "It's not just chilly. It's downright cold."

Pelicans and gulls were their main attraction on the trip over. The clouds had lifted, and the sun was shining bright in the sky by the time they reached the island. When the boat landed at the pier, they ascended a steep ladder up the cliff on the north side of the island.

"Barry, look! There's an Island Scrub-Jay. Look at the big bill and dark brown back, and see the blue undertail. The mainland Western Scrub-

Jays are white," Grant said, pointing to the bird's undertail.

"That's cool."

They continued walking with the other members of the group until they passed a eucalyptus tree, and Barry yelled, "Hey, there's another one of those freakin' Scrub-Jays perched in the tree."

"Good for you. I'm gonna grab a picture if I can," Grant said, pulling his camera out of his pocket. "Here, take the binoculars, and see what you can see." Grant quickly snapped several pictures.

Suddenly, Grant stopped and stared at the sky. Barry looked up and saw an enormous bird soaring above them. "What's that?" he asked. "Is it a hawk?" He grabbed the binoculars to get a closer look.

"The Golden Eagle, the King of birds," Grant answered, taking more pictures as fast as he could snap them. "Now, that's one magnificent bird. See the distinctive golden brown nape feathers crowning its head and neck, and that smooth chocolate brown color covering the rest of the body? They're a symbol of beauty and power all over the world. Damn, we're lucky to see one. They've been a problem on this island because they eat the island fox, and now, the island fox is becoming extinct."

"That's not good," Barry said.

"Well, actually what happened is pigs were introduced to the island when there were ranches here. Now, the pigs are wild, and the piglets attract the Golden Eagle. Eagles have excellent hunting abilities. They soar down and catch their prey. They can tuck their wings and swoop and plunge at speeds up to two hundred miles an hour. When they can't find piglets, they move on to the fox. Nature Conservancy owns about seventy five percent of the island, and they're trying to relocate the Golden Eagles to the mainland. I think there're only a few left." Grant snapped several pictures while he was talking. "Here, see if you can find one in this field guide."

He passed the book to Barry who quickly glanced through the guide. "Here it is. They're a lot prettier in real life than in the picture. They sure are cool...so graceful." Barry handed the guide back to Grant.

"Yeah, they really are. You know, they're monogamous. They keep the same mate for life. And both parents share responsibilities for raising the young. They usually build their nest high on a rocky crag or cliff. Their worst enemy is people," Grant said.

Several members of the group were standing about, listening to the conversation when one man spoke out, "You sure know a lot about Golden

Eagles. But, you did forget one thing. Don't forget to tell the kid about their keen eyesight. And they really have large eyes for a bird."

"You're right. Did I miss anything else?" Grant asked, looking at the group.

A woman said, "Don't forget the huge flight muscles in the breast, and that they protect themselves by their sharp beak and claws."

"Hey, I didn't know there was so much freakin' stuff to this bird watching thing," Barry said, scratching his head.

"We're just really fortunate to get to see a Golden Eagle today. They'll be gone from here soon. I understand they're reintroducing the Bald Eagle," a man said.

Grant turned to Barry, "They only eat fish."

They headed back to the pier and left for home around three, watching the brown pelicans circle above the high cliffs. Some of them were plunge diving and skimming over the water as they pulled away from the island.

As Grant drove Barry back to Santa Barbara he said, "You know, you got a good start today on bird watching. All it is, really, is learning how to identify birds and understanding what they're doing when you watch them. To me, they're fascinating creatures."

"Thanks for taking me. I can see why you like it. That Golden Eagle was something." Barry flashed a grin.

Grant pulled up in front of his folk's house and let the car idle, dropping Barry off in the driveway. He shoved a couple of tens in Barry's hand. "Use this for your next date."

"Thanks, Grant. That was fun. You comin' in?" Barry asked, getting out of the car.

"No, I've gotta get home, but say hello to the folks for me. Good to have you with me. See ya," Grant called, backing out of the driveway.

CHAPTER SIX

WAITING FOR ARMON'S ARRIVAL, TAMARA SAT on one of the ornate chairs adorning the hotel's lobby. She didn't want to be classified as the typical fashionably late female from the United States. While she waited, she admired the elaborate ceiling, date palm trees, and fascinating statue. She didn't have to wait long. Moments after sitting down, she heard Armon's voice next to her.

"There you are, Tamara. I do like a punctual woman." His eyes swept over her from head to toe.

Tamara stood up and responded, "I think it's a good trait for both sexes. We women don't appreciate waiting either." She noticed that Armon wore the traditional dress of the dishdasha, a long collarless dress shirt. A knotted tassel hung from the top of the shirt. Adorning his head was a turban, known as a massac.

After living in the Middle East for a while, Armon had forgotten how U.S. women tend to speak out about what they think. He liked that quality. It made the woman more interesting to him. "I'm taking you to the Tuscany Italian Restaurant for dinner here in the hotel. I think you'll enjoy it immensely. Shall we go?" He held out his arm, and Tamara hooked her arm through his.

They stepped through the wrought iron gate of the entrance to the restaurant. Tamara's eyes turned to the life size statue of a roaring lion and the open kitchen with a wood-burning stove. The room was warm and cozy. Mouth watering smells emanating from the kitchen filled the air.

When they were seated, Armon said politely, "And how are you feeling this evening?"

"Quite well, thank you. And you?" Tamara understood that it was important in Omani culture to exchange pleasantries to be considered polite. Even though she knew that Armon was raised in the United States, she observed that he followed the customs of Oman.

"I'm quite well, thank you. I hope you enjoy the restaurant. It's my favorite Italian restaurant. Would you care for wine, or would you prefer a cocktail before dinner?" Armon asked.

"Wine would be nice," Tamara responded, spreading the napkin across her lap.

"They have a marvelous dish called Stinco di Angelli. It's a braised lamb shank that's considered their specialty. If you like lamb, I highly recommend it."

"Sounds good. I do like lamb," Tamara said, opening the menu the waiter handed her. "It's fun to look at the menu, even though I think I'll have the specialty." Romantic dinner music echoed throughout the room. Tamara wondered why they called it dinner music...probably because it was soft and easy on the ears. But, what about elevator music? Who ever came up with that term?

Armon turned to the waiter and ordered a bottle of wine. "How long will you be in Muscat? Do you know?" He asked Tamara.

"Oh, probably not more than a week or so. It's a fascinating city. Have you lived here a long time?"

"For a few years, but my heart's in the United States."

Tamara thought to herself. Yeah, right. But she said, "Oh, I don't know. I'm pretty happy to be away right now. I'm sick to death of American politics. I hate us always interfering, and I really wish we'd pull out of Iraq. Oh well, I better not get started on that...enough about politics." She picked up her glass and took a sip of wine.

"That's all right. I like to hear your views."

Sure he does, Tamara thought. Her thoughts now turned to looking at the Omani women, although she was discreet with her glances. She noticed the jewelry most of all...the many rings, bangles, heavy earrings and necklaces. One woman had a ring on every finger. Many had their hands and feet dyed with henna. She also noticed that most women in Oman didn't wear a veil, but she had seen several face masks. They continued making small talk during dinner. "These vegetables taste like they're in a red wine sauce. They're delicious. And I love the lamb shanks," Tamara said, taking another bite.

"I had hoped you would enjoy it. The chef goes to extensive efforts in preparing his culinary creations. That's why it's such a popular restaurant in Muscat," Armon said, taking a sip of wine.

"Armon, I'd invite you to my room for an after dinner drink, but I'm afraid if my partner or someone saw you they would think it would be inappropriate." Tamara flashed a smile at Armon.

"I've already taken care of that. I'm staying here in a suite tonight. You can slip up to my room for a drink, and no one will be the wiser." Armon held out his glass for a toast. "To the beginning of a beautiful friendship."

Tamara put her glass to his and said, "Yes, I'd like that." Like that's all he wants, Tamara speculated.

Armon paid the bill and walked Tamara to the elevator where he made a big show of saying goodnight. Tamara got in the elevator, and Armon walked to the bar and ordered a drink before going to his room.

After a discreet amount of time, Tamara walked up three flights to Armon's suite, making certain no one saw her. She tapped gently and then let herself in the unlocked door.

Armon arose from the chair and saluted her with a drink in his hand. "What would you like to drink? I'm having brandy, but I have most anything you'd like."

"Brandy's fine for me. What an elegant room. Do you play the piano?" Tamara asked, taking in the room with a glance.

"Unfortunately, no," Armon said, while pouring a drink and handing it to Tamara. He sat down next to her on the couch. "I don't want to offend you, Tamara. I want very much to kiss you. May I?"

Tamara turned her face toward Armon and said, "I'd like that." It crossed Tamara's mind that she had the perfect setup to kill Armon now. It sickened her when she thought of all the vile acts this monster had committed. No one knew she was in his suite. But, she also knew she could obtain more information from him if she waited and bided her time.

The kiss was long and deep. Armon pulled back. "I want you, Tamara. You're so beautiful. Please stay the night with me." Armon looked intently into her eyes, waiting for her reaction. She gave a small smile of approval. He stood, taking her hand and led her toward the bedroom.

Tamara reflected on Grant. She tried to shut the thoughts off. She couldn't think about Grant now. It was too important to her country that she remain dedicated. She shut the door on Grant like a solid prison door slamming shut with no sign of a window. Her thoughts returned to the task at hand. She was determined to make Armon want to empty his soul to her.

She awakened around three in the morning and quietly slipped out of bed. Armon appeared to be sleeping as Tamara pulled on her clothes, but suddenly she felt his hand on her arm as she reached for her shoes by the side of the bed. She let out a gasp and jumped.

"You're leaving me without a word?" Armon asked, frowning, his dark brown eyes flashing.

"I planned on leaving you a note. I need to be in my room before daylight for appearances. You know that. I had a lovely evening." She leaned down and kissed him gently on the lips. "Thank you."

He relaxed and fell back on the bed. "It was

my pleasure. I hope you enjoyed it as much as I. I want to see more of you, Tamara. Tonight?"

"Why don't you call me later today. I'll know more what the plans are by then. I need to check in with Hani," Tamara said, kissing Armon once again. She walked to the door and quietly left the room. Tamara understood that although Armon appeared to be a pussycat, he was much to be feared.

During her stay in Oman, Armon never took Tamara to his residence. He always managed to stay in a different hotel room. She could only presume that he didn't want her to have access to his activities. Plus, she surmised that he wanted no one to know they were intimate. He was always discreet. There was no public display of affection. Tamara never forgot for a moment that if he suspected her, he would slit her throat without blinking an eye. He told her she was unlike any woman he had ever met and was fascinated with her. Even so, with his history, she knew there'd be no hesitation. She needed to be extremely careful. She had obtained no information from him and was beginning to get discouraged. There were only a few days left before she and Hani would be returning to the United States. She needed to contact Christopher York and see what he advised.

When Tamara reached her room, she took out

one of her disposable cell phones and called Christopher. "I'm not sure what to do, Christopher. I've gotten nowhere. Do I still wait and try to get more information on the plan? I'm returning to the United States tomorrow. Our company has gotten the contract we were after, so our job here is finished for now."

"Do you think he'll contact you in the U.S.?" Christopher asked.

"I'm pretty sure he will. He's wanted to see me every night I've been here and has already been making inferences about future meetings," Tamara said.

"Then I think you should wait. It's worth the risk."

Tamara put her bag on the bed, took off her clothes, and pulled on walking shorts and a sweat shirt.

God, it feels good to be home. Seems like I've been away forever. I've got so much to do, but maybe I'll take a run before I get started.

Walking by the telephone, she noticed the red message light blinking and proceeded to listen to her calls. Her friend, Lance, called, two solicitation messages, and Grant. She thought to herself she'd return the two calls as soon as she got back from her run. By now, it was late afternoon, and the jet lag was setting in, so it was necessary to do a little forceful self talk. She realized if she didn't run now, she'd never do it. She headed down the path to the beach below, with Toby at her heels, and started running. It was chilly. The salty sea air filled her nostrils. The sun was hiding behind the billowy clouds, but Tamara knew she would soon be warm from running.

A lone woman walked along the shoreline. She watched the woman reach down, roll up her pant legs, and wade deeper into the water. Tamara observed that she was picking up shells and placing some in her pocket. Then, she noticed a man farther down the beach putting bait on his hook and casting it in the ocean. As she got closer, he reeled the line back and cast it again as he walked against the tide. The sun suddenly broke through and cast its last welcome warmth of the day. Tamara continued to run.

Tamara's heart was pounding, and she felt invigorated when she returned to the house. She took a quick shower and sat down on the couch ready to make her calls. Lance was first on her list. Wanting to savor Grant's call, she would save it for last.

"Hey, Lance, good to hear from you. Sorry to hear you got fired too."

"Oh well, if that's the kind of bullshit they pull, who needs 'em. I've got some good leads going, so I'm feeling okay. Sure good you got hired at Excel Media. They're lucky to have you. How do you like their company?" Lance asked.

Tamara responded, "They're good...good benefits and all. Haven't gotten to know all the people yet. I went out on an assignment right away. In fact, I just got back from Oman. I've known Frederick Mason for some time though, and he's a really good guy. You interested in this company? I could put a good word in for you."

"I'd appreciate that. You know if they have any openings?"

"I don't really know, but I'll find out."

"Hey, that'd be cool. Where's Oman? I've heard of it, but I don't really know where it is." Lance questioned.

"It's in the Middle East. It's below Dubai, next to Yemen and Saudi Arabia."

"Guess I'll have to look at a map. I'm not really familiar with that area. Hey, I miss seeing you. When can we get together?" Lance asked.

"Let me check with Frederick, and I'll get back to you. Maybe we could meet for lunch next week. Okay?"

"Great, I'll talk to you soon then."

Tamara liked Lance right from the get-go. She felt as if she needed to take care of him, sort of like a kid brother. He always tried to watch her back, so maybe that's why she felt the same way about him. Plus, he was always supportive. He made her feel better about herself. She was glad he had called.

Tamara walked to the kitchen, poured herself a glass of wine, settled back on the couch, and picked up the phone to call Grant.

Grant answered the phone on the third ring. "Hello, Grant speaking."

The deep resonance of Grant's voice emitted a strong sensual sensation flowing through Tamara's body. She hadn't expected that reaction.

"Hi Grant. It's Tamara."

"You're back...finally. God, I missed you," Grant said.

"I missed you too."

"I'm dying to see you. Could you possibly come down to Santa Barbara for the weekend? I really want you to meet my family," Grant said excitedly.

"I'd love to. Tomorrow's Friday, so I could leave in the late afternoon," Tamara said as she took a sip of wine, slipped off her shoes and socks, and tucked her feet under her.

"Bring Toby with you. There's lots of room for him to run at my place."

The sun was setting the following day as Tamara's foot pushed stronger on the gas peddle on the way to Santa Barbara. Glancing in the mirror, she noticed a police car in the far distance. Her foot instantly lightened on the gas as she settled to a comfortable pace. When the police car passed her, she breathed a sigh of relief. Tamara found Grant's home without much difficulty and drove through his open gate.

Grant saw the headlights coming down the driveway and rushed out to greet Tamara. She looked beautiful, stepping out of the car in an A-line skirt and scoop neck top with appliquéd sequins around the neck. He grabbed her around the waist and pulled her to him in a deep embrace, inhaling her fresh fragrance. She felt so good to him. He released her, taking her by the hand and leading her into the house. Toby leaped out of the car and put his paws up on them as if he wanted to join in their hug. "Okay, Toby, I'm glad to see you too. Let's go on in, Tamara. You've gotta be tired from the long drive. I'll get you something to drink. You hungry?"

"No, I picked up something at a Taco Bell along the way. I could use a drink though...maybe a glass of water."

As she stepped into the house, Tamara looked around the comfortable room, surrounded by large picture windows facing the ocean. Flames were licking fresh logs in the fireplace, creating a crackling noise. Bookcases filled with books lined one wall. The room had a warm masculine feel to it. It was surprisingly neat for a bachelor's home. She noticed he had placed a bowl of water in the corner for Toby, as well as a dish ready for his food. Grant handed Tamara a glass of water and walked to the fireplace, stoking the logs with a poker. Tamara took her glass and sat at the bar.

Grant twisted the cap off his beer, sat down on the stool next to Tamara, and leaned forward with his elbows propped on the bar. "How was the trip to Oman? Did you get the contract you were after?"

"We got it. Isn't that great? So yes, it was a very profitable trip."

Grant chuckled. "I bet your boss was happy. Plus, that's a feather in your cap. You must have given a good presentation."

"It went well, but Hani, my associate, did a really good job too. I don't think I would have won them over all by myself," Tamara acknowledged.

"Tell me about Oman. What was it like?" Grant probed.

"It's a fascinating country. I discovered that Muscat's comprised of towns and neighborhoods sprawled along the Gulf of Oman for around fifty miles. I really felt its beauty was in the barren and sandy, yet rocky soil. Plus, I didn't see the commotion of most large cities, maybe because everything was so spread out. And then, the culture and dress are very different from ours. They can have four wives, although not many men do. It's way too expensive." Tamara laughed. "Can you imagine having to have several houses and support four women equally?"

"It'd be a good juggling act," Grant agreed. "I think one wife would be enough for me."

"I certainly hope so."

"I haven't been to the Middle East, but I've read a lot about it," Grant said. "Oh, by the way, tomorrow is dinner at Mom and Dad's. My brother and sister are both coming, so be prepared for the inquisition. You're the first woman I've brought over since Malika, so I know they'll be full of questions."

Tamara frowned. "Well, that makes me feel great."

"Oh, don't worry. They're all going to love you." Grant laughed softly.

"Oh, sure. I'm good with company stuff, but families...I know nothing. Now, you've made me really nervous." Tamara shook her head.

Grant took Tamara's face in his hands, looking directly in her eyes. "Relax, you'll feel you've known them for years after just a few minutes. I'm sorry, I shouldn't have said anything."

It was almost noon on the following day, and Tamara hadn't awakened. Grant tried making noise, even dropping a book, but there was no response. He finally decided to try a more subtle approach. Tamara's eyes opened and closed, she stretched her arms, yawning a few times before she grabbed Grant around the neck and pulled him to her.

Tamara's eyes popped open. "What was that I felt on my neck? I want more."

"I didn't think you'd ever wake up," Grant groaned in her ear.

"I'm awake now. Be careful what you wish for." She laughed, pinning him to the bed. Suddenly, she let go and sat up straight. "What's that I smell? Is it bacon?"

Grant leaped to his feet. "I forgot I was cooking it. Look what you do to me," he said, running to the kitchen, almost tripping over his own feet.

Tamara climbed out of bed, wrapped a sheet around her, and followed him to the kitchen.

"Well, it looks like I made a mess of that," Grant said as he turned and saw Tamara draped in the sheet. "What a sight you make. You look like a Greek goddess."

"Which one?" Tamara laughed.

"Aphrodite, of course. Breakfast can wait."

In the early afternoon, Tamara and Grant took a walk down to the beach. Grant's home was on a hillside about a half a mile from the ocean. They strolled along hand in hand, enjoying the beautiful clear day. Toby ran along the shoreline, chasing birds and dodging waves, but sometimes getting caught. The sun was shining, but there was a chill in the air. Sitting down on a log, they watched two young men getting ready to go spear fishing. The boys were outfitted with wet suit vests, gloves, and rubber boots. They watched them throw their poles into the sand as they sat down on the wet sand.

"Gosh, now they have to pull their fins over the rubber boots. How hard is that," Tamara said, watching in fascination.

"Some fins have velcro or buckles on the back, so that makes it a little easier," Grant responded.

The boys stood up, backing into the water, holding a weight from their buoy with a red and white flag attached. Then they washed out their masks and snorkels, sliding them over their heads.

"Look at all the work they have to do just to get ready," Tamara said.

"Looks like they're ready now. They're

starting to swim. See the water pushing out of their spouts."

Later in the day as they pulled up to Grant's parent's home, Tamara felt her stomach tighten.

Why am I so nervous? It's only Grant's family...his mom and dad, and brother and sister. What's scaring me? I guess it's just that I never really had a real family...maybe the fear of the unknown, or is it that I really want them to like me? I don't know.

"Okay, we're here." Grant cut the engine and opened the door, hopping out. He came around to the other side to help Tamara out.

Barry came bounding out of the house, calling to Grant, "Hey, Grant. Guess what? I saw one of those big eagles the other night." Suddenly, he saw a woman getting out of Grant's car. "Oh, hey, I'm Barry."

"Hi Barry. I'm Tamara. Nice to meet you." Tamara closed the car door.

"Well, I see you two met. I've told you about my little brother." Grant turned to Barry. "So you saw a Golden Eagle?"

"Yeah, that's it...the one you like so much--your favorite bird," Barry responded.

"You were lucky. You don't see many of them."

Grant smiled, patting Barry on the back.

"What's it look like?" Tamara asked.

"Well, they're magnificent...beautiful...smooth chocolate brown color with golden highlights crowning their heads. They remind me a lot of you. Grant pointed to her hair. Look at the gold in your hair. The sunlight brings out the shimmering golden highlights. And another similarity...they often make their nests high up on a rocky cliff, and look where you live."

"So you're comparing me to a bird?" Tamara laughed.

Grant sported a cocky laugh. "No, it's just that the Golden Eagle is my favorite, and so are you...graceful and beautiful."

"Come on now. Now you're trying to charm your way out of it." Tamara pointed a finger at him.

Grant took Tamara's hand and said, "Okay, okay, let's go on in." They walked up the few steps to the entrance of the house.

Barry followed them. Grant opened the door and called to his mom, "Hey, Mom, we're here."

It was a cheerful home with comfortable bright furniture. Grant's mom came from the kitchen with a big smile on her face. She walked over to Grant and gave him a quick kiss on the cheek. Then, she turned to Tamara, taking hold of both of her hands before Grant had a chance to introduce them and said, "I'm so happy to finally get to meet you, Tamara. I've been after Grant to bring you over ever since he told me about you. I'll go and tell your dad that you two are here. I think he's out in the backyard."

"Thank you, I've been looking forward to meeting you too, Mrs. Larson."

Hurrying toward the door, Grant's mom called over her head, "Please call me Patty, Tamara. I'll be right back."

Within minutes, Kathleen stormed into the house, her long dark hair streaming behind her, shouting, "Mom, where are you?" Getting a glimpse of Grant, Barry, and a woman standing in the room, she stopped in her tracks, "Where's Mom? I need to talk to her." Kathleen panted, throwing her sweater and purse on the chair.

"I don't know. I think in the backyard looking for Dad," Grant said.

Kathleen took off without waiting to meet Tamara.

Grant looked at Tamara and shrugged. "Sorry, that's my sister."

Barry laughed.

Meanwhile, Kathleen found her mom in the backyard, waiting for her husband to finish cleaning his hands.

"Mom, you won't believe this. I think Sam's been cheating on me. Some girl had the nerve to call at my apartment asking for him, all sweet and everything. Then, she said she'd check at his work when I said he wasn't there. When I told Sam about the call, he got all flustered and then wouldn't discuss it." Kathleen's breath caught in her throat.

"Okay, calm down. Maybe it was just a marketing call. We get so many of those," Patty said.

"No, Mom, she knew Sam. I could tell. I'm just so upset. He acted like I'm just suspicious of everyone because I'm jealous. He tried to throw it on me and acted like he was mad at me for being jealous." Kathleen's eyes welled up with tears. "Why is he doing this to me? I've waited so long for him to ask me to marry him."

"Honey, maybe it's time to stop waiting. But first, you need to find out if this is an innocent thing. Don't condemn him before you know he's guilty," Patty said pointedly.

"I suppose you're right, but there's been a couple of other things lately that have made me wonder. He's staying later at work, saying he has to work overtime, and he's just not being as affectionate. I don't know. You know, it's just a feeling. Something's different."

"So, what do you want to do?" Patty asked, placing a hand on her shoulder.

"I want him to want me. I want him to ask me

to marry him. I'm getting older, and I want a baby. I've waited three years," Kathleen cried dejectedly.

Ryan spoke, putting his two cents in. "Well, if you ask me, I'd ask him directly if he wants out. It would be better to know now than to waste any more time on him...enough of this pussyfooting around."

"You always tell it how it is, don't you, Dad. Actually, you're probably right," Kathleen said, looking at her dad.

Ryan turned off the water, putting the rag and can down where he was cleaning his hands. "Hey, Baby Girl, don't you shed any more tears on this guy. You're way too good for him. If he hasn't asked you to marry him by now, he's probably never going to. What's he waiting for? No husband is a hell of a lot better than a bad husband." Ryan walked over to Kathleen. "Nail the bastard. All I know is where there's smoke, there's usually fire."

"That's not what I want to hear, you know. I guess I'd better go back in the house and apologize. I didn't even say hello to Grant's girlfriend. I just had to talk to you guys first," Kathleen said.

"I'll go in with you. Dad'll be cleaning up for a while," Patty said, turning around and heading into the house.

Kathleen entered the house somewhat

sheepishly. Walking over to Grant, she gave him a quick kiss and playfully tapped Barry on the head.

Turning to Tamara, Kathleen said, "I'm sorry. I apologize for being rude when I came in. I had a personal problem and needed to see Mom. Sorry, I'm Kathleen."

"That's okay. I understand. I'm Tamara."

Patty joined them saying, "Anyone hungry? We'll be eating in about ten minutes."

Ryan entered the room, walked over and took Tamara's hand. "Sorry I took so long cleaning up. I had a hard time getting the grease off my hands. So, you're Tamara. It's about time we get to meet you. A pretty one you are. No wonder that son of ours was keeping you hidden."

"Thank you. It's wonderful to get to meet Grant's family."

Grant's mom called, "Food's ready. Why don't you all sit down."

Ryan went to the kitchen and helped his wife carry the food to the dining room table, saying, "God, Patty, you've got enough food for an army here."

Tamara looked around at the siblings joking with each other, thinking how fortunate Grant was to have the love and camaraderie of a family. After all the dishes were cleared away, Grant's dad strolled over to the piano and started playing.

Soon the three kids and Grant's mom gathered around the piano, and they all began to sing. The melody of "When Irish Eyes are Smiling" filled the room. Tamara noticed Ryan giving Patty a wink as their eyes met, feeling the deep seated love between the two of them.

Grant walked to the couch where Tamara sat, took her hand, and led her to the piano, whispering, "Join us."

Tamara hesitantly sang a few bars. Grant's mom looked at her and smiled. Song after song filled the air for about an hour until Ryan got up from the bench and walked to the kitchen for a glass of water.

As Ryan walked back to the living room, he said, "Okay, it's time to get to know Tamara. Let's all sit down and have a chat."

Grant led Tamara to the couch and sat down next to her. Trying to take the pressure off Tamara, he turned to his sister and asked, "How's school, Kathleen?"

"I've got some really cute first graders this year. They're full of personality and mischief. They'll settle down. First grade is a big transition for them," Kathleen said, sitting down on the big easy chair.

"How many do you have this year?" Patty asked.

"Only twenty two, so that's a help. How are

your classes going, Barry?" Kathleen asked, pulling her legs under her.

"Well, now that I have most of my required classes out of the way, I just have my major and electives. I like that. I'm even taking a class in wood shop this semester. That's totally fun," Barry walked over and sat down on the floor, his legs crossed in front of him.

"You like U.C.S.B.?" Grant asked.

"Yeah, it's cool," Barry said.

Ryan returned to the room and joined them. "Yeah, ask him what he likes best about it. I'm sure he'll tell you it's the girls."

Barry shrugged, looking embarrassed, but recovered quickly with a retort. "Well, what else is there?"

Tamara looked around the room and again felt the warmth of the family, making the void in her own life more blatant.

Ryan turned to Tamara and said, "Grant told us he met you at a conference and you're sort of in similar fields."

"That's right. We're both in the computer industry. I think Kathleen probably gets more satisfaction out of her job though. It must be exciting to see the growth in the kids, particularly in first grade," Tamara said.

"It really is. I love it, but you all have the advantage with salary, that's for sure," Kathleen said.

Tamara frowned. “That’s true. It’s not fair. Children are our greatest resource. You’d think the pay would be much greater for teachers.”

“Well, nothing’s fair. At least I’m doing something I really enjoy and getting paid for it, even if the pay isn’t all that good. What about you, Dad? Are you having any fun since you retired, or do you miss your job?” Kathleen asked.

“Oh, your mom’s managed to keep me pretty busy with all the things I’ve let go or put off because I was working. You know, the ‘honey do’ list. I haven’t had time to miss the job yet. I’m sure I’ll miss the excitement, but I’m looking forward to taking some trips and pursuing some things I’ve always thought about doing, but didn’t have time to do.”

Grant turned to Tamara. “Dad was on the Police Force for thirty years...worked as a detective.”

“Oh, that must have been interesting work,” Tamara said.

“It was, but I promised Patty I’d retire so she could have a playmate. She retired from teaching three years ago,” Ryan said.

“Grant didn’t tell me you were a teacher too. What did you teach?” Tamara asked.

“I taught elementary too, mainly third grade, but I also taught first and fourth for a while. I’m liking retirement better now that Ryan's retired. So, Tamara, tell us about yourself. Where'd you grow up? Do you have any siblings? Grant hasn't told us much other than how wonderful you are," Patty said, pulling a chair up next to Tamara.

"Not much to tell. I was raised by my grandmother in Los Altos Hills after my mother abandoned me. I never knew my dad, and I don't think I have any siblings. I left home after high school when I went to college at M.I.T. I've never married, and I'm sort of a workaholic. I bought my first house, which I dearly love, about three years ago. That's about it," Tamara said.

"You must be really close with your grandmother."

Tamara smiled and nodded. "Umm. She took good care of me." Tamara's thoughts ran rampant.

If she only knew. She did take good care of me financially. I had everything I could ever want, except love.

Grant looked at Tamara and said, "I hate to break this up, but I think it's time we head out. I know you have to get up early to head back to Aptos."

Tamara stood up and walked over to Grant's mom and said, "I had a wonderful time. Thank you so much. The dinner was delicious."

Patty hugged Tamara, telling her to come again soon. Kathleen and Barry both hopped up, saying their goodbyes.

Kathleen spoke up, "Tamara, next time you're here, I'd love to show you around Santa Barbara. There's so much to see. Maybe Grant would let you go to lunch with me one day."

"I'd like that," Tamara responded, making her way over to Ryan for a hug. "Thank you so much for your hospitality, Ryan. I loved the singing. I had more fun than I've had in a long time."

Placing her overnight bag in the trunk of her car the following morning, Tamara turned to Grant, wrapping her arms around his neck and kissing him softly on the lips. He helped her into the front seat. "Toby and I had such a good time. I hate to leave. I loved your family. They made me feel right at home." Tamara turned the key and let the car idle.

"I could tell. They loved you. Of course, not as much as I do, but...well, you made an impression. I wish you could stay longer," Grant said, pulling her to him for another kiss.

"I know. Me too. I'll call you when I get home," Tamara said.

"Bye." She blew him a kiss.

Grant watched her car fade into the distance.

CHAPTER SEVEN

ARRIVING AT HER SEACLIFF HOME, TAMARA inserted the key in the lock and opened the door. She turned on the lights, threw her things down on the kitchen counter, and went to the refrigerator, pulling a carton of mint chocolate chip ice cream from the freezer. As she scooped it to a dish, the phone startled her.

She saw from caller ID that it was Grant and responded, "Hi Grant."

"Hey. You no more than pulled out the driveway and I missed you."

"Good, I miss you too. I just came in the door."

"How was the trip back?" Grant asked.

"Fine, no problems. Actually, the time went fast. I was thinking about you."

A beep sounded on Tamara's phone, and she said, "Could you hold a minute, Grant? I have another call."

"Sure."

"Tamara? At last you answer. I've been trying to reach you. It's Armon. I'm here in San Francisco. I want to see you before I go back to Oman."

"It's good to hear from you, Armon. How long are you here for?"

"I only have a few days left. Can you come up and join me for dinner tomorrow night, and perhaps stay over?"

"I'd love to see you. I'm not sure what time I can be there yet, but I'll be there," Tamara assured him.

"Good, I'll e-mail you the directions."

"I'm on the other line, Armon. Sorry, but I'll see you tomorrow night." Tamara signed off, and switched back to Grant.

"Sorry, Grant. That was a business call."

"That's okay. I just wanted you to know how much I miss you. Sleep tight. I'm glad you're home safe."

"Night," Tamara said, slowly putting the phone down. She sat motionless for several minutes, looking at the phone.

Tamara crossed the expansive classic lobby of the old downtown hotel, heading for the elevator.

When she reached Armon's floor, she walked to his door and rapped softly. She had arrived earlier than expected. When he didn't answer, she tried the door and found it unlocked. Standing in the entry hall, she heard male voices arguing loudly in the room to her left. She unconsciously held her breath, listening intently to the conversation. If she were discovered, she could be in deep trouble. She heard bits of the conversation, enough to tell they were talking about the President's arrival in San Francisco tomorrow...something about the airport. She recognized Armon's voice saying they had to be precise on the timing of the bomb. She sucked in her breath.

Oh my God. They're talking about killing the President. I forgot the President's coming here tomorrow. No wonder Armon's here. Who's the other man in the room?

Tamara cautiously backed up, her heart thudding as she silently opened the door, making her escape. She walked quickly, looking over her shoulder, to a bend in the hall near the elevator and waited. She breathed a sigh of relief. Beads of sweat appeared on her forehead. She took a deep breath and realized she was holding it. A moment later, she heard the door open and muffled talking. She pushed the elevator call button and waited. Someone came up behind her as the elevator arrived. She got in, glancing out of the corner of her eye at the man who entered behind her. When she recognized him, her stomach lurched. Without looking back, she got out of the elevator and walked to the bar.

The warmth from the brandy, sliding down her throat, was a comforting feeling. She must calm down and think clearly! A quick call told Christopher of her discovery, then she headed for the elevator. It was clear now what she needed to do.

This time, when Tamara knocked on the door, Armon answered immediately. She took in the room with a glance.

"Tamara, you're early. Come on in." Armon stood aside and ushered her in.

"I'm a little early. I hope it's okay. I was able to escape work early and thought I'd surprise you." Sauntering over to the chair, she took off her sweater and dropped it along with her purse. The room smelled of cigar smoke.

"Yes, yes, it's a wonderful surprise. Come sit down, and I'll make you a drink. What would you like...whiskey, scotch, brandy or vodka?"

Tamara sat on the love seat, crossed her legs, and threw her head back. "Thank you. I'll have brandy on the rocks, please."

Armon handed Tamara the drink, taking a sip of his own, before placing it on the small table and sat down next to Tamara.

He moved closer, putting his arm around Tamara and pulling her toward him. He whispered, "I missed you more than I thought I would. I'm afraid you've gotten under my skin." He kissed her neck and cheek, making his way to her lips. She couldn't betray her true feelings. She allowed him to kiss her deeply, her lips parting and matching his ardor.

Tamara pulled back and whispered, "I missed you, Armon. I'm so happy you're here." She took a swallow from her drink and held it up for a toast. Armon lifted his glass.

Before Tamara could make the toast, Armon said, holding up his glass, "To us." He finished his drink and stood up. "Let me make us another drink before we retire to the bedroom. There's time for dinner later."

"No, it's my turn. Let me take care of you," Tamara said, picking up Armon's glass along with hers, and walking to the bar. "You were having scotch over rocks, right?"

"Right. It's nice being waited on, but I want to do for you. I want to shower you with riches beyond your wildest dreams."

Tamara skillfully slipped the powder into Armon's drink and stirred. She gave a slight jump when she felt his hands on her shoulders behind her. Turning quickly around, she handed him the drink.

Armon placed the drink on the bar and took Tamara in his arms, kissing her passionately.

Not wanting to arouse suspicion, Tamara wrapped her arms around Armon's neck and kissed him back.

Armon took hold of her arm to lead her into the bedroom. Tamara picked up her drink and said, "Patience is virtue. Isn't that what they say?" She walked back to the love seat and sat down. "Let's finish our drinks first." There was a strained silence.

"So, you're going to tease me?" Armon asked with a frown.

"No, I don't tease. Isn't the anticipation part of the fun?"

"If you say so." Armon sat down, picked up his drink and studied Tamara.

"Tell me about yourself, Armon. I really know nothing about you." Tamara matched his level gaze.

After a long pause, Armon said, "There's not much to tell. You know where I work. What would you like to know?"

"Oh, what you want out of life...what you like or dislike...that sort of thing," Tamara said, taking a sip of her drink.

"I guess I want to live life to the fullest, and that means having money to buy everything that life has to offer...living the good life. I believe in going after what I want when I want it. I guess you can see that from me pursuing you. From the first moment I saw you, I knew you were what I wanted. I believe in actions. No one gets what he wants if he sits back and waits for it to happen." Armon leaned back against the back of the love seat and took a swallow from his glass.

"Well, those are all good things. Let's toast to the good things in life," Tamara said, holding up her glass.

Armon raised his glass and took another large sip. "You know, I feel sort of strange." He started to stand up, but sat back down with a quizzical look on his face. He looked at his almost empty glass. "I can't believe–Did you...put..." Armon slid to his knees, then fell onto his face. It looked as if he were dead before he hit the carpet.

Tamara took her glass to the bathroom and washed it carefully with soap and water, placing it back on the tray on the bar. She knelt over his prone body and felt for a pulse. Nothing. Looking into his empty eyes, she walked out, closing and locking the door behind her.

Meanwhile, Grant stood out on his deck holding a drink in his hand. He couldn't take his eyes off the magnificent Golden Eagle with its enormous wingspan, gliding and circling, taking advantage of the air currents. Suddenly, the eagle tucked its wings and plunged at high speed, soaring through the sky and captured its prey.

Christopher impatiently sat in Union Square, San Francisco, waiting for Tamara. The bench was getting harder by the minute. A mother chased after her son, trying to divert the motorized car the boy powered from ramming into Christopher's foot. Her attempt failed. Christopher leaned down and handed the car to the mother. Apologizing, the mother took the boy by the hand and headed for a different area for the boy to play.

Christopher's thoughts wandered. He had always been fairly much of a lone wolf. He thought how he loved playing war games on the computer, barely tall enough to peck at the keyboard. He had never married, although he came very close once. Many years had passed since then. He didn't have to blot out Amber's image from his mind quite as often. He knew she had long since moved on with her life and was now married with two children. He wondered what his life would have been like if he had made a different choice. Oh well, it wasn't as if he were lacking a women's companionship. Hell no, he had lots of women. Amber did manage to slip into his mind once in a while though, and he'd wonder what it would have been like having her sleeping next to him every night...sharing little jokes that only had meaning to the two of them. It wasn't that his life was bad. He had the adventure and excitement he always felt he wanted. So, why did he sometimes feel the lack, this empty hole? He scratched his head and shook it, as if trying to shake the thoughts free from his mind. He jerked himself back to the task at hand.

Shivering from the damp chill air, he pulled the collar of his shirt around his neck. At last, he spotted Tamara coming up the steps toward him.

"Hi Christopher. Have you been here long?" Tamara sat on the bench next to him and wrapped the scarf, which had come loose, tightly around her neck.

"No, not really. It just felt long," Christopher said, offering Tamara a peanut from the bag in his hand. "How'd it go?"

"Fine, but now we have an additional problem, right?"

"Nothing you can't handle. I've done some checking, and I'm amazed he's been able to slip under the radar all this time. It's good detection on your part. We've diverted the President, and we have the airport covered." Christopher looked intently at Tamara. "I need to talk to you about something though. We're a little concerned about this man you're seeing, Grant Larson."

"What do you mean? He's a great guy." Tamara threw her head back defensively.

"I know, we've checked. But, we're concerned you're getting too involved with him."

"What's wrong with that? Aren't I entitled to a private life?" Tamara asked, with a frown on her face.

Christopher hesitated, then spoke slowly and deliberately, "Not if it reflects on your work."

Tamara flashed a scowl at Christopher. "How's it reflecting on my work? Haven't I been doing my job?"

"Yes, for now you are, but, if your thoughts are preoccupied, it could reflect on your work. You can't afford preoccupation. Also, there's always the chance of a slip of the tongue when you get too close to someone. That was the good thing about you. You had no one you were close to."

"Well, I have no intention of getting rid of Grant. He's the best thing that's happened to me in my entire life. I won't give him up for anyone." Tamara glared, hands on her hips.

"Give it time, Tamara, and think it through. I'm sure you'll see our point."

Tamara shook her head and sighed. "I'll think it through, but you're wasting your time with this one. My private life is my own. Let's get back to the problem at hand. What about the Secretary of Energy?"

"We've discovered that he's tied up with some big wigs in Saudi Arabia. It appears money is his nemesis. He's not happy with the President trying to wean the U.S. off Middle Eastern oil, looking at alternative fuels and easing the high oil prices. Just take care of the problem. We'll tie up all the loose ends on the Saudi Arabian side ourselves," Christopher said.

"Done, but lay off my private life." Tamara stood up, giving one last look at Christopher, looked away and walked off.

Christopher watched her carefully as she faded into the distance. There was no doubt in his mind that she didn't know who she was dealing with. She should. He thought he made it real clear to her when she joined them. She'd been one of their best agents. He didn't want to lose her.

Meanwhile, Grant had only been home from work for a short time when his sister, Kathleen, knocked on his door.

Finding the door unlocked, Kathleen shouted, "Anyone home? It's me."

Grant came out of the bedroom where he was changing into a pair of shorts and t-shirt. "I thought I heard your voice. What's up?"

"I went by Mom and Dad's, but no one was home. I needed to talk to someone. Hope you don't mind," Kathleen said, throwing herself on the couch.

"What's wrong? You look awful. Have you been crying?" Grant questioned.

"I can't believe I'm such an idiot. How could I not see what was going on right under my nose? I'm so stupid," Kathleen cried.

Grant sat on the couch next to Kathleen. "Tell me what happened."

"Sam's been seeing someone else, and now he's going to marry her. Can you believe I've been waiting for three years for him to marry me. Like how stupid is that?" Kathleen cried in despair, gnawing the corner of her lip. "What's wrong with me, Grant? Why didn't he want to marry me?"

Grant pulled Kathleen into his arms and held her. "Nothing's wrong with you, Kathleen. It's Sam who has something wrong. He's been stringing you along all this time. It's his loss. You're a wonderful person."

"I don't know what I'm going to do, Grant. Sam's been my life for so long." Tears streamed down Kathleen's cheeks.

"He's not worth it, Katie. Just cut him loose, and get on with your life. You've wasted too damn much time on that lowlife."

"I know, Grant, but how do I do that? It's not easy."

"You want me to go punch him out? I could, you know. I can't stand the guy." Grant stood up and started walking toward the door.

"Come back here. That's not what I want," Kathleen blurted. Grant walked back to her, and Kathleen grabbed hold of him. "Oh, Grant, I don't know what I want. I know I don't want Sam back after what he's done...even if he crawled back. I need someone I can trust. I'll be okay. I just needed to unload, I guess. I'm sorry." She looked down at the bracelet on her wrist, ripped it off as if a monster spider were on her and threw it in a waste basket.

"What's that all about?" Grant asked, raising his eyebrows.

"Nothing, just something that jerk of a boyfriend gave me. Sorry again."

"Don't be sorry. That's what I'm here for. What good's a big brother if you can't unload on him?" Grant asked. "You'll find someone, Katie...someone a whole lot better than Sam."

"Thanks, Grant, I guess I'll get going. I've got so much to do for school. I love you." She reached up and kissed him on the cheek.

Tamara walked into a restaurant, on Steven's Creek Boulevard in San Jose, for the promised lunch with her friend, Lance. She strolled past the counter with the display of fresh fish. Scanning the tables, she scooted across the leather fabric on the bench seat at an end booth. The restaurant was almost empty, but she knew that within a half hour it would probably be filled to the brim with people. A waiter approached the table and asked if she'd like something to drink.

"No, thank you, but I'd like a glass of water, please. I'm waiting for a friend," Tamara responded.

"I'll bring it right away."

Before the waiter returned with the water, Lance arrived.

He slid into the booth. "Sorry I'm late. I got held up in traffic."

"That's okay. It's good to see you."

Lance looked at Tamara. "You're looking good. I've missed our talks." He laughed. "I don't have anyone to complain to anymore."

The waiter, carrying the water, arrived at the table. Setting it down, he asked, "Would you like to order, or do you need a few minutes?"

"My friend just arrived, so we need a little more time," Tamara said, picking up the menu.

"No problem." The waiter turned to Lance, "Would you care for water too or something else to drink?"

"No thanks," Lance said, placing his napkin on his lap.

Tamara leaned forward, put her menu down, and said, "One of the reasons I called you is that I talked to Frederick. He has an opening that's right up your alley."

"That's great. I'd love to have a chance to work at Excel Media. It's a fast growing company, and I've heard really good things about it. I think I have a job offer coming in Friday, but I'd sure prefer this. What's the position?" Lance asked.

"Our company is fairly small, so your job would be a programmer-analyst. You'd be responsible for both the systems analysis and the programming work. But, you're used to that. You've done both jobs. That's why I thought you'd be so good for the job."

"Sounds great. Should I call Frederick Mason?"

Tamara pulled a piece of paper and a pen out of her purse. "Yes, I'll give you Frederick's number. Just tell him that you're the one I spoke to him about." She handed the paper to Lance.

"I really appreciate this, Tamara. Thank you for putting in the good word," Lance said, smiling.

"You're welcome. I'd be really happy working with you again. I guess we'd better look at the menu. The waiter's going to be back, and we haven't even looked at it." Tamara laughed. "They have great fish here, if you like fish. I love their salmon. Then again, if you like spaghetti, they make great spaghetti. Gosh, I can't decide what to have." Tamara studied the menu.

"Well, I think I'll have spaghetti and a salad," Lance said. "I'm going to make this my dinner so I don't have to cook tonight."

"Still no girlfriend to make dinner for you? Knowing how you hate cooking, I'd think you'd get one just to have someone to see that you get something to eat." Tamara smirked at him.

"Oh, come on now. I'm not that bad. I do cook once in a while. I just tend to eat a lot of fast food. It's easier. And no, there's no girlfriend. I've had a hard time getting back in the dating game since Cindy walked out on me. I guess she hurt my ego. My confidence is shot," Lance said.

"If I can do it, so can you. I'm seeing a great guy, finally. His name is Grant."

"How'd you meet him?" Lance asked.

"At a conference where I was speaking in Philadelphia. I guess he liked the way I spoke. Anyway, we hit it off right from the start."

"It's about time. I'm really happy for you. When can I meet him?"

"Soon."

Chapter Eight

TAMARA WAS STEPPING INTO THE SHOWER WHEN she HEARD the phone ringing. Grabbing a towel off the rack, she wrapped it around her and answered it on the fourth ring.

Grandmother's voice, sounding strained on the other end of the line, echoed on the bathroom's marble. "Hello, Tamara? It's Grandmother."

"Yes, I know your voice, Grandmother. How are you?"

"I'm not calling about me. It's your mother. I had a call from the treatment center, and Robin's dead. She died this morning. I thought you should know."

Tamara sucked in her breath. "Oh, God, Grandmother. I'm sorry, but at least she's out of pain. How're you holding up?"

Grandmother responded with a shaky voice, "I'm okay. Parents don't expect their children to die before they do. I really loved her, but she never thought I did. She ran from everything...from me...from the world. She didn't have a good life."

"But, she loved you, Grandmother. She told me you knew what to do. She said she knew you'd take care of me. She entrusted her child to you. That had to mean something."

"Yes, it does. I don't think your mother or I were cut out to be mothers. Maybe you'll do better, Tamara. I have to go make arrangements. We'll do a small memorial here at the house. I don't even know her friends or who to call. Well, I'll call you about what day."

Tamara asked, "Can I help you, Grandmother?"

"No, Gracie's here. Goodbye."

The phone went dead before Tamara could say goodbye. She looked at the phone she was holding, staring at it, and slowly placed it in its holder.

I know I should feel worse about my own mother's death. I do feel bad, but I also feel as if I lost her a long time ago. I never really knew her. It's still strange to think she's gone.

Tamara placed a call to Grant. "Hi Grant, it's me."

From the tone of Tamara's voice, Grant could

tell something was wrong.

"What's the matter?" he asked.

"My mom died this morning."

"Oh, Tamara, I'm so sorry. Want me to come up? I can be there in a matter of hours."

"No, I'm okay. I feel so strange. I hardly knew my mother, but I feel a loss knowing she's gone. Isn't that crazy? I just needed to hear your voice. You always make me feel better."

"I'm glad. I wish you'd let me come be with you," Grant pleaded.

"I think I'll be ready to get away in a few days. If it's okay with you, I'll come see you then."

Grant responded, "Of course it is. I always want to be with you. I thought you understood that."

"Good, I'll let you know. I better go."

"Okay. Call me if there's anything I can do to help you. I'm sorry, Tamara."

"Thanks."

Exhaustion washed over Tamara. Thoughts of her mother had been exploding in her mind for hours. She sat motionless and suddenly realized she hadn't moved from the couch since her grandmother had called her earlier in the evening. She forced herself to go into the bedroom. Sitting on her bed, she pulled open the drawer of her night stand and took out a picture. Peering at the photograph of a pretty young woman and a very small girl on a swing, a lone tear ran down her cheek. She lay on the bed, staring at the ceiling, with little memories of her mother flashing through her mind.

Tamara awakened with the morning light shining in her eyes, the picture still resting on her chest. The memory of her mother's death washed over her. She noticed the picture on her chest and gazed at it. It was difficult to remember what life was like with her mom.

I was pretty little, maybe four. I remember my mom kissing me goodbye and walking out the door with her suitcase. She told me to call my grandmother, then play with my doll. But, I couldn't remember how to call my grandmother. I was scared...shivering, curled up in a ball against the wall, clutching my doll to my chest. It seemed like I cried forever, but every once in a while I'd stop, thinking I heard my mom coming home. When it started to get dark, even at four, I knew I had to do something. I remember...that's when I went next door to the neighbor's house. She called my grandmother. God, it was so scary.

Thinking she had been brooding for too long, Tamara dragged herself out of bed and showered. After emerging from the shower, she noticed the red light blinking on the answering machine. When she pushed the button, her grandmother's voice came over the speaker, "Tamara, aren't you home? I wanted to tell you the memorial is set for Sunday afternoon at two. I'll see you then."

Tamara learned via Christopher's sources the Secretary of Energy was in Dubai. Since making it clear that time was of the essence in concluding the assignment, Tamara noted it was Wednesday, which gave her time to get to Dubai and back before Sunday afternoon. She'd see if she could get a flight that night if possible. When she called Frederick at work, he told her to take a few bereavement days off. At first, she was going to turn the days down, but then she thought she could use them to her advantage. Discovering she could get a flight out that afternoon, she packed a bag in preparation for the trip.

After one stop in New York, Tamara arrived at Dubai International Airport. She caught a taxi, which took her to the hotel where Christopher had told her the Secretary was staying. As she arrived at the hotel, soaring sixty meters short of the empire state building, the magnificent sail-shaped structure was a dramatic sight. Standing in awe in the main foyer, watching the water cascading down the lobby entrance and admiring the tall interior atrium, visions of a sultan with his harem running through the water exploded in her head. Surely, she must have been transported here by a magic carpet. A bellman interrupted her thoughts, asking to escort her to the room. Floor to ceiling windows surrounded her as the bellman walked her through the suite, explaining how to operate the TV, DVD and the electronic curtains. Her eyes unconsciously moved to the panoramic view of the waters of the Arabian Gulf. She was led to a sweeping staircase leading to the bedroom and dressing area, all furnished in red, blue and gold. "What a magnificent suite!" she exclaimed.

"We are an all suite hotel, and this is only a standard suite," the bellman explained.

"I can't imagine what else one could want."

She would expect this extravaganza to be in Vegas, not in the middle of the Arabian desert.

When the bellman left, Tamara checked the room. She opened and fished in the back of the dresser drawer, discovering a briefcase. Opening it carefully, she saw a PSG-1 semiautomatic rifle. She pulled it out of its safe haven and skillfully put it together, attaching the scope. Her support team, as she often called them, always made certain she was well equipped. With the exception of Christopher, she had never met any of them. She had no idea how they had managed to get the rifle into the room. But then, she never knew how they managed to do many things. Since she was informed through her sources the Secretary would be attending a conference at the U. S. Embassy in the morning, Tamara decided to get a good night's sleep to be alert for tomorrow's assignment.

The following morning, Tamara situated herself on top of a prearranged roof outside the main gate of the hotel. As she knelt down to wait, she thought about the Secretary sitting in the back seat of the Ambassador's car. Construction work was everywhere, assisting in camouflage to enable her escape. Checking her watch, the Secretary should pass this point in precisely five minutes.

Her thoughts drifted off to Grant. *What am I doing getting involved with him? I shouldn't be involved with any man, much less a really good man like Grant. All I can do is hurt him. I know I'll have to leave him eventually. I can't stay. It's even harder because I've met his family and see what I've been missing. Sometimes we're our own worst enemy. I got myself into this mess. There's no one I can blame except me. I know what that means. I'm the one who has to get myself out of it. Okay, enough of this, or I won't have to worry about anything again. I'll be dead.* She shook her head and let out a disgusted laugh. *In the past, nothing could distract me. I need to get myself together and concentrate on the task at hand.*

Even though her contacts had assured her the embassy car would not be armored, when she spotted it making its approach across the causeway, she struggled to determine if it was. Her heart picked up its beat, pounding in her chest. She thought of the Secretary smugly making deals with the Saudis. Remembering his friendly alliance with Armon, she knew it was time to put him out of business. She lowered the rifle, rubbed her eyes, and concentrated on closing in on the approaching car. It slowly came through the guard's gate and rounded the corner. The scope was focused and aimed at the Secretary as she held her breath. Her finger remained steady on the trigger. The shot silently sliced the air with deadly accuracy, the bullet shattering the rear window. Tamara's marksmanship skills paid off. The bullet pierced the Secretary directly in the temple, his head exploding like a ripe melon. She placed the rifle on the flat gravel rooftop and calmly walked away. When she was a safe distance from the area, she slipped out of her jumpsuit, stuffing it in her briefcase and pulled on a skirt, once again an average business woman.

After arriving home and catching a couple of

hours sleep, Tamara readied herself to attend the memorial at her grandmother's house. Slipping on a navy blue empire waist dress with lettuce edge trim around the neck, she gave herself one last appraisal in the mirror and walked out the door.

Tamara tapped on Grandmother's door and stepped in. "Grandmother? Gracie? I'm here. Anyone home?"

Gracie bounded out of the kitchen. "Hi Honey Girl. You holding up okay?" she asked, giving Tamara a hug.

"Yes, you know Mom wasn't my favorite person, but it's hard to think of her gone. I think I've been mad at her most of my life. Sort of a waste of energy, wasn't it. The last time I saw her she looked so fragile. I think I can let it all go now and be happy for her that she's out of pain."

"I know. That's good. I hope you can let it go. She wasn't a happy woman."

Tamara replied, "I think she looked for happiness in the wrong places."

"Your grandmother's in the living room waiting for you. Why don't you go say hello. She needs some cheering up. I'll finish up with the hors d'oeuvres." Gracie walked toward the kitchen.

"Okay, the minister here yet?" Tamara asked.

Gracie turned and said, "Not yet. Soon, I hope."

Entering the living room, Tamara called out, “Hi Grandmother. I didn’t want to startle you.”

Tamara’s grandmother looked up from the couch, with the Bible open in her lap. “Hello, Tamara, I’m glad you’re finally here. You can help me choose a verse for the minister to read. He asked me to pick something your mom liked. I have no idea what she liked.”

Her strong self-assured grandmother suddenly looked very fragile. Tamara sat down next to her. “You’re asking the wrong person, Grandmother. I hardly knew my mother.”

“The one thing I ask you for help with, and you turn your back on me. I should have known. You never could do anything right. Just forget it.” Grandmother’s eyes returned to the Bible.

Tamara’s foot nervously danced. “I’m sorry. I’ll try to think of something.”

“Thank you, but, you’d better do it quickly. It’s time for Pastor Dillingham any minute.”

“How about ‘Father forgive them for they know not what they do?’ You’ll have to look it up. I know it’s in the New Testament, and I think it’s John, but I’m not sure. I think my mom was sorry for a lot of things in the end, but I don’t think she ever knew how much pain she caused people by her actions. I know what she’s done to me, and I see the pain in your eyes, but who knows who else she’s hurt.”

Pastor Dillingham entered the room, escorted by Gracie. He walked over and stood in front of Tamara and her grandmother.

"Hello, I'm Tamara. Robin was my mother." Tamara stood up, shaking the pastor's hand.

Pastor Dillingham smiled. "Yes, your grandmother said you'd be here. Are there any others coming, or will it just be the four of us?"

"No, this is it," Grandmother confirmed.

"Okay then, let's get started. Would you like to share some memory of Robin?"

Grandmother shared several memories of her daughter when she was young that Tamara had never heard before. Tamara strained her brain trying to think of something to say, but nothing came. When Pastor Dillingham looked in her direction, all she could say was that her mom drew a picture for her once when she was a little girl. She told her it was a picture of herself with blond hair. She still had it tucked in a drawer at home.

When the service was over and Pastor Dillingham left, Tamara turned to her grandmother. "That was real nice, Grandmother. Mom would have liked it."

"Thank you, Tamara. At least you picked a passage, even if it wasn't a particularly good one."

"Will you be okay, Grandmother? Would you like me to spend the night?" Tamara asked, ignoring the remark.

"If you'd like. You could stay in your old room, but it's not necessary. I have Gracie here with me."

For the first time, Tamara saw a real chink in Grandmother's armor. She didn't think her mother knew how much Grandmother loved her. She placed a hand on her grandmother's shoulder and said softly, "I think I'd like to stay over."

"Good, I'll have Gracie prepare your room." She patted Tamara's hand, now resting on top of her shoulder.

"No need. I'll run up and put some sheets on the bed."

Scowling, Grandmother cautioned, "Tamara, that's Gracie's job."

"I thought I'd help her. She's getting older and doesn't need to do something I can do easily myself." Her eyes sought out her grandmother's for confirmation.

"Oh, do as you like," Grandmother said, falling back into her usual pattern.

Tamara turned and went up the stairs to her old room. Nothing had changed...same bedspread, even some of her old dolls sitting on top of the cedar chest. Tamara took sheets out of the closet and began to make the bed. Gracie entered the room. "Let me do that, Tamara. You're doing my job."

"Why don't you come help me. Then we can have a minute to talk," Tamara persuaded.

Gracie walked to the bed and picked up one end of the sheet. "You helped your Grandmother get through today, Tamara. It was a difficult day for her."

"I should have come sooner. I didn't realize," Tamara admitted.

"How did you happen to think of that passage?" Gracie asked.

"I only went to Sunday School twice, Gracie, and both times were when you took me with you to church when I was young. I remember wondering how Jesus could ask his Father to forgive the people who were killing him. It made an impression on me. But, do you think that God really could forgive someone who has killed someone?" Tamara asked, directing her attention to Gracie.

Gracie paused before replying. "That's what the Bible tells us. But, I think they have to be repentant, or honestly be sorry for what they've done...not just go out and do the same thing again."

Tamara mulled it over in her mind while they continued to make the bed.

The next morning at breakfast, Tamara sprang to her feet. "I have a great idea. Why don't you and Gracie come to my house for a visit.

You've never been there. It would be fun. I could show you all around the area."

Grandmother contemplated the contents of her coffee cup before replying, "I don't know. I haven't been out of the house in the last few years, except to see Robin when she was dying."

Tamara was almost speechless. She didn't know. Her grandmother had always been going to charity functions, bridge and all those activities. When did it stop? She cupped her hands around the coffee cup, warming them. She took a small sip before speaking cautiously, "I'll be with you, Grandmother, and I'll bring you right back home if you're uncomfortable."

"Let me think about it, Tamara." Grandmother sighed, and gave her a small smile.

Tamara vowed to herself that she wouldn't let it slide. She would diligently pursue a visit. For better or worse, this was her family.

CHAPTER NINE

WHEN TAMARA ARRIVED HOME, SHE IMMEDIATELY called Grant. Hearing Grant's strong masculine voice answering the phone, she took a deep breath. As her body relaxed, she said, "Hi Grant. I'm so happy to hear your voice."

"Tamara, I've been worried about you. I should have come straight up. I've been trying to reach you. I didn't know how to get in touch with you. I mean–I shouldn't have listened to you. I was so stupid." Grant berated himself. "You needed me, and I wasn't there for you."

"I told you not to come. It was my fault," Tamara assured him. "Anyway, I just needed to hear your voice. I have to go to work for the next couple of days, but I'll come down on Friday if that's okay. I've had a few Earth shattering revelations which have really shaken my world. I'm starting to look at life in a different way."

"Is that a good or bad thing?" Grant asked cautiously.

"Good, I think...I hope, anyway."

Grant didn't want to pry. He knew Tamara would share with him when she was ready. "Why don't I come up now and drive back with you," he asked hopefully. "I'm sure I can get a couple of days off."

"No, that would be silly. I have to go to work, so you'd be wasting your time off. I'll be there on Friday. I promise."

"Okay, I suppose you're right. How're you holding up? I can hardly wait to see you...to take you in my arms."

"Me too. I'm holding up okay. I made it through the memorial. That's a plus."

"What about your grandmother? Is she okay?"

"I'm trying to get her to stay with me for a few days. I don't know if she will though. Anyway, I'm anxious to see you."

At last Friday arrived and Tamara was on her way to Santa Barbara. It was a beautiful clear day when she hit the coast, passing Pismo Beach. It was early evening, and it wouldn't be long until the sun would be setting. She no longer wanted to break it off with Grant. She wanted more, much more. It was the first time ever that Tamara wanted one man, and that man was Grant. She longed for the feel of his arms holding her, shielding her from the outside world. Suddenly, she started laughing, laughing at herself for imagining an assassin, someone who kills for a living, wanting to be protected by a man. She laughed until her stomach hurt. Stopping abruptly, she felt foolish. It wasn't funny at all.

Approaching Grant's gate, she observed he had left it wide open for her. Toby was excited. He paced back and forth to each side of the car. Tamara was sure he could sense where he was. She pulled through the gate and drove up to the house, turning her engine and lights off and got out of the car. Grant hurried out the door to greet her. She hastily walked up the single step. Catching her in his arms, he murmured into her hair, "I didn't think you'd ever get here." Toby ran past them and bounded into the house.

Tamara wrapped her arms around Grant's neck, whispering in his ear, "I couldn't wait," and kissed him passionately. Grant kissed her back with the same intensity. Swiftly moving into the house, Tamara kicked off her shoes and threw her purse on a chair.

Grant grabbed her hand and prompted her urgently, "Let's go in the bedroom."

Tamara observed his plain old denim Levis,

faded and tight. He seemed virile and male to her. She thought it was a funny thing to think, but some men just didn't exude that strong masculine quality. She thought probably only women would understand that. Once inside the room, Grant turned and took her into his arms, placing light kisses on her neck. She groaned with delight. She wanted this man, not any man, only Grant, with the intensity of a volcano about to erupt. Tamara locked eyes with Grant as she pulled her cotton tee over her head, her hair cascading over her shoulders. Unsnapping and stepping out of her shorts, she stood in front of Grant with only her bra and panties. His gaze seemed to burrow into her flesh. She looked at him expectantly as he unzipped his Levi's and tossed them across the room. He unbuttoned his shirt one button at a time, as if prolonging the wonder of the moment. Tamara said nothing, but her heart began to pound.

Grant could wait no longer. He pulled Tamara to him and fell back on the bed, with the warmth of their combined bodies searing his insides. Grant groaned, murmuring, "Oh God, Tamara, I've never wanted a woman like I want you. I think I'm in love with you. I really feel this is right...us...we're right."

Tamara pulled back, looking directly into his eyes. "You don't really know me, Grant. You're only infatuated. I'm feeling the same way," Tamara confessed. "But for me, it's the first time in my life I've felt this way."

"Don't be afraid, Tamara. Let yourself go. I won't hurt you. I promise. I do love you. It's not only infatuation. Sure, I'm infatuated, but it's more than that. I love the way you look at me, your smile, the way your leg dances when you're nervous or not sure what to say. I love everything about you."

Tamara's thoughts turned to visions of the Secretary's head exploding. *What am I doing? I think I'm in love with this man. I'll ruin his life. I can't ever tell him what I've done. He wouldn't understand. I did it for my country. But, I killed people, real people. What do I say to Grant? These people deserved to die? They're terrorists or drug dealers? Oh sure, but, I still killed them. What would he say? He'd run. He'd run as fast and as far away from me as he could. He'd be shocked...terrified. Would he still want to protect me then?* She gave a feeble laugh.

"What are you laughing at? Did I say something funny?" Grant asked innocently.

"Of course not. You just told me you loved me. I'm laughing because I'm scared. Women tend to do that, you know. They laugh when they're happy, sad, scared, you name it. Many times it's a cover up for their true feelings. Grant, I care for you very much. I just think we need to slow this down a little. Give me time to work things out in my head."

"I'll give you all the time you need, Tamara." He pulled her to him, kissing her, trying to make her reluctant thoughts go away. They continued their love making, but the complete joy of the moment didn't return.

When Tamara awakened in the morning she turned over, exploring the bed with her hand, but was disappointed when she didn't find Grant. Lying back on the soft sheets, Tamara thought about her feelings for Grant. She felt confused. She checked the clock and discovered it was nine o'clock. She couldn't believe she had slept so late. The sun was already streaming in the window. Climbing out of bed, she reached into her suitcase and pulled out her robe. She walked down the hall, calling softly, "Grant, are you here?"

"I'm in the kitchen. I was going to surprise you with breakfast in bed." He pouted. "You woke up too soon."

"I'm sorry. It smells so good," Tamara exclaimed. "What're you making?"

"I have a cheese omelet casserole in the oven. I can give you some fresh fruit and coffee while we're waiting."

"Sounds good, particularly the coffee. I can smell it brewing. I can't believe I slept so long."

"I tried not to wake you. You looked so peaceful...and beautiful. I love watching you sleep."

Tamara wrinkled her nose at him. "So, are we going to see your folks while I'm here?"

"I asked them all over for a barbecue this afternoon. I hope that's okay."

"Of course, I want to see them. I'd love to, in fact. I thought I'd see about getting together with Kathleen before I go home. I don't have to be back until Monday night, and I thought you'd be working Monday. Is that okay with you? I'll leave in the afternoon and drive home."

"Sure, that'd be good. I think you two will be great friends, and Kathleen needs a friend now. That stupid Sam dumped her for another woman after stringing her along for over three years. Now, he's going to marry the other woman. Can you believe that one?"

"Sounds par for the course. Poor Kathleen, she waited all that time because she thought he was afraid of commitment. It's doubly hard when he's ready to jump into marriage immediately with this new one. She has to feel like a fool, besides being hurt," Tamara sympathized. "Is she coming over today too?"

"I hope so, unless she's still moping around her apartment."

The family began their arrival in the

afternoon, with Ryan and Patty being the first to arrive. Barry pulled right behind them in his new Honda Insight, bringing a girlfriend with him.

Grant walked out to greet them. “Come on, Tamara. Let’s go see the new jalopy. My folks are already inspecting it.” He called to Barry, “Whoa, that’s sweet. When’d you get it?”

“Last night. Thought I’d surprise everyone,” Barry shouted proudly.

Ryan spoke up, “Well, you surprised us all right. I knew you’ve been saving up, but wow. They let you buy it without a co-signer...only your part time job?”

“Dad’s just worried about you working too many hours with school and all,” Patty chimed in.

“I know. Don’t worry. I’ve got it covered. Isn’t it awesome?” Barry said enthusiastically.

Patty interrupted, “Aren’t you going to introduce us to your friend?”

He turned to his girlfriend, taking her arm. “I’m sorry, I was so excited about the car, I forgot to introduce you. Everyone, this is Monica. Monica, my mom, dad, brother Grant, and his friend, Tamara. I guess my sister’s not here yet.”

Patty stepped up to Monica and said, “Welcome, it’s so nice to meet you. You go to college with Barry?”

“Nice to meet you too, Mrs. Larson. Yes, I do go to school with Barry. I met him in a computer class we're both taking," Monica said in a small voice.

"That's good. I enjoy meeting Barry's friends. It's nice you could come." Turning to Tamara, Patty said, "Tamara, Grant told me about your mom. I'm so sorry for your loss. Cancer's a terrible thing."

"Thank you. At least she's out of pain."

Patty stroked Tamara's back and turned her head toward Grant. "Shall we all go inside, Grant?"

"Sure Mom," Grant replied. I want to check out Barry's car a little more, but why don't you all go on in. I'll be in in a minute."

The three women walked in the house while the men stood admiring the car. Patty immediately walked to the kitchen and opened the refrigerator door, examining the contents. She removed some tomatoes from the bin and began slicing.

Tamara spoke up, reaching for a knife, "Here, let me help. What can I cut up? What about the pickles or lettuce or something?"

"Sure," Patty responded. "How about some pickles and cheese, and I'll do the onions."

Kathleen pulled in the driveway and parked behind Barry. As she got out of the car, she called, "Nice set of wheels, Bro."

"Yeah, nothing but the best," Barry replied,

giving her a wink.

"Where's Mom? Is Tamara here?" Kathleen asked.

Grant replied, "Mom went in the house, and yes, Tamara's in there too."

After quickly giving each of them a hug, Kathleen hurried into the house, calling, "Where are you guys?"

"In the kitchen, Dear. Come join us," Mom answered. Kathleen entered the kitchen and discovered her mom slicing tomatoes.

"Hi Honey. Come meet Barry's friend, Monica. They go to school together. And you know Tamara."

"Hi Monica. I'm Barry's sister, Kathleen." She turned to Tamara. "I'm glad you made it down, Tamara."

"Me too. By the way, are you free for lunch Monday? I thought maybe we could have lunch together before I head back home."

"I'd love to. I know I can meet you for lunch, but maybe I can get the day off, or at least half day and show you around the area. Let me check."

"Great," Tamara responded.

The three men sauntered into the house chatting about the car.

"Anyone hungry?" Grant asked. "I'll start the barbecue." Seeing his mom working in the kitchen, he called, "Hey, Mom, what're you doing taking over my job? Go relax. You're not supposed to be working. You're company today."

"You know I love to help. I saw you already had the meat made into patties," his mom responded.

"You trained him well," Ryan chimed in.

After everyone had their appetites satisfied and had time for socializing and joking, it was time to say goodnight.

Tamara was amazed how much "at home" she felt with Grant's family. She was completely at ease. They made her feel as if she belonged. On Monday morning Tamara kissed Grant goodbye, and he promised to come up to her house the following weekend. She was almost convinced that she was ready to introduce him to her family. As she placed some dishes in the dishwasher, the phone rang. It was Kathleen. She was able to take the morning off and would pick her up shortly.

After finishing cleaning up the kitchen from breakfast and packing her few things in preparation for the drive home, Tamara sat out on Grant's porch. Above her head, she noticed two large birds with enormous wing spans, gliding with the air currents. They looked majestically graceful circling the skies. She wondered if they were the kind of bird Grant liked so much. She could see why he liked them. They were beautiful creatures. Her thoughts were interrupted when

Kathleen's horn tooted. She waved as she pulled up in front of the house, the stereo blaring an old Elvis classic, "Are you Lonesome Tonight."

"Morning," Kathleen called. "You ready, or should I come in?"

Tamara grabbed her purse. "I'm ready. How're you doing this morning?" Tamara walked around the car to the passenger side, opened the door, and got in.

Kathleen turned the stereo down a notch. "I'm okay, just feeling sorry for myself. I'm afraid that's been my usual thing these last few weeks. I'm glad I'm having a change of routine today. Did Grant tell you about Sam dumping me for another woman?"

"Yes, he did. I'm sorry," Tamara said sympathetically. "It has to be really difficult after being with him so long."

"It's not just that. It's the fact that he wants to marry her right away. I kept thinking I had to give him time because he was afraid of commitment, but it wasn't that. He didn't want me permanently."

"You'll meet someone who's right for you, Kathleen. Give it time. This guy definitely was not the one. You're better off without him."

"Yeah, but I'm thirty years old, and I want to start a family. I don't have a lot of time." Kathleen heaved a sigh.

"I'm the same age as you, Kathleen, so I can sort of understand what you mean. Those thoughts were never important to me before, but lately I've been changing," Tamara admitted.

"I wasted way too much time with the son of a bitch. But, damn, I really thought he was the one." Kathleen slammed her hand on the steering wheel. "Sorry, I guess I'm really angry at myself for being such a fool and believing all his lies. Let's change the subject. I can't think about that idiot any longer."

"Good idea. This might be a little too soon, but I work with a really cool guy who I think you might like. Would you like me to see if he's interested in getting together? I know he doesn't have a girlfriend right now. He's around our age, has a good job, and is a really great guy. I think you'd like him. He's nice looking too...not drop dead gorgeous, but a good looking guy."

"I don't know, maybe, but, give me a couple of weeks. Right now, I wouldn't be very good company for anyone."

"Good, not this time, but maybe next time Grant comes up to see me, he could bring you with him, and we could double. That way, you wouldn't feel threatened. He had a girl he'd been going with give him a 'Dear John' a few months back, so you have something in common. Incidentally, his name is Lance."

"Tamara, Mom told me about you losing your mom. That had to be really hard. I'm sorry."

"Thank you. It's strange to think she's really gone. We weren't close. I don't know if Grant told you, but Mom left me when I was little, and my grandmother raised me."

"No, he didn't tell me that."

"Oh well, that's another story. So, where're we going?" Tamara asked.

"I thought I'd show you a little of Santa Barbara before we go to lunch. I have until one o'clock to be back to school," Kathleen said. "You know, Santa Barbara is a unique town. I'm afraid I'll only be able to show you the tip of the iceberg. There are so many outstanding small museums, great restaurants and shopping arcades. There's Stearns Wharf and the botanical gardens. But, today I'm taking you to Mission Santa Barbara. I've brought my classes there for years."

"Sounds good. I see red tile roofs everywhere I look. I really like the Spanish influence. I know there's a lot of old money in Santa Barbara," Tamara reflected.

When they arrived, Kathleen exclaimed, "Here it is, the 'Queen of Missions.' You can see why. It's really the centerpiece of the entire town. I guess you could say it sets the theme because it reflects Santa Barbara's past and present. It kind of sits here like a queen overlooking all of her subjects. Look at the magnificent twin bell towers."

"I love the stone facade on the walls," Tamara said.

"They're patterned after an ancient Latin temple."

"It's the tenth mission in the chain of the twenty-one Franciscan missions in California. The 1925 earthquake severely damaged the original mission, but the restoration completely reflects the original appearance. Isn't it great? Well, you can see, I really love it."

"It is beautiful," Tamara agreed.

After spending time touring the grounds, the water fountain with the lily pads, the cemetery, and the chapel, Kathleen suggested they leave for lunch.

She drove them to a quaint Spanish style restaurant which had always been one of her favorites. The hostess ushered them to a small corner patio table. Kathleen and Tamara were forced to silence in order to concentrate on the extensive menu.

"I can't decide. There are so many good things. What're you having?" Tamara probed.

"I'm not sure, but I'm leaning toward the spicy chicken salad with toasted almonds and avocado."

"That does sound good. I was looking at that salad. The taco salad with grilled chicken or fish sounds good too."

"Yeah, it does. Think I'll have that...with chicken," Kathleen declared.

"Tamara laughed. "You sold me on the spicy chicken salad." Kathleen joined her laughing.

"This is such a cute place. I love the bougainvillea and nasturtiums growing up the lattice work," Tamara said.

Kathleen lowered her voice and asked, "Have you noticed the woman at that table over there? She keeps getting up and putting chips on the wall for the birds?"

"I did, and the man she's with is breaking chips up and throwing them on the ground for the smaller birds. I don't know if the owners appreciate that, but it's fun to watch."

Kathleen reached across the table and placed her hand on top of Tamara's. "Tamara, I'm so happy you and Grant are seeing each other. I've been really worried about my big brother. Ever since his wife died, it seemed as if a part of him died too. He's like another person now. He's full of life and happy. I don't know if he told you how his wife died or not."

"Yes, he said she died from a car bomb explosion," Tamara responded. "And that she was a stewardess on an airline."

"Right, well, she wasn't in her car. It was a man's car, and he died in the explosion with her.

It was the man the bomb was probably aimed at, and Malika was only an innocent bystander. Well, not so innocent. They discovered she had spent the night at a hotel with the man before the explosion. Someone apparently wanted him dead. He was involved in some way with the Russian mafia. Anyway, both Malika's death and her being unfaithful were quite a shock to Grant."

Tamara sat silent, allowing Kathleen's words to sink in. "Thanks for sharing this with me, Kathleen. It helps me understand Grant better. Besides the loss of someone he loved, he felt betrayed. And then he had no release. He couldn't confront Malika, or have any of his questions answered because she was gone. How awful for him."

Kathleen shook her head and glanced at her watch. "He went into a shell and buried himself in his work. We didn't see him much for a long time. When we'd ask him why he hadn't been over, he'd only say he wasn't good company right now and needed time alone. Anyway, you've changed all of that."

Tamara responded, "It's not only me. I think time helps to heal wounds of the spirit."

After lunch was finished, Kathleen drove Tamara back to the ranch, hugged her goodbye, and promised to consider a date with Lance.

Chapter Ten

Tamara knew she would see Lance the following day. She had heard he'd had a favorable meeting with Frederick Mason and had been hired by Excel Media last week. She thought she was right in telling Kathleen that Lance was nice looking. He certainly wasn't ugly. He looked a little like Tom Hanks. He had dark curly hair and a great personality. Tamara enjoyed having lunch with Kathleen and getting to know her a little better. She hoped Lance would be agreeable to meet Kathleen because she felt they'd be good for each other.

Arriving home, her first chore was calling her grandmother. Hearing her voice, she responded, "Hi Grandmother. It's Tamara. I've given you several days to think it over. How about me picking you and Gracie up tomorrow after work and bringing you to my house for a couple of days?"

"I don't really think–"

Tamara interrupted. "It would be a little vacation for you. You've never even seen my house."

"I'd like to see where you live. I really would, but I don't know if I could handle it," her grandmother said honestly.

"Why don't we try it. If you're too uncomfortable, I'll take you home the next day. Okay?"

"Well, maybe I'll try it. What time will you be coming for us?"

"I'll be there around five. I'll come straight from work. Thank you, Grandmother. It'll be fun. I know it will."

The first person Tamara saw the next day when she entered the Excel Media building was Lance.

"Lance, it's so good to see your smiling face. I've missed working with you," Tamara exclaimed.

"Me too...with you, that is. How was your weekend?"

"Great. How's the new job coming? You like it?"

"Yeah, it sure beats Innovative Insights. I like the people I'm working with. It makes all the difference."

"I have a meeting right now, but I'll call you. I have something I want to talk to you about. Talk to you later," Tamara called on her way into the conference room.

"Hey, Tamara," Frederick said, the leather chair squeaking as he got up. "Take a seat and we'll get started shortly."

Tamara pulled out a chair and sat down, crossing her legs.

Hani entered the room and sat across from Tamara. The rest of the seats around the conference table quickly filled, and the meeting commenced.

The shapely knee over the other one didn't go unnoticed by Hani. Tamara felt his watchful eyes on her and glanced in his direction. His eyes penetrated her, and he gave her an odd smile. Tamara shifted in her seat, her eyes avoiding contact with Hani. Her foot commenced dancing, and her pencil tapped against the desk.

The meeting ended, and Tamara went to her office. Within minutes, Tamara heard her office door open. Digging in the bottom drawer, she looked up and saw Hani entering, closing the door behind him.

He walked over to her and spoke, "Tamara, I've made up my mind. You're the woman I want. I wanted you to know that."

Slapping a folder down on her desk, Tamara took a deep breath and responded, "Excuse me. What are you talking about? You're a married man."

"I told you my wife left me. I no longer want her. I want you. I've given it much thought, and you're what I need."

"Hani, we're friends. I like you very much, but only as a friend. Can you understand that? I have a man I'm seeing. In fact, I think I'm in love with him."

"Well, that's disappointing." He paused a minute before continuing. "Maybe you'll change your mind now that you know how I feel," Hani pressed.

"I'm not like that, Hani. I don't just change my mind. Is your wife completely out of your life? Have you filed for divorce yet?"

"I don't need any papers to get rid of her. We're divorced in my mind. The thought of her makes me sick." He grimaced.

"Well, in this country it's not that simple. Either you or she needs to file for the divorce."

"So, what do you care if I'm divorced? Would it make a difference in how you feel toward me?" Hani probed.

She wanted to wipe the smirk off his face. "No, I was only talking to you like a friend."

Hani gave Tamara a hard stare and walked

out of her office, his footsteps echoing on the hard wood floor.

Happy to get home after work, Tamara stepped out of her shoes, feeling the cool oak wood floor on her bare feet. Sensing a presence, she stopped in her tracks, listening. Christopher walked through the kitchen door with a glass of juice in his hand.

"What the–are you crazy? I'm sick to death of you coming in my house and scaring the wits out of me." Tamara took a deliberate breath, attempting to steady her nerves. "What if I had a gun? Then, you'd be sorry."

"If you had a gun, I wouldn't have a chance to be sorry." Christopher laughed. "Okay, I didn't mean to scare you."

Tamara rolled her eyes and gave him an annoyed look, but said nothing. Then she looked at Toby wagging his tail. "Fine watch dog you are."

Christopher continued," So, have you broken it off with your friend?"

"I told you to butt out of my personal life." Tamara glared at him.

"You have no private life, Tamara. Your life belongs to our agency. I thought you understood that when you agreed to join us."

"My relationship with Grant has nothing to do

with my job," she snapped.

Christopher released a big sigh. "It affects everything you do. We've had this discussion before. Fortunately, this last job went well. But, you need to know how serious the matter is. The consequences could be huge."

Tamara turned and made eye contact. "What do you mean the consequences could be big? What are you talking about?"

He took a sip and put his glass down before speaking. "The separation from the agency isn't that easy. It could become quite complicated, and you'd be at the short end."

She almost choked the words out. "What–what's that supposed to mean?"

"How about you'd be six feet under."

Tamara arrived at her Grandmother's home the following day right after work. She found both Gracie and her grandmother upstairs still placing things in a small suitcase.

"Hi, can I help?" Tamara asked.

"No, I'm having a hard time deciding what I'll need at your house."

"You won't need much. It's only for a few days."

"You don't understand my needs, Tamara. I

have things I must have with me," Grandmother said with irritation clearly showing in her voice.

"Okay, are your things ready, Gracie?"

"My bag's all set downstairs. I'll go take it out to the car." Gracie turned to Tamara's grandmother. "Is there anything else I can help you with?"

"No, Gracie, I think I'm almost ready."

Tamara decided to go downstairs and talk with Gracie in order to stay out of her grandmother's hair. It was obvious her grandmother was dragging her feet in leaving the house. All she could do was wait until she was ready to leave.

When they finally arrived at Tamara's home, Grandmother stepped into Tamara's living room, taking in the sight of the ocean and said, "I must say, this is a wonderful view you have."

"Yes, it is. I never get tired of looking at it. Toby raced into the room to greet them. Her grandmother stood frozen. "Get this creature away from me. You didn't tell me you had a dog." Gracie reached down to pet him. Tamara took Toby by the collar and put him outside.

"Let me show you your room upstairs." Tamara led her grandmother and Gracie up the stairs. The second bedroom wasn't quite as large as the master bedroom, but it also had a balcony overlooking the ocean below. "Gracie, this room is for you."

"Oh my, this is nice." Gracie put her things down and walked out on the balcony.

"Good, now, Grandmother, let's go into the next room where you'll be staying." She led her grandmother into her own bedroom. Tamara planned on sleeping on the couch downstairs.

"Thank you, Tamara. I think I'll rest until dinner," her grandmother said, sitting down on the edge of the bed.

"That's a good idea. I'll call when dinner's ready." She knocked on Gracie's door. "Anything I can do for you? Grandmother's going to rest while I'm fixing dinner."

"Why don't I come help," Gracie suggested.

"No, you're my guest. You just relax, or come and visit with me...whatever you'd like."

"I think it's great that you got your grandmother away from the house. This is a first in a long time. I've been worried about her. She forced herself to fly to Seattle to see Robin, but we only stayed a few hours and came right home. It was a difficult trip for her."

"I'm glad too. I hope she enjoys it." She should have known her grandmother wouldn't like dogs.

"She's been keeping the blinds closed with everything dark. It's depressing. She's refused to leave the house until today. This is a big stride for her," Gracie assured her.

During dinner, Tamara's grandmother brought the conversation around to a personal level. "So, do you have a special male friend?"

"Well, actually, I do. I was going to tell you about him. This is the first man I've ever felt I wanted as a part of my life."

"What's he like? Does he come from a good family?" Grandmother probed.

"His family's wonderful. If you mean what I think you do by good, I don't know, and I could care less," Tamara shot back, tossing her hair back over her shoulder.

"Those things are important, Dear," Grandmother cautioned.

"I wanted you to meet him, but I have no intention of having him grilled." Tamara counted silently to five, struggling to control her temper. There was an uncomfortable silence in the room.

"You have never liked the men I introduced you to. I thought you were being selective by waiting. Was I wrong?"

"Oh, come on, Grandmother. Get off your high horse. What makes you think we're any better than anyone else?" Tamara glared for a minute and sighed. "Okay, I don't want our evening ruined. Let's change the subject. But first, let me say one more thing. I think you'd actually like Grant very much if you gave him a chance. He's a wonderful man."

Gracie sat silently through the entire conversation. At this point she broke in, "Did your grandmother tell you she's ordered all new drapes for her house?"

Tamara laughed to herself. Gracie always knew how to calm a potential explosion.

They continued to avoid the subject of Grant. Tamara managed to keep them for two entire days before returning to Grandmother's home. She cut the engine and came around to open the door on Grandmother's side.

"Thank you, Tamara. We had a lovely visit," Grandmother climbed out of the car.

Tamara pulled the back door open as Gracie chimed in, "We really did, and your house is wonderful. We're both proud of you."

"It was so good having you. We'll have to do it again."

When Tamara returned home and apologized to Toby for having to stay outside, she reflected on the past few days. Except for the altercation with her grandmother the first evening, the rest of the visit had gone well.

Tamara picked up the phone. "Hey, Lance, how's it going?"

"Great, I just fixed myself an egg sandwich. Not very creative, but it'll have to do."

"I know I'll probably see you at the office, but I wanted to see if you might be interested in something. You remember I told you about my friend, Grant?" Tamara asked.

"Yes, how could I not remember that?" Lance chuckled.

"Well, he has a younger sister who was recently dumped by her boyfriend. I thought she was in need of cheering up, and I thought of you. Maybe we could double or something because I know blind dates can be uncomfortable. She's cute and has a great personality, so I think you might really like her. What do you think?"

"I don't know. I usually make a policy to avoid blind dates at all costs."

"So, the policy's carved in stone? You might be missing out on someone wonderful all because of a policy."

"I suppose I could try it once. But, if she's a dog, you're dead meat." Lance chuckled.

"You won't have to worry about that. I'll see what I can do to get something set up for a week from Saturday, okay?" Tamara pressed.

"Sounds good, but is she still hung up on the boyfriend?"

"I don't think so. She's just angry, mostly at herself for wasting so much time on him. You know the feeling. I thought that's something you both have in common. She's a teacher, by the way...first grade, and her name's Kathleen."

"Oh–"

Grant arrived on the weekend, and Tamara surprised him by telling him she was planning to take him to meet her grandmother and Gracie the following day.

"Just remember, Grandmother thinks she's Mrs. Astor...better than anyone else. You'll have to be ready to be grilled, not just about you, but your family as well. Get yourself ready to take the stand. That's why I've put this off."

"Don't worry about it. I'm not made of glass. I won't crumble. Your little old granny isn't going to scare me away. Anyway, look what I put you through."

"Yeah, but your parents were nothing compared to my grandmother. In fact, they were great."

The following morning Tamara smiled as she lay back on the soft sheets and listened to Grant singing in the shower. It was nice having a man around the house. But, she told herself she better not get used to it after the lecture Christopher gave her. She trusted Christopher was her friend and had difficulty believing he was serious. However, something told her she shouldn't take it lightly. She filed his little talk into the far corner of her mind, not wanting to think about it.

Grant walked out of the bathroom, with nothing but a towel wrapped around his middle, and abruptly stopped singing when he saw Tamara staring at him with an amused smile on her face.

He laughed, suddenly embarrassed. "I guess I thought I was Harry Connick, Jr. for a minute there. I wasn't too bad, was I?"

"You were absolutely wonderful." She looked him up and down. "I especially like your singing outfit." She tugged at the towel, causing it to drop. Grant grabbed the towel and pulled it back, snapping it at her as he dropped to the bed. She reached up and ran her fingertips across his cheek. "You are pretty gorgeous, you know."

"Tell me more," he said as he gathered her into his arms.

Later in the day, they pulled into the driveway at Tamara's grandmother's home. Since they were arriving unexpectedly, Tamara rang the bell.

"Tamara," Gracie said, answering the door, "What a pleasant surprise. You've brought your friend." She turned to Grant. "Hi, I'm Gracie. I've heard good things about you."

"Well, I see Tamara's been telling fibs again. Kidding aside, I've been looking forward to meeting you. Tamara has told me how important you are to her."

Gracie smiled and led them to the library, saying to Tamara's grandmother, "Look who's here. Tamara has brought her gentleman friend to meet you."

Grandmother looked up with a start from the corner of the room where she sat with a book in her lap, giving Tamara a look that would melt an iceberg. She held her words before she spoke slowly, "I wasn't expecting you, Tamara. I wish you had called."

"I'm sorry. I didn't know I needed to. I'd like you to meet my friend, Grant Larson."

"How do you do Mr. Larson," Grandmother responded, with a chill in her voice. "Won't you take a seat." She motioned to a seat across the room.

"Thank you," he said. "You have a lovely home. Is this where Tamara was raised?" Grant sat back in the chair. Tamara walked over and took a chair next to him, reaching out and patting his arm.

"Yes, it is. I've lived here for close to forty years. And where do you live, Mr. Larson?" Grandmother inquired, stiffening her shoulders and sitting up straight in the seat.

"I have a house in Santa Barbara. Actually, my whole family is from there." Grant smiled, thinking of his family.

"I presume your family is from the 'old money'

crowd of Santa Barbara."

Grant laughed. "No, not really. My mom was a teacher, and my dad a police detective. I'm very proud of both of them."

"Oh." A poignant silence followed. "And what do you do for a living, Mr. Larson?"

"I work in a similar field as your granddaughter...the computer field."

"Umm. Well, I tried to get Tamara to chose a more worthwhile profession, but she never listens." The silence was deafening until Grandmother continued the grilling. "What university did you attend?"

Tamara tried to hold her temper, but finally broke in. "Okay, that's enough. The interrogation is over. Besides, you're being too modest, Grant." Turning to her grandmother, she said, "He has a lovely ranch house on twenty acres. But, we're not here for Grant to impress you, Grandmother. I wanted Grant to meet my family."

"I see. Well, I'll just call Gracie, and we'll have some tea. What would you like to talk about, Tamara?" Grandmother asked, disdainfully.

If Tamara was going to have any kind of a relationship with her grandmother, she would have to speak up. She had played the obedient silent granddaughter far too long. Keeping a distance for ten years had been her solution. But, it wasn't any solution at all. She loved her grandmother. After all, she and Gracie were all the family she had.

Ignoring her grandmother's arrogant attitude, Tamara responded, "How about what fun we had together at my house? The three of us even played cribbage, and Grandmother won."

"I must say it was a good time," Grandmother relented.

Gracie interrupted their conversation by appearing with a tray of goodies. Tamara observed her grandmother leaning back like a queen on her throne, waiting for her servant to pour the tea.

Tamara quickly stood up and said, "Gracie, let me help. Why don't you sit down and join us for a minute. We'd like you to get to talk with Grant too." Turning to her grandmother, she continued, "Don't you agree, Grandmother?"

Flustered, Grandmother studied Tamara for a moment, and responded, "Of course, Gracie, please join us."

Grant winked at Tamara over the tea cup, giving her half a grin.

CHAPTER ELEVEN

TAMARA THOUGHT SHE SHOULD BE USED TO Christopher scaring the living daylights out of her, but she wasn't. Once again, she jumped a mile when he surprised her as she entered her house after Grant left for Santa Barbara. It bothered her that he seemed to appear out of nowhere. It didn't exactly help her feel safe in her home if Christopher could get in so easily. Unfortunately, Toby seemed to love him.

Tamara glared at Christopher. "So what do you want now? I thought we discussed last time that you'd let me know you were coming." She didn't wait for an answer. She pushed past him and walked into the kitchen, took a glass out of the cupboard, and got herself water from the refrigerator.

He grabbed her shoulder. "Okay, stop for a minute, and listen to me."

Tamara spun around and shouted, “Why should I? You don’t listen to me.”

Endeavoring to keep things low pitched, Christopher spoke slowly in a quiet voice, “Let’s go into the living room and sit down.”

“If you’re here to rag at me about Grant, forget it,” Tamara snapped. She turned and walked back to the living room.

“Look, I’m only here because I’m your friend. I want what’s best for you,” Christopher said, attempting to disarm her anger.

“Okay, so spit it out,” Tamara said, sitting down on the couch. She kicked off her shoes and drew her legs up under her.

“Have you thought at all about what I told you last time?” Christopher asked as he sat down beside her.

“I’ve tried not to.”

“Well, have you?” Christopher probed.

Tamara clutched the arm of the couch, her voice wavering. “Yes, how could I help but think about it?” She winced and gave a deep sigh. “I don’t know, Christopher. What if I stay away from Grant for a while? If I cool it down, will the agency, or whoever they are, leave me alone?” She waited a full minute for a response.

“I think it would help,” Christopher conceded. ”Now, let’s talk business. I have an assignment for you.”

Tamara deliberated on the best way to handle the situation. She'd try cooling it down with Grant, but she knew she needed to see him the following weekend because they had already set up a meeting with Kathleen and Lance. It wouldn't be the best time to talk to Grant because Kathleen would be staying at Tamara's house too. She cogitated on how she would tell Grant she wouldn't be seeing him for a while. Christopher had always been a friend, as long as she did what he wanted. She needed to regain his confidence in her. Then, she'd make her decision on Grant.

The full work week flew by. Plus, Tamara completed the assignment Christopher had given her. Grant and Kathleen were due to arrive any minute. The coffee was brewing, and she had some super chocolatey brownies in the oven. The smell was making her stomach growl with anticipation. A pair of headlights flashed through the window announcing their arrival.

Tamara opened the front door and called out, "It's about time you two got here. My stomach couldn't wait much longer for the brownies."

"Brownies? Whoa, aren't you Miss Suzie homemaker." Kathleen laughed, as she got out of the car and hugged Tamara.

You know what they say, the way to a man's

heart is through his stomach," Grant said. "And I do love brownies." He pushed the car door shut and walked around it, taking Tamara in his arms.

"I thought I already had your heart." Tamara pulled back and made a pretend pout.

Grant's mouth came down hard against Tamara's lips. "I hope that pout's gone from those beautiful lips now."

"Oh, come on, you two. Enough of this talking about brownies. How about let's go have some." Kathleen smiled, reaching in the back seat to grab her bag.

Tamara thought to herself. *What am I doing? Flirting, that's what. What a jerk. And I'm supposed to be putting him off.* "Sure, let's go inside."

Grant popped the trunk lid, pulled out his overnight bag, and walked up the step to the house. "Wait 'til you see the view from her deck. It's really something, Kathleen."

Kathleen set her things down by the door, her eyes roaming the room, and walked outside to the deck. The full moon cast its glow on the waves, crashing on the rocks and sand below. "How do you ever drag yourself away from this deck? I could stay out here forever," Kathleen squealed, leaning over the deck and looking down.

"Come on, Kathleen. You need to see the rest of the house," Grant urged.

When Tamara and Grant were finally able to retire to the bedroom, Tamara took Grant's hand and led him out to the deck. Grant placed his hand around her waist and pulled her close.

Searching her eyes, Grant uttered, "You know, I'm in love with you, Tamara. I've been counting the minutes until we could be together."

Tamara's heart pounded in her chest with excitement. She yearned for Grant's touch, wanting to smother him with kisses. Her mind was in complete turmoil. She pulled back, seeking to gain control of her emotions.

She touched her fingertips to his arm. "Grant, I've wanted us to be together too, but I think we're going a little too fast for me. I think we need to cool it down and take it a little slower."

His mouth flew open. "What? Why? What's wrong with what we're feeling? What's going on? Talk to me."

"Well, nothing, but I've never been in love before. This whole thing is new to me. You've been married before. I've never had feelings like this...ever. I need a little time to understand what's happening to me. I want us to...well,...not see each other so much, just for now." Tamara placed her hand on his forearm and stroked it. "Please understand, Grant."

Grant ran his fingers through his hair. He couldn't conceive where she was coming from.

"Yeah, right. You need time to be away from me. I understand, all right."

Tamara gripped his arm and leaned against him. "Why can't you understand? This is a major commitment I'm considering. I have to be sure. It scares me."

"Yeah, well, it's big for me too, and I don't seem to be running away from it." He glared at her.

She returned his stare. "You say I don't understand where you're coming from, but you certainly don't understand where I'm coming from."

Grant's arms were crossed over his chest. "You're right, I don't. But, hey, you say you need your space. You've got it." Grant turned and walked away.

Tamara ran after him, grabbing his arm. "Why are you taking it like this? You know I care for you very much. I just need time to sort out my feelings. I mean...can we agree on that much?" She narrowed her eyes at him. "You know I have feelings for you." Tamara looked at Grant with a question in her eyes.

Grant stood looking at her for a long minute, shaking his head. "You're making it really hard for me, Tamara. Yes, I know you care for me. At least I thought you had feelings for me, but, I guess things are always black or white for me. I either love you, or I don't, so it's difficult for me to make sense of not being sure."

Tamara touched her fingers to Grant's cheek. "Kathleen told me about Malika cheating on you. I want you to know I'm not being unfaithful and I never would be. All I'm asking for is a little time."

He turned away and shook his head. "She didn't need to tell you that."

"I know she didn't, but I'm glad she did. It helps me understand where you're coming from. I–"

Interrupting, Grant struggled with his words. "I've never told anyone some of the things about Malika. This wasn't the first time she had an affair. I had the nightmare of catching her in the act with some guy in my own bedroom."

Tamara stopped him. "You don't have to tell me this Grant."

"I know I don't. I want to. I want you to hear it all. I came home unexpectedly. I wasn't due back until the following morning. I let myself in and called out to Malika. There was no response so I walked down the hall to the bedroom and heard the shower running." He paused and took a breath. "Not wanting to scare her, I called out again before opening the bedroom door. There was Malika on the bed completely naked."

"Oh my god, how awful." Tamara gasped.

"It took me a few minutes to process the scene.

After recovering my senses, I asked her who was in the shower. Before she could respond, the door opened and a man appeared with only a towel wrapped around his middle."

Tamara's jaw dropped. "What...you must have been furious."

Grant nodded without smiling, acknowledging an observation that was self-evident. He shook his head. "I don't know what I was...bewildered, hurt, angry as hell, and I felt terribly betrayed."

"What'd you do?"

"I didn't say a word. I turned and walked out."

"But you took her back?" Tamara asked.

"Yes, probably a stupid thing to do, especially in hindsight after seeing what happened at the end. She was so repentant and swore it would never happen again. I kicked her out at first. It was months before I let her move back." He looked away, suddenly embarrassed. "It's hard to explain without sounding like a naive jerk."

"I understand. You loved her and wanted to believe her." Tamara sympathized.

"I really think I was just too much of a straight arrow for her...too boring. She craved excitement."

"Well, it seems she got it." Tamara shook her head.

"Then when she was killed in the car crash and it came out that she had been having an affair with the guy in the car, I felt betrayed again. I really thought it was a one time thing, and here I was duped again." He paused. "Besides having her die, I felt foolish and stupid."

"She was the foolish and stupid one, Grant." Tamara patted his arm.

Grant gave her a half smile. "I don't understand any of it. The whole thing is still hard for me to believe. It shows you how naive I am. I want you to be as sure of us, Tamara, as I am. I don't want any uncertainties on your part. So, I guess what I'm saying is take your time and be sure."

"Thank you. I'm sorry, Grant, I didn't mean to ruin our weekend. Let's try and have a good weekend and put this aside for now." Tamara leaned over and kissed him lightly on the lips.

Grant rubbed his chin slowly. "Okay, Tamara. We'll put it aside for now."

"Thank you for understanding," Tamara said, patting his hand.

Grant pulled back. "I didn't say I understood. I said we'd put it aside for now."

She nodded. "Okay, I guess that's all I can ask."

The following morning while Grant was in the shower, Tamara's thoughts turned to the night before. Grant had said they'd put it aside, but there had been a definite change in both his attitude and behavior. He hadn't even attempted to touch her and had turned over and gone to sleep. There was no conversation, no cuddling, no passionate love making...nothing. This morning, they made polite conversation, but something was missing. Tamara cursed Christopher for forcing her to cool it with Grant.

Tamara opened the bedroom door, and the smell of bacon drew her down to the kitchen. "Something smells really good." She dropped into a chair at the table.

"Morning," Kathleen said. "I made coffee if you want some."

"Hey, I'm supposed to be the hostess. How come you're doing all the work?" Tamara asked.

"Oh, I got up early. I don't know, I guess I'm nervous over meeting Lance. I have to stay busy when I'm nervous. I hope you don't mind. How do you like your eggs?"

"Over easy is good...just one, please. And, of course, I don't mind." Tamara got up and poured a cup of coffee.

"Is Grant coming out soon?" Kathleen asked.

"I think so. He was getting out of the shower when I came out. This is really a treat, Kathleen. I'll have to have you up more often."

"What time is Lance coming over?" Kathleen asked.

"I think he said around eleven. Don't be

nervous. You're going to feel as if you've known him forever."

Grant walked into the room. "What are you two up to? I couldn't stand it. The smell was driving me crazy."

Tamara chimed in, "Kathleen's making breakfast for us."

"Sure has my stomach turning flips. Glad Mom taught you to cook." He smiled at Kathleen, picked up a piece of the bacon and placed it quickly in his mouth.

Kathleen gave his hand a playful slap. "Stop that. Everything's almost ready. What are you talking about? She taught you to cook too. In fact, you're a great cook."

"God, you remind me of Mom." Grant laughed.

Close to eleven o'clock, they were sitting on the deck when the door bell rang and Tamara said, "Oh, that must be Lance." She saw Kathleen suck in her breath. Tamara patted her hand and said, "Calm down," on the way to the door.

Tamara came back to the deck with Lance at her side. "Kathleen, Grant, I want you both to meet my good friend, Lance."

Lance clasped Kathleen's hand and said with a smile, "Kathleen, you're every bit as pretty as Tamara said you were."

Kathleen laughed. "Well, thank you. I see you have a bit of the blarney in you."

Lance flashed her an innocent smile. “You don’t know me yet. I only tell the absolute truth.” He turned to Grant and held out his hand as he said, “I’m happy to meet the man who’s finally stolen Tamara’s heart.”

The two men shook hands and Grant spoke up, “I’d like to think so. Nice to meet you, Lance.”

After the initial meeting was over, Tamara could see Kathleen relaxing. She hoped something would click with them because they both deserved some happiness after the jerks they’d been going with dumped them. She thought she was doing all she could by playing cupid and introducing them. She’d have to butt out now and let nature take its course. Tamara planned to take them to lunch on the municipal wharf, and it turned out to be a good decision. They appeared to be having a wonderful time together.

"There are so many sea lions. It’s like they’re talking to each other,” Kathleen said.

“They really bellow. I’ve come down here when there weren’t any sea lions around. It’s a lot more fun when they’re here,” Lance responded. “I love watching the way they get up on the crossbeams under the wharf.”

They strolled past the little shops selling surfing and tourist goodies. It was a beautiful clear day, and the air was thick with the smell of fish as they walked past the fish market near the end of the pier. They stopped a few times to watch and see what the fisherman had on the end of their poles. Tamara noticed that Lance and Kathleen were chatting with each other as they walked, while she and Grant were noticeably silent. She thought she'd made a mistake bringing up the needing time bit before the end of their visit. It felt as if there was a chasm between them. Lance and Kathleen were a fair distance ahead of them when Tamara pulled Grant to a halt. Tamara shaded her eyes with her hand as she looked at Grant. "I can't stand this wall between us. I thought we were going to put it aside and have a good time."

Grant's eyebrow went up. He leaned down and tied his shoe before he spoke, "I'm sorry. I guess I've just been deep in thought. I'll try and do better."

Tamara brushed him lightly with her lips, searching his eyes. She took his hand and rushed to catch up with Kathleen and Lance.

They went into a restaurant near the end of the pier for fish and chips. They figured they couldn't go wrong on their choice of restaurants. All the restaurants had fresh fish and great views of the ocean.

Lance spoke up, "You know. This is funny. I only live a half hour from here, and I haven't come to the pier in ages. I don't know why, because I love it."

"That's usually the way it is. We go miles to see things and ignore the things that are right under our noses," Tamara said with a smile.

Kathleen piped up, picking up a piece of fish, "How true. Gosh, this fish is sure good. I love it when you can find halibut and chips. It's usually cod with the chips."

Lance pointed out, "Look at that seagull perched on the railing. Someone must have left some food. He's working like crazy trying to get something off the rail."

They left the restaurant and walked over to the railing, looking at the Boardwalk in the distance. They could hear the screams of fear and excitement emanating from the Giant Dipper and other rides.

Lance said, "Did you know this is the last of the seaside boardwalks on the West Coast? They're all gone now, except for this one. The Dipper has a classic wooden track and was built way back in 1924."

"It begins in a dark tunnel," Tamara added. "That's really scary."

Grant said, "Sounds like fun."

"I like the carousel," Tamara said.

Kathleen agreed, "I'm with you."

"You should take Grant over and at least look at the carousel," Lance said to Tamara. "It's a classic, and the antique pipe organ is wonderful. The guy who hand carved the carousel horses really had a sense of humor. He carved some horses with big smiles and some showing their teeth. It's something to see."

"My folks used to come up here over twenty years ago to watch the Miss California pageant," Grant said. "They said they loved it."

"It was held right out there on the beach in front of the boardwalk. I think it's held in Fresno now." Lance pointed and then continued, "Thank you so much for getting us together. I'm going to take Kathleen over to see my place, and then I'll bring her back to your house, Tamara. That'll give you two a chance to be alone. Is that okay with both of you?"

Grant responded, "It's fine with me, if it's okay with Kathleen."

"I told Lance I'd love to see his place," Kathleen responded quickly.

"Let's go over and look at the carousel before we go back to the house," Tamara suggested. "I've been there so many times and never paid attention to what the horses looked like."

"Sure, I'd like that."

"Okay then. We'll see you later." Lance and Kathleen strolled off hand in hand toward Lance's car.

"Well, I guess that went well." Tamara

laughed.

"Looks like it."

After checking out the carousel, Tamara and Grant drove back to Tamara's home and were happy they had a little time to themselves. They had both been feeling the strain of their relationship. They made love, but they left it unspoken that something was missing.

Kathleen called that she wouldn't be home until around eleven in the evening. Arriving at Tamara's house, she couldn't contain her excitement.

"I can't believe it. He's everything you said he'd be, Tamara. I feel like I'm sixteen again, instead of thirty."

"I'm really glad you hit it off."

"Hit it off...we more than hit it off. It's like we've known each other forever. He's coming to Santa Barbara to see me next weekend," Kathleen boasted.

Grant rolled his eyes and sighed. "Come on, Kathleen. You not only feel like sixteen, you sound like sixteen."

"Oh, you don't want me to be happy? Some brother you are."

"Okay, okay, I'm not going to go there. Sorry, I liked Lance, and I'm glad you two got along. I'll leave you two girls to talk. I'm going to bed."

"I'll be up shortly," Tamara said.

Kathleen turned to Tamara. "It feels good to have someone want to be with you after getting dumped. And it's not only that, I like Lance. He's really fun to be with."

"I know, we've become really good friends." Tamara gave her a reassuring look.

The next morning, Grant and Kathleen left for Santa Barbara, and Tamara returned to work. Lance beamed when he saw Tamara. "God, Tamara, thank you so much for talking me into meeting Kathleen. She's wonderful. I haven't felt this good in ages. Let's meet for lunch so we can talk, okay?"

Tamara smiled. "Sure, see you then."

When lunch time came around, Tamara and Lance went to a little cafe around the corner and slid into a corner booth.

"So, I was right that you'd like Kathleen." Tamara smiled smugly.

"You're not kiddin'. I've been walking around functioning like a real person these last several months, but I was really a walking dead person. I feel as if I've come alive. I can't really explain it."

"I do understand." Tamara nodded her head.

"What's going on with you and Grant? You both seemed so distant. Am I wrong?"

"No, not really. I don't know. I told him I thought we were moving too fast...that we needed to slow down, and maybe not see each other for a while."

"What? Are you crazy?" Lance raised his voice. "I've seen the difference in you, Tamara...talk about coming alive. You've been a different person since Grant came in your life. Why would you wanna cool it?" He said with exasperation.

A waitress stepped up to the table, interrupting them. "Have you two decided what you'd like?"

They placed their order and continued their conversation.

"You know, Lance, it's just like I told Grant, I've never been in love before, and it scares me. I need time to sort out my feelings."

"Sometimes you need to grab love and happiness when you can get 'em. They just might not hang around. Grant makes you happy. I've seen it. Why would you want to give that up?"

"I don't know. Maybe I'm crazy. I need to be sure, and he's pushing love and commitment."

"We all get scared that maybe we're not making the right decision. But, you have to take a risk some time to be happy. Real love doesn't come by every day, you know. It's few and far between. When it does, you need to accept it and cherish it...not run away from it. Okay, I'm sorry I came on so strong, but I only want what's best for you. I also want to thank you for Kathleen."

The waitress arrived at the table, placing

their meals in front of them.

CHAPTER TWELVE

IN THE MIDDLE OF THE WEEK, TAMARA RECEIVED word of another assignment. She was to fly to New Mexico on Friday, receiving more information as needed.

On the airplane heading for New Mexico, she didn't feel the adrenaline rush she usually felt on her way to an assignment. In fact, she was dragging her heels, not wanting to go at all. Grant had made several calls to her answering machine, which she had not returned. She was avoiding any contact, but the avoidance appeared to be making missing him worse. She couldn't shake Grant from her mind.

Her thoughts returned to her assignment. She was given a picture, but nothing else. Why were they waiting to fill her in? She was on her way to Albuquerque, where she'd rent a car and drive to some small hayseed town barely on the map. After landing, on her way to pick up the rental car, her cell phone rang. “Yes?” she responded.

“Your target is a man named Travis Johnson. He’s a rogue agent. We don’t know what name he’s going by now, but you have his picture, and it’s a small town,” the voice said.

Tamara’s jaw dropped. Her stomach tightened as she mulled over her words carefully before responding, “Any other instructions?” she asked, trying to keep her voice calm.

“No, let us know when the assignment’s completed.” The phone displayed “call ended.”

Tamara pulled the car to the side of the road, cutting the engine. She leaned her head against the back of the seat and closed her eyes. At last, she picked up her cell phone and punched in Christopher’s number.

“Hello,” the voice on the other end answered.

“It’s me. Are you aware what my assignment is?”

“Of course I am.”

“This isn’t what I signed up for...a fellow agent? You’ve got to be kidding. No way.”

“I can’t discuss it now. Just do your job, and we’ll talk later.” The phone went dead.

Tamara sat in silence looking at the phone.

Arriving in the town, she saw there was no way of getting lost. It was maybe six blocks long. Tamara pulled into a parking spot and sat back to wait. She didn't have to wait long. She spotted the man in the picture coming out of the barber shop. Slipping out of her car, she followed him. Suddenly, he disappeared. Where'd he go? How could she lose him? Her eyes roamed the surrounding area. The next thing she knew, he was standing directly in front of her, staring into her face. Her heart jumped into her throat. She felt her face flush. Her heart pounded. She forced herself to remain immobile.

He grabbed her by the wrist. His mouth was drawn. His eyes squinted at her. "Why are you following me?" he asked with a voice surprisingly devoid of emotion.

She licked her dry lips and spoke in a calm voice, wishing she were anywhere but there. "You look like a man I dated a few years ago. I wanted a closer look, but I see you're not that man." She frowned at him and then gave a slight smile. "Do you always grab the wrist of women who follow you?"

He looked down at his hand and quickly released his grip. He noticed she was a strikingly beautiful woman, wearing a pair of tight jeans and a loose fitting shirt that couldn't cover up the shapely breasts beneath the cloth. "I'm sorry. Did I hurt you?"

"No, not really. Please listen to me carefully. I made that story up. I know you're Travis Johnson, and you're a run away agent. You have to get out of here."

Before Tamara could say another word, the man looked at her with startled eyes as he slumped to the ground. Someone had shot him. Where did it come from? Tamara scoured the area, but no one was in sight. Travis Johnson was dead. There was nothing she could do. She turned and walked to her car, got in, and drove away before anyone discovered Travis Johnson was lying dead on the sidewalk. When she believed she was a safe distance away, she pulled over and collapsed against the seat. Tears ran down her cheeks.

What am I going to do? This is what they do to agents who quit? They didn't trust me to do the job. They sent someone else. Oh God, I'm so screwed. Why'd I ever get into this in the first place? I thought I was doing some good for my country. I've got to talk with Christopher. He got me into it. He's gotta get me out.

Tamara was absorbed with her thoughts and didn't see the car that pulled up behind her until a man knocked on her car window. She sprang up in her seat as the man leaned his head forward and said, "We got him."

Tamara spun her head around and blurted, "What do you mean, we got him?"

"You set him up, and I nailed him." He smiled.

"...our first job as a team."

A look of astonishment flashed across her face. "Who said we were a team? No one told me."

"Christopher said you might be a little surprised. But, it's the end result that counts, right? Where's your sense of teamwork? My name's Josh, by the way." Josh held out his hand.

Tamara gave him a long hard stare, and he dropped his hand. "I guess that means you're not happy with the partnership?" Josh smirked.

"Why'd you shoot him? He was one of us."

"He was a rogue agent. That's all you needed to know. He wasn't one of us. You know...bad guy, good guy. We're the good guys, in case you didn't know."

Tamara frowned and said, "I need to talk to Christopher."

"Fine with me, Lady," Josh blew her a kiss as he walked off in the direction of his car.

On the plane home, Tamara had time to think. Her thoughts returned to Grant. She loved him and wanted nothing more than to spend the rest of her life with him. But, what could she do? She couldn't drag him into this mess. She called Christopher and got his answering machine, leaving a message to come and see her.

Tamara arrived home exhausted and extremely nauseated. She thought the nausea and exhaustion must be from everything she had been through. She fell into bed and slept fitfully, wild dreams of a man's head exploding in front of her. Sometimes it was Tyler Johnson's face, which would suddenly transform into Grant's face.

When she awakened in the morning, the nausea had returned. She went into the bathroom, and a dreadful feeling washed over her. She quickly got dressed, drove to a nearby pharmacy and returned home. When she came out of the bathroom and sat down on the side of the bed, she didn't know whether to laugh or cry. She was pregnant. She couldn't believe she hadn't suspected it before now. She'd missed a period, but had marked it up to stress.

Oh my God, a baby. How can I have a baby now? But, a baby would be someone all mine to love. What kind of a mother would I be? I wouldn't be like my mother, that's for sure. I'd love my baby more than anything in the world. Oh, who am I fooling? I'm an agent, and they're going to try and kill me if I leave. I can't tell Grant he's going to be a father. It would put him right in the middle of it, and he'd feel it was his duty to stick by me. I can't do that to him. What'll I do?

Tamara was deep in thought when the doorbell rang, interrupting her. "Just a minute," she called, running down the stairs. She pulled open the door, and there stood Christopher. “What? You actually rang the doorbell?”

He flashed her a grin and walked through the door. His eyes roamed the room as he walked over and sat down.

Tamara strode across the room and stood in front of him. “How come you sent me to do a job, and then someone else did it?”

He hesitated, looking off in space, apparently considering something. At last, he looked at Tamara and asked, “Were you going to follow through?”

“I told you I didn’t sign up to kill fellow agents. What does it matter what I say? You’ll never know what I might have done. I didn’t have that opportunity.” Tamara glared at Christopher. “You sent some jerk to be my partner...and didn’t even tell me?”

Christopher stood up and walked slowly over to the window, looking out. “I planned to tell you, but there wasn’t time. We weren’t sure what you were going to do. It was the perfect time to introduce Josh in the equation.”

“Christopher, I need to retire. I’ve put ten years in this job. I know you wanted me to see first hand what happens to people who want out. But, damn, Christopher, I’ve been a good agent. That should mean something. I think I deserve a life."

"The agency is the one who tells you when it's time to retire," Christopher replied stiffly.

"Has any agent been able to retire, or is what I saw today your way of retiring agents?" Tamara asked pointedly.

"Your target today was a rogue agent. Do you know what that means? It means he was operating out of agency control. This particular agent was doing non agency business on his own... hunting off the reservation." Christopher shook his head. "Plus, this guy was warned many times, and he gave away information that could put us all in jeopardy. Tamara, we don't just pop off agents who want to quit. How many agents would work for us if that's the way we operated? I was the one who recruited you. I've been your control for the entire ten years, but I'm not the one who makes these decisions."

"What am I going to do, Christopher? Please help me," Tamara pleaded.

"Tamara, give me some time to think this out and talk to the people above me. I'm going to do this on the Q.T. In the meantime, I think you need a little time off from agency work. I'll get back to you in a couple of weeks."

"Thanks, Christopher. I really appreciate it."

He placed a hand on her shoulder. "Don't get me wrong. I'm not promising you anything. But remember, you aren't a rogue agent either."

"What's the deal with Josh? Am I assigned a partner now?"

"Not all the time, but yes, Josh and you will be working together on some of the assignments. Is there a problem with that?"

Tamara heaved a sigh. "No, no problem."

Christopher paused before he spoke, "Well, sleep on it. You'll see it could be a good thing. It's kind of nice to have your back covered. I've gotta go." He turned, winked at her, and walked out the door.

Tamara went to the kitchen and pushed the answering machine's button. She stood with her elbows on the counter and her eyes closed, listening to the messages from Grant which she couldn't bring herself to erase. She hadn't heard from him in the last few days. He had stopped calling. Tamara punched in Grant's number and heard his masculine voice answer the call.

"Hello Grant," Tamara said, her mouth dry and her hands clenched.

Grant bolted from his reclining position and sat up. "Tamara, where've you been? I've called you so many times."

"I'm sorry, Grant. I should've called you sooner."

"So, you were just cooling it, so to speak, and didn't answer my calls on purpose?"

Tamara could hear the anger in Grant's voice. "All I can say is I'm sorry. I made a mistake."

"Okay, so what now?" Grant probed flatly.

"I want to see you...that is, if you want to see me." Tamara unconsciously held her breath, waiting for his response.

After what seemed an eternity to Tamara, Grant replied, "Yes, Tamara, I want to see you. I felt like my heart was torn out by its roots when you didn't return my calls all week. It made me realize how much I care for you. I probably shouldn't be saying this to you because you run when I let you know how I feel, but I want you to know."

Tamara felt a wave of relief spread through her body. "Oh, Grant, I do want to see you. I'm sorry. I didn't mean to hurt you. I care too much about you to do that."

"I'll be gone for a few days. I'm flying over to Hawaii for a first birthday luau for my cousin's baby. The Hawaiians make a really big thing of the first birthday. It's a significant milestone in the life of the child. Traditionally, the parents give thanks with a luau for the child's survival. The custom still continues today. Is there any way you can come with me? Could you take a few days off work?" Grant urged.

"I'd love to, but I'll have to ask Frederick in the morning. When are you going?"

"I'm flying over on Friday and coming back on Tuesday. You'd only miss a couple of days of work."

"I'll check first thing in the morning. Bye Grant. I love you."

Frederick was good about her taking a few days off. In fact, he told her to take the entire week if she needed it. He said he was very aware of all the extra hours she put in when it was called for.

She and Grant agreed to meet Friday afternoon in the Honolulu airport at the baggage claim area by the Hertz car rental booth. Their planes landed about a half hour apart.

Tamara arrived first and sat waiting on a cement bench in sight of the Hertz booth. She spotted Grant walking toward her, looking handsome in a pair of navy shorts and powder blue t-shirt, trailing a small carry on bag behind him. A large grin spread across his face when he saw her.

Without saying a word, Grant drew her into his arms and gave her a kiss she wouldn't forget easily. He pulled back and looked deeply into her eyes. "You know what you said to me on the phone. Did you mean it?"

Their eyes locked as if in a tight embrace. "Of course I did. I love you, Grant Larson." She didn't want to withdraw from the eye embrace, but she needed to feel his lips on hers.

It was close to dinner time when they drove into the parking lot of the condo on the windward side of Oahu. “What a beautiful spot,” Tamara cried. “Look at those mountains. They look like giant canoes were dragged up their sides.”

“They’re called the Ko’olau’s.”

They took the elevator up to the sixth floor and walked down the outside corridor until they reached the end apartment. Tamara squealed with delight when she saw the magnificent view through the windows. “This is so beautiful. We’re right on the ocean. Look at the water. It’s such a gorgeous color of aquamarine.” The salt air and trade winds penetrated her nostrils.

Grant pointed. “See the coral reefs out there about five hundred feet. There are three reefs, and they make the water here much more protected for swimming with no big waves. The high surf is way out by the reefs. There’s really good snorkeling too.”

“That’s so great. And I don’t see a lot of people like in Waikiki.”

“No, you won’t. You’re lucky if you see four or five people on the beach,” Grant said.

“This is really a hidden treasure away from all the tourists.”

Tamara made the decision not to talk about anything serious until after tomorrow’s luau. She didn't know how Grant was going to react to what she had to say. The next morning they decided they had time to go to the beach before they had to get ready for the luau. Tamara walked out on the deck to get two beach chairs to take down to the beach. While she was on the deck, she saw a man shimmying up a tree to cut the coconuts. She could almost reach out and touch him. She yelled, "Grant, you have to come and see this."

Grant joined her and said, "Oh, right, if you haven't seen them cut off the coconuts before, it's something to watch."

"It's scary. He has to come up so high."

They walked down to the beach below and placed their beach chairs on the fine sand. Tamara's eyes scoured the beach, and all she could see was one lone swimmer. With the sweet fragrance of plumeria and the palm trees waving in the wind, Tamara thought she had truly found paradise. She looked out at the deep aquamarine water and the blue sky with the billowy white clouds.

Tamara pointed upward. "Do you see the big snowman with his arms outstretched?"

"No, but I see a dog running with one leg out and the other one bent. He has a big fluffy tail."

They continued playing the cloud game until they tired of it.

"Oh, just when I thought no one was around

except the baby crabs, here comes someone running down the beach." Tamara laughed. The man waved as he ran by.

"The water is so calm," Tamara continued.

"It's mostly always calm in the morning, but as the trades come up, by afternoon there are usually strong ripples in the water," Grant explained.

Sprinkles of rain came down on them, and by the time they made it back to the building, it was pouring.

"That happened so fast. It was beautiful and sunny," Tamara said.

"It's these daily showers on the windward side that makes everything so green. By the way, the luau is being held at a ranch on the windward side of the island. My cousin came to Hawaii about five years ago on a vacation. A girlfriend from college, who was visiting family over here, invited her to a barbecue at their house. That's where she met her husband. She's lived here ever since. My cousin's husband is Hawaiian on his mother's side, and he's very into the native customs of the island. This is my mom's sister's child. Did I tell you her name's Michelle...I think she's about five years younger than I."

"What's her husband's name?" Tamara asked.

"Hanalei, but he goes by Hana."

As they pulled up the long driveway to the

ranch at the base of the Ko'olau mountains, they could hear the music vibrating in the air. The site overlooked Chinaman's Hat, a cone shaped island that resembles a coolie cap.

"You didn't tell me about the birthday child. What's her name?"

"Kaliko. This'll be the first time I've gotten to see her," Grant said. "Mom and Dad have already been over. You know Mom. She couldn't stand it. She had to see her new grandniece."

"How come they didn't come over for the luau?"

"I guess I forgot to tell you. Dad was in the hospital last week with appendicitis."

"You didn't tell me. How's he doing? Is he okay?" Tamara asked anxiously.

"Yeah, he's doing fine. Dad's pretty resilient."

A very pretty young lady with long blond hair ran up to Grant and threw her arms around him. "I'm so happy you came, Grant. I was really excited when Mom said Auntie Patty told her you were coming."

"I'm glad I could come too. Hey, I'd like you to meet my girl, Tamara."

Michelle reached up and hugged her. Tamara felt like a giant along side of Michelle. Michelle was maybe five feet one next to Tamara's six feet.

"So happy to meet you, Tamara. I'm glad you could come." Michelle picked up two beautiful fragrant leis made out of tuberose flowers and put one on Grant and one on Tamara.

Tamara said, lifting the lei to her nose. “Thank you. It smells so good.”

“Come meet my baby girl. I think Hana has her. I’m not sure. She’s been passed around so much,” Michelle said. Then she pointed her finger. “There they are.”

Grant hadn’t seen Hana for several years, but he still looked the same. “Hey, Hana, good to see you. So, this is my new cousin. Hi, Kaliko, I’m your cousin, Grant.”

Hana held Kaliko up to Grant. “Give your cousin a kiss, Kaliko.” She stared at Grant and immediately pulled back to her daddy.

“Oh, Hana, I’m sorry, this is Tamara. She’s with me,” Grant said.

Hana leaned over and gave Tamara a hug. “Glad you could come. Why don’t you take a seat. Some of the family are sitting up in the front area.”

“Don’t worry about us. We’ll be fine. We know you have things to do. See you a little later,” Grant said.

“There are pu pu’s and a salad bar over there if you’re hungry,” Michelle said, pointing in the direction of the table area.

“You wouldn’t believe what they go through preparing the pig. My mom told me it took them three days. First, they dug a large hole in the yard and lined it with river rocks. Then, they built a big fire out of wood from a keawe tree. After that, they cut up banana trees. The banana stumps were used to line the imu so that the pig wouldn't burn. Next, they put the pig in the ground and wrapped it completely in banana leaves enclosed with chicken wire. Finally, they covered it with wet burlap bags and a large sheet of plastic, heaping soil all around the edges of the plastic. The pig was left in over night and not taken out until the next morning. That day they worked at shredding the meat, adding Hawaiian salt. They sent my mom pictures of the whole process by e-mail. It's some job."

When Tamara and Grant arrived at the buffet line to take a plate, neither of them recognized the dishes. Fortunately, Michelle came by and walked through the line with them, explaining the food. First, she pointed out the poi, which was made from crushed taro root. Next was the lalulau, or steamed pork wrapped in taro leaves. Then came the kalua pig, the famous shredded pork dish, and the lomilomi salmon. They recognized the pineapple, rice and purple sweet potatoes.

"Why do they call it lomilomi?" Tamara asked.

"Well, lomilomi means massaged," Michelle answered. "They massage the salmon with Hawaiian salt, and then add diced tomatoes and onion."

Finally, there was the squid luau, chicken long rice, which sort of looked like clear spaghetti, and raw fish dishes.

A little later in the evening the hula dancers performed, accompanied by drums and chants, followed by two male Samoan fire knife dancers, a man and a boy of around age ten. "Wow, that's scary." Tamara winced. "They're so good. I don't know how they catch the torches and knives they throw."

Next, the Chinese lion dancers arrived. Two men dressed as colorful lions, with one in the head and one in the body, danced through the crowd to the beat of the music. Their mouths opened for money to be placed inside, which would go to the baby for good luck.

"They're so funny. There goes a little boy's head inside the lion's big jaws." Tamara laughed.

Tamara and Grant danced and socialized, having fun with the family until the party ended.

It was now Sunday, and Tamara understood she needed to talk to Grant soon. She decided she'd wait until afternoon. They had breakfast on the deck, overlooking the ocean on one side and the magnificent mountains on the other. Grant was fascinated watching the different birds. Of course, he knew all of their names. He pointed out the Hawaiian coot and the noisy myna bird, with its beady yellow eyes. He even saw some frigates and Hawaiian stilts. After relaxing on the deck for a while, they walked down to the beach to take a swim.

"Look at this water. It's so clear," Tamara said.

"I forgot to tell you. We need to look out for Portuguese men-of-war. They're a type of jellyfish and have long purple string-like tentacles trailing behind them that can wrap around you and sting."

"Oh, great. Now you tell me when I'm in the water," Tamara blurted, her eyes anxiously scouring the water.

"You probably won't see one, but at least you can be on the lookout. They're easy to spot floating on top of the water like a bubble," Grant explained.

Grant got out of the water to get their fins and snorkel masks. Bringing them to Tamara, they headed out toward the reefs. Tamara swam close to Grant and pointed to a large green sea turtle. Grant spotted an eel and motioned for them to swim the other way. When they returned to shore, Tamara said, "There were so many colorful fish out there. Several schools of fish completely surrounded me."

"Too bad we don't have time to scuba dive while we're here. Oh, I never asked you. Do you scuba?" Grant asked.

"Yes, actually, I do. I haven't gotten to go for a while though."

"Next time," Grant said. "Damn, I almost stepped on a spiny sea urchin. They can really hurt. I jumped even though I had fins on."

After showering, they drove North to Kahuku and stopped at a shrimp truck near the fresh shrimp ponds.

"Ooh, is this grilled shrimp ever good. Don't think I can eat all the rice though," Tamara said.

Tamara thought Kahuku was a really charming plantation town with its old turn of the century sugar mill. Now, it has the machinery of the old mill, but it has been turned into a museum and shopping area. On the way back to the condo, she noticed the brightly hued red and pink hibiscus and the purple and scarlet bougainvillea vines along the highway.

Tamara felt her stomach tightening as they pulled into the driveway of the condo. A nagging inner voice told her it was time to talk to Grant. She could wait no longer. When they entered the apartment, Tamara suggested they sit outside and enjoy the view. Grant went to the refrigerator and poured himself a glass of water. "Would you like something to drink, Tamara?"

"No, thank you."

Grant joined Tamara on the deck, taking a seat next to her. "See how the ocean has strong ripples in it in the afternoon. It happens almost every afternoon when the trade winds come up."

"Umm," Tamara said, her mind elsewhere. She turned to face Grant. "I need to talk to you, Grant... about something I've wanted to tell you for a long time."

"Okay, I'm all ears," Grant said, looking at her intently.

Tamara took a deep breath. "I've been working for a covert government agency for ten years. My job at Excel Media is only a cover." She paused. "I could be in terrible trouble telling you this, but I have to if I want any kind of a relationship with you. I kill people, Grant. I always thought I was doing a great service to my country, like being in the service, but I'm not feeling good about it any longer. I want out, and I don't know if they're going to let me out yet." Tamara stopped and looked at Grant.

He was staring off into space with his head back. She couldn't tell what he was thinking. He swiveled around and looked at her as if he had never seen her before. "I don't know what to say, Tamara. You got me on this one. I didn't see it coming. I guess I need time to take it in." Suddenly, Grant began to laugh.

"What's so funny?" Tamara asked.

"Oh, only that I discover that the woman I love...the woman I was about to ask to spend the rest of my life with, is a hit woman. No, nothing funny about that. I guess I'm just getting a little hysterical, or maybe a whole damn lot hysterical." He shook his head and stared off into space. "I can't believe it."

"I'm not a hit woman. I only eliminate people who are threats to our country, like terrorists or thugs from the drug cartel...people who are our enemies. How is it different than if I told you I was in the army and had killed people in Iraq in service to our country?"

"They going to give you an honorable discharge... or what?" Grant gave her a hard stare. "God, I don't know, Tamara. I've gotta think about this one."

Tamara looked at the ground dejectedly. "I know, but I want to be truthful with you. I guess I understand you need time to think it through."

The remainder of the day passed in strained silence, other than the few times when they made small talk.

As they were parting to fly their separate ways home, Grant looked with searching eyes at Tamara. "You meant it when you said you were quitting, right?"

"Absolutely. That's why I thought I could tell you. I want a life. I want that life to be with you. So, the ball's in your court, Grant."

"I don't have to worry that you might get shot,

do I?" Grant asked.

"No, you can relax. That's all behind me."

CHAPTER THIRTEEN

IT WAS LATE WHEN TAMARA PULLED IN THE driveway of her Seacliff home. She was tired and eager to climb into bed after the plane ride. Fumbling to turn on the lights as she entered the house, the hair on her arms stood at attention like an animal with a predator approaching. She felt a presence. Before her eyes had time to completely adjust, her hand found the light switch and light flooded the room. Christopher smiled at her from where he sat on the couch.

"What are you doing sitting here in the dark?" Tamara stormed, stopping dead in her tracks, nearly tripping over Toby. "Do you enjoy scaring me?"

"Well, now that you mention it, yeah. It's kind of fun. A guy has to get his kicks somewhere." He gave her a wink.

Tamara gave him a hard glare and gritted her

teeth. "Don't do this to me again, Christopher. I don't like it. I've told you before." Her fists clenched and her jaws tightened.

He gave a couple of stifled snorts. "I think you'll like what I have to say. I'm here to offer you a hefty bonus, and you only have to stay with us for five more years. Then you'll be free as a bird with all the money you'll need to enjoy life." Christopher leaned back and smiled smugly.

"What about me getting out?" Tamara asked. "What did they say?"

"Oh, you can get out now, but it would be foolish with what they're offering you to stay...and for only five more years. You could retire a wealthy woman."

"Money isn't everything." Tamara shrugged.

"No, but it sure makes life easier," Christopher responded.

"They'll give you a new identity and relocate you if you choose to opt out, but I think you'd be making a huge mistake."

"How much are you talking about?" Tamara asked.

"One hundred thousand right now and an additional hundred each year for four years. The fifth year, they'll double the total amount. That's nothing to sneeze at." Christopher winked. "Don't forget, this is just a bonus in addition to your salary." He didn't tell her that he was offered a bonus if he talked her into staying.

"I must say, it's tempting. I'll have to think about it."

"Well, don't think too long." He glanced at his watch. "I've gotta go. I'll be in touch." Christopher stood and walked to the door.

Tamara closed the door, picked up her things and started up the stairs. Her mind was spinning.

What's wrong with me? I can't consider their offer. I'm pregnant. Besides that, I promised Grant I was getting out. But, damn, that's a lot of money. It would really give us a nest egg.

She set her bag down, opened it, and unpacked a few things, placing them on her bed. She stopped, decided to unpack in the morning, and fell back onto the bed with clothes still stacked alongside her. The ringing of the phone startled her.

"Hello."

"Tamara, it's your grandmother. Where have you been? I've been calling you for days."

"I'm sorry. I should have told you. I went away for a few days. Is something wrong?"

"I thought you'd want to know that Gracie's in the hospital, and I'm all alone."

"What's wrong with Gracie?" Tamara gasped.

"She had an infection and went to the doctor, but the antibiotics weren't picking it up. Her temperature stayed up high, so the doctor said to take her to emergency. They decided to keep her for tests, but she seems to be doing a little better now. They said the infection's in her kidneys and bladder. It's been hard on me not having her here. She's never sick."

"Now you know how much she does for you. She's not a spring chicken anymore, Grandmother."

"I understand that, Tamara. I'm not stupid, you know, and I'm getting older too." The irritation was showing in Grandmother's voice.

"I guess I'm only saying that maybe you could require her to do a little less, and enjoy her companionship a little more."

"Oh, Tamara, you're such a child. What do you know? You're never around. I didn't call to argue with you."

"I'm sorry. I'm just worried about Gracie."

"What about me? You don't think about the fact that I'm all alone and having to take care of myself."

"What do you need, Grandmother? Do you need me to come and stay with you?"

"Well, that would be nice, if you can tear yourself away from that boyfriend of yours."

Tamara heaved a sigh. "I'll be there in an hour or so. Anything you need me to pick up?"

"Good. Yes, would you please stop at the store and pick up a few things for breakfast?"

Tamara was exhausted from the flight and the emotional stress of telling Grant about her secret life. This was the last thing she wanted to do, but she felt an obligation to her grandmother. She had to go. She yawned and stretched her arms before dragging herself out of bed. She dumped the rest of her Hawaii clothes in a pile on the floor and threw a few things in the bag. She planned to stop at the hospital to see Gracie before going to her grandmother's.

When Tamara arrived, Grandmother's first words made her wonder why she had come. "Why do you stay at that job when they're always sending you here and there?"

"The job didn't send me, Grandmother. I went to Hawaii for a few days with Grant to his cousin's luau."

"Why are you getting so involved with that man?"

Tamara's body stiffened. "I'm in love with that man, Grandmother."

"He's not good enough for you, Tamara. Oh, come on in. I might as well be talking to the air."

Why do I even try? I never seem to be able to please Grandmother. She's never satisfied. She finds fault with whatever I do or whoever I see.

Whatever it is, she's always against it. I should be used to it. She's been that way as long as I can remember. I'm glad I went to see Gracie. At least she makes me feel good about myself. She's always so happy to see me.

Tamara heard her grandmother calling her. "Tamara, aren't you settled yet? I need you to do a few things for me."

Tamara called back, "I'll be down in a minute." She stalled as long as she could before going downstairs. "Yes, Grandmother, what can I do for you?"

"Well, first, I'd love a cup of hot chocolate before going to bed. Then, if you could get the box in the kitchen, I'd like you to pay a few bills for me."

"I'll be happy to make the hot chocolate. Would it be okay if I get the box and pay the bills tomorrow right after work? I'm really bushed. I'm afraid I'll have a hard time getting up for work in the morning if I stay up much longer. We can go over and see Gracie together tomorrow after dinner. Okay?"

"Yes, that will be fine." Grandmother sighed.

Tamara awakened early, wrote a note for Grandmother, reminding her that she'd be home early to fix them dinner and go to the hospital to see Gracie. She left the note on the kitchen table and quickly left the house, hoping not to have an encounter with her grandmother before she made her escape.

When she arrived at work, Hani stepped in front of her, blocking her movement.

"What is it, Hani? I need to get to my office." Tamara stared into his dark eyes.

"What makes you so anxious to get away from me? Am I not worth your time?"

Tamara shook her head. "I'm not trying to insult you, Hani. I need to get to my office, and you're blocking the way."

"When can I talk to you?" Hani persevered.

"Come to my office at eleven, and we can talk," Tamara said, knocking Hani's arm off the wall as she pushed past him.

A little later in her office, Tamara checked her e-mail messages. There was a message from Frederick, telling her to drop by his office when she had a minute. Tamara turned away from the computer and walked down the hall to Frederick's office. His door was open, so she poked her head in and asked if he had a minute to talk. "I got your e-mail. What's up?"

"Come on in and pull up a seat. I haven't gotten to talk to you for a while. How's your grandmother?"

"She's fine. It's not my grandmother who's sick. It's Gracie. She pretty much raised me because my grandmother was always busy."

"Well, how's Gracie?"

"She's in the hospital with an infection in her kidneys and bladder."

Frederick winced. "That has to be painful. By the way, how was your little vacation?"

Tamara smiled. "It seems like it was a long time ago, but it was great. Hawaii's a wonderful spot to rejuvenate." Tamara continued to tell him about the luau. Then she said, "Okay, Frederick, I think I know you well enough to ask you. How come you like to be called Frederick instead of Fred or Freddy?"

"Well, if you must know, Freddy sounds like I'm two years old, and Fred was my dad's name. He wasn't my favorite person. In fact, I thought about changing my name, but I kind of like Frederick. It sounds sort of noble."

"That's a good answer. Frederick has taken on a whole new flavor for me now. Thank you, Frederick," Tamara said as she made a deep bow.

Frederick laughed. "You're planning on doing that every time, I hope."

Promptly at eleven, Hani knocked on Tamara's office door and poked his head in. "Are you free?"

"Yes, come on in," Tamara called, looking up from the papers on her desk.

Hani walked across the room and sat down in the chair next to Tamara's desk. "Why are you avoiding me? I told you how I feel about you."

"I, too, told you how I feel. Maybe I didn't make it clear enough. I'm happy to be friends, Hani, but I'm seeing someone else."

"He's not right for you, Tamara. He can't take care of you the way I can," he stated emphatically.

Tamara gave him an annoyed look. "I think I should be the judge of that."

"You've given me signs that you're interested in me. Why are you spurning me now?" Hani heaved a sigh, silently regarding her.

"I'm sorry if I misled you. I thought since we were traveling together, we could be friends...nothing more than that."

"That's well and good, but I want to be more than friends," Hani persisted.

"I understand you come from a culture where the man plays a dominant role, but I thought you'd been here long enough to know that women have a say in things in America. I'm in a happy relationship, and that's the end of the discussion as far as I'm concerned."

"Okay, Tamara, but that's not the end of the story. I happen to know that you had something going with Armon Hadad, and isn't it strange that he was killed in San Francisco shortly after we returned?" Hani gave her a knowing look as if he had a secret he was dying to share.

"So, what is it you're trying to say, Hani? Are

you accusing me of involvement in Armon's death?" Tamara took a deep breath.

"Let's just leave it for now. We'll continue our discussion at a later date when you're more receptive to me. I'll give you time to reevaluate." He turned and started for the door, looked back, and gave her a wicked grin.

Tamara sat at her desk for a long moment, staring off into space. She felt totally bewildered at what had just transpired. She couldn't imagine what Hani knew about Armon. It certainly sounded like a threat.

Later in the day, Tamara received a disturbing message from Christopher, saying it was urgent that he see her. She was to meet him at four that afternoon at a restaurant near her work.

Christopher wasted no time when he saw her. "I'm sorry to have to tell you this, Tamara, but we have word through our sources that there's a price on your head for killing Abdul Alhmad. Somehow, information has been obtained that points to you. there's a contract out to kill the person responsible, and you're at the top of the list."

Tamara's mouth went dry. She stood perfectly still, taking it all in before responding, "How do you know this?"

"Our sources are very reliable, Tamara. We need time to investigate further, and you need to be protected. It's not the time to leave us. The best way for us to help you is for you to stay in the organization until we've seen this thing through."

"Christopher, I have to tell you. I'm pregnant. I haven't told Grant yet, but that's beside the point. That's the most pressing reason for me to get out of what I'm doing. It doesn't look as if I have a choice right now though. I need you...at least until I'm safe. I hope you're going to throw suspicion elsewhere."

"We're already working on it. We're not going to leave you out in left field." Christopher scratched his nose and shook his head. "That does throw a monkey wrench in the equation with the development of the baby."

"I know," Tamara said.

"Are you planning on keeping it?" Christopher asked.

"I want to...very much. I don't know how Grant will feel about it, but I'm used to doing things on my own. Plus, I won't be alone. I'll have my baby."

"I hope it works out for you."

"I had a situation arise at work a few minutes before you called. Hani Alradi, a coworker who went to Oman with me, is stalking me. He's insinuating that he knows I was involved in

Armon Hadad's death in San Francisco. I think he's trying to get me to leave Grant and be with him. He told me when I had time to think it over, I would be more responsive to his advances. In light of what you just told me, I thought you should know about it."

"We'll get on it right away. He could be the source, but I rather doubt that he would use his trump card before getting the response he wants from you," Christopher said.

Tamara arrived at her grandmother's home after stopping at a local Chinese restaurant where she picked up some take out food. She didn't know if her grandmother would like it that she wasn't cooking, but after the developments of the afternoon, she was in no mood to cook. She remembered having Chinese food as a child, but she didn't remember what her grandmother liked. Although it wouldn't make much difference, her grandmother wouldn't be satisfied with whatever she got.

Grandmother caught sight of Tamara entering the door and said, "I was getting worried. You're late."

"I'm sorry. I thought to save time, I'd stop and pick up some Chinese food for dinner. I hope that's okay with you."

"I guess it'll have to do," Grandmother replied stiffly.

Tamara placed the cartons on the table and went to the kitchen to get the plates and utensils. "Have you talked with Gracie today?"

"Yes, I think she may be coming home soon. The culture came back, and now they know what meds they need to use to treat the infection. She should start feeling better soon," Grandmother said.

After finishing dinner, Tamara and her grandmother went directly to the hospital. Gracie gave them a weak smile. She reached out for Tamara's hand and squeezed it. "You look tired, Tamara. Are you trying to do too much?"

"Stop worrying about me. I'm fine. What about you? I hear they've found the source of your infection. Maybe you can finally start to get better."

"I'm already feeling a little better, just weak. I feel like a limp noodle." Gracie smiled.

"Are you getting along okay without me, Mrs. Lake?" Gracie asked.

Grandmother responded simply, "I miss you."

Tamara wanted to ask, but didn't, if she missed Gracie or what Gracie did for her. When Grandmother got up and walked out to the desk to talk to the nurses, Gracie took advantage of being alone with Tamara. "How's that nice gentleman friend of yours, Tamara?"

"He's wonderful, really. I went to Hawaii with him for a few days for his cousin's baby luau."

Gracie took her hand. "Tamara, you have to grab happiness in this life, and don't let it go. You don't want to end up a lonely old woman like me. Don't let your grandmother or anyone else keep you from having a life. If you love him, go for it. Don't let anything stand in your way."

Tamara had never really thought about how lonely Gracie's life must be. She was always there for her when she needed her. Tamara looked at Gracie with compassion. "I love you, Gracie. You've been the closest thing to a mother I've ever had, and I love you for it. Thank you for being there." Tamara reflected on all the little things Gracie had done for her. She remembered the after school snacks and the little presents she'd tuck under her pillow. And most of all, she remembered Gracie's listening ear. Gracie looked into Tamara's eyes, enclosing both of Tamara's hands in hers and smiled, pulling her close with a lengthy hug.

Meanwhile, in Santa Barbara, Grant worked late and stopped at the grocery store to pick up a few items to make a stir fry. His thoughts were on Tamara as he walked back to his car. He planned to call her as soon as he got home and tell her he didn't care what she had done. He still loved her and didn't want to be without her. He never saw it coming. Suddenly, something came over his head from behind and there was complete darkness.

When Grant awakened, his head was pounding. He tried to open his eyes, but couldn't. Something was tightly covering his eyes. He tried to move, but discovered that his feet were tied and his hands were bound tightly behind his back. He rolled on to his back and felt around with his fingers. It felt like grains of sand. His senses came alive, and he heard the sound of the ocean.

I must have been dumped on a beach. Why? Did they want money? I didn't hear any voices. Was I drugged or did they hit me? Why didn't they put tape on my mouth?

He called out, "Is there anyone there?" His voice was met with a kick in the face. He could feel the blood spurting out his nose. "What is it you want? Is it money? You're welcome to whatever I have."

"Shut the fuck up. We'll tell you when to speak," a voice blurted.

Grant was silent, assessing the situation. There must be more than one. The voice had said "we". His eyes were covered, so they obviously didn't want him to see them. That was good. If they were going to kill him, they wouldn't care if he saw them. What were they waiting for? Grant heard a car pull up and cut its engine. The car door opened. He heard footsteps approaching and muffled voices. His heart pounded. Beads of sweat trickled down his forehead.

Grant felt the hot breath on his face. "So, you're the infamous Grant Larson. You don't look so formidable now," a voice echoed with a smirk.

Grant said nothing. He had thought maybe they had taken the wrong person by mistake. That possibility ended. He was the one they wanted. The silence was deafening.

The same voice said, "This will be your one and only warning. Stay away from Tamara Mantz. There will be no second warnings."

Grant felt hands lifting him to his feet. A fist landed on the side of his head, and at the same time he felt the jab to his stomach. He folded and slumped to the ground. When he awakened, he found himself on the front seat of his car, unbound, with no signs of the assault, aside from the blood on his face, a headache, and the developing bruises. Who was this man who was so interested in Tamara? He couldn't imagine she'd be involved with a man like that. But, how much did he really know about Tamara? He only knew what she allowed him to know. He never thought of himself as a coward, but he liked things up front. He had been on the boxing team in college. He fought as good as anyone in a fair fight. But, this, this was sneaky...tying him up when he was unconscious and beating him when it was impossible to fight back. He didn't know who the enemy was. He felt frustrated, demoralized and angry.

Chapter Fourteen

GRANT STOOD IN THE SHOWER, ALLOWING THE water to wash over his wounds. He didn't really know how long he stood there, his mind in turmoil. He wanted to call Tamara and tell her what had happened and see if she could shed some light on it. But, he wanted to get his head clear before he called.

How did I ever let myself get mixed up with a woman who made a living from killing the "supposed" bad guys? What's wrong with me, anyway? Am I crazy? Why wouldn't she be involved with thugs like the one who beat me up? Damn. Why'd I have to fall in love with her? No matter how he tried to talk himself out of it, he was hopelessly in love. *So now what? I get killed by some thug, and I don't even know who he is? No way. I'm not going to be caught with my pants down again. I have to at least know who the enemy is.*

Grant grabbed the phone and punched in Tamara's number. No answer...only the machine with her throaty voice. He didn't leave a message. He called her cell number, and this time heard a live voice respond.

"Hi Tamara, it's Grant."

"I'm so glad you called. I've missed you."

"Are you alone? Can you talk?"

"Yes, I'm at Grandmother's house, upstairs in my room. Why?"

"I need some answers. I was attacked tonight after I left work. I don't know who they were, but one of them knew you, and I was warned to stay away from you."

Tamara gasped. "Who would do such a thing? Are you okay? Were you hurt?"

"I'm okay. I have a few bruises, but I'm okay." Grant reassured her.

"What'd they look like?" Tamara asked anxiously.

"Something was put over my head from behind. I was knocked unconscious. When I awakened, I was blindfolded and tied up, so I never saw them. There was more than one because I heard one voice first. Then, a car drove up, and another voice made the threat. Next, the beating began, and I woke up back in my car."

Tamara sucked in her breath, realizing she

was holding it. She took another breath, attempting to calm herself. “My God, Grant, that’s terrible. I’m so sorry you were hurt because of me.”

“It’s not your fault. You didn’t have me attacked. Do you have any idea who it could have been?”

Tamara sat silently for a full minute, her foot tapping the air unconsciously. She ran her fingers through her hair and said, “I have an idea who it could be, but I can’t imagine he would go to that extreme. His name is Hani Alradi. He’s a coworker of mine. He’s expressed love for me, but I’ve given him no reason to think I’m the least bit interested in him.”

“Have you been involved with him or dated him in the past?”

“No, he was sent to Oman with me on assignment. I thought we were just friends. He received news that his wife was leaving him when we were there. It was after that that he told me I was the woman he wanted. He comes from a different culture, you know. He knows about you because he told me you weren’t right for me.”

Grant silently took it all in and responded, “Sounds like he’s a good possibility. Anyone else?”

“Not that I can think of.” Tamara hesitated. “...unless the agency I work for wants you out of the way, so I’d continue working for them. Maybe they think they can scare you away. I guess that sounds a little far-fetched though. This is scary, Grant. I don't want you hurt. Maybe we should stay away from each other for a while until we can find out who's responsible."

"I'm not going to let them win, Tamara. They can't scare me off that easily."

Tamara's temper flared. "So, what would it take? Getting you killed? Then who wins?"

Grant laughed. "Calm down. I'm not crazy. I'm not going to get killed. I need to flush this guy out though."

"What're you going to do?" Tamara felt an uneasy feeling in the pit of her stomach.

"I don't know yet. I need to do some thinking."

"Just be careful, Grant. I do love you, you know. I want you alive." Tamara frowned and shook her head.

"I want me alive too, Tamara. I'll let you know. Good night. By the way, I love you too." Grant put the phone down.

After making a stop at the hospital to see Gracie, it was noon when Tamara arrived at work. The first thing Tamara saw when she entered her office was the lovely vase of beautiful yellow roses on her desk. She walked across the room and opened the card tucked in between the stems. Grant had sent a message requesting that they meet for cocktails at seven that evening at a restaurant not far from her work. He hadn't told her that he was coming up. She was happy, but wondered why he hadn't mentioned it when they talked.

A knock sounded on Tamara's door, and Hani entered the room. "Do you have a few minutes to talk?" he asked.

"Certainly. Please have a seat," Tamara said, motioning to the chair.

Hani looked at Tamara in silence for a moment before speaking, "Have you had time to reevaluate, Tamara? Are you ready to be more than friends?"

Tamara stalled, taking time to collect her thoughts. She didn't want to give away the fact that she believed Hani was the one who had Grant beaten.

"I really haven't had much time to think about anything, Hani. I've been busy with family problems."

Hani observed the roses, and his eyes glanced down at the card on the desk. Tamara noticed his observation and quickly placed a paper on top of the card. She didn't know if he had had time to read it or not.

"I'm sorry to hear you've had family problems.

Have they been resolved?" Hani asked, making a mental note that Tamara had not wanted him to see the card. He chuckled to himself. She was too late.

"Not completely, I'm afraid, but things are getting better."

Hani stood up and said, "We'll talk in a few days when things have calmed down for you." He turned and walked out of her office without looking back.

Grant arrived at the restaurant early and discovered a message was waiting for him that Tamara would be about twenty minutes late. He thought to himself that would work out to his advantage. He ordered a drink and settled back to wait. Two men approached his table and sat down, one on each side of him.

The man on his left spoke, "I see you don't listen well, Mr. Larson." Grant immediately recognized the voice as that of the man from the night of the attack.

"I listen to what I want to hear," Grant said.

"You're a brave man, but a foolish one," Hani responded. "Perhaps you didn't believe what I told you before. You were warned to stay away from Tamara." He turned to the man to the right of

Grant. "Take Mr. Larson out to the car, and I'll be out shortly."

Grant felt the butt end of a gun in his side.

"This will probably be the last time we'll meet. I should have finished you off the first time. I shouldn't have given you another chance." Hani turned to the other man. "Go ahead and take him out to the car." With a contemptuous smile, Hani picked up Grant's drink, saluting him before he downed it.

Grant walked forward out the exit with Hani's henchman at his side. As soon as they exited the building, two men surrounded them, taking control. Grant spun to the side as one of the men said, "I suggest you drop your gun. I don't think you're paid enough to get killed." Hani's henchman's gun dropped to the ground.

Grant spoke up, "Good job, fellas. Let's take him over to the car."

They quickly taped his mouth, spun him around, placed his arms behind his back, snapped the handcuffs around his wrists and threw him in the back seat with precision and ease. Pete, one of Grant's men, said, "I made certain I heard the threat before I went outside, Mr. Larson."

"Good. Charlie, you wait here with our friend. Pete and I'll be back in a few minutes," Grant said.

Grant strolled back in the restaurant with

Pete at his side. Hani did a double take when they sat down next to him at the table.

"What the–" Hani mumbled.

"Did you enjoy my drink, Mr. Alradi?" Grant smiled. "So, we meet again."

"You think you outwitted me. You don't know who you're dealing with. I have friends," Hani said.

"They're not doing you much good right now." Grant grinned as Pete shoved his gun in Hani's ribs.

Pete looked Hani in the eye and said, "Put your hands on the table...now." He cuffed him, pulled him to his feet, and frisked him.

Hani looked at Grant with contempt. "You think you've got me, but I'm not done with you yet."

Grant turned to the maitre'd and said, "Please leave the table as it is. I'm sorry for the disturbance. My guest will be arriving soon. Could you please seat her, and I'll be right back." He threw a credit card on the table.

They led Hani out to the car and shoved him in the back seat along side of the other man. Then, they called the police.

When they arrived, Grant gave the police an account of what had transpired and said he'd come to the station to file charges. He then turned to Pete and Charlie. "You two are awesome detectives. I'm really glad I hired you this morning."

"Thanks," Pete said. "We're only doing our job." Next, Pete spoke to the police detective, "I can corroborate the threat on Mr. Larson's life. I overheard exactly what was said to him."

Grant returned to the restaurant and spotted Tamara sitting in the booth he had reserved. He leaned down, brushed her lips lightly, and slid in across from her. She looked at him intently. "What's going on? You look harried."

"Nothing much. I told you I needed to flush out my attacker. Well, I did. He's taken care of," Grant said calmly.

Her eyebrows arched, and her eyes went wide. "What do you mean? Was it Hani?"

"Yes, it was. But don't worry, it's handled."

"Why are you being so evasive? For God's sake, tell me what happened. You act like I'm some fragile doll or something. Stop pussyfooting around. I'm really getting angry now," Tamara stormed.

"Okay. I was only trying to keep you out of it. I know you were friends with Hani. He–"

"Not that good of friends," Tamara interrupted.

"That's good. He's not a good person. I recognized your coworker's voice as the man from the night of the attack. Anyway, he came after me tonight with a henchman at his side. He planned to have his man do away with me. But, I was ready for him. I had hired two private detectives who took care of the situation pretty easily."

"How'd he know where to find you?" Tamara asked.

Grant said simply, "The yellow roses."

"You mean you sent them to me as part of the set up?" Tamara asked with a frown on her face.

"Well, yes. I'm afraid I did. I'm sorry."

Tamara shook her head. "What if he hadn't read the note? You might have told me. I tried to hide the note from him."

"That was a chance I had to take."

"So, where's Hani now?"

"The police have him in custody, but I suspect he'll get out on bail," Grant said. "At least he knows I'm not an easy mark."

"That does a lot of good. He'll try again, Grant. The one thing I've learned about Hani is he's persistent. He doesn't give up. I'm sure he thinks if you're out of the way, I'll come running to him. He doesn't realize how mistaken he is," Tamara paused. "Grant, I have to tell you something you're not going to like." She took a deep breath before continuing. "I may have a contract out on my head." Tamara looked at Grant for his reaction.

His mouth flew open. "What? Who? Certainly

not Hani. He's in love with you." Grant sat forward in his seat.

"I was told that I'm a prime suspect in the killing of a terrorist, and their people are out to get the person responsible. I don't know who leaked information to them, but I know Hani suspects me because he threatened me with the information as leverage for me to dump you." She kept her watchful eyes on Grant.

Grant heaved a sigh. "Wow, that's scary information. Were you involved?"

A few seconds of silence followed. "Do you really want an answer?"

"I need to know," Grant prompted urgently.

Tamara silently regarded Grant before replying. "Yes, I was." She watched his face.

Grant winced. "Oh."

Tamara grabbed his hand. "Grant, you know what my job is. I was only doing my job."

Grant placed his other hand over hers. "I'm sorry. I know you don't need me making things worse, but you've gotta understand this is really hard for me. So, what now?"

Tamara took another deep breath while her foot danced in the air. Grant wondered what was to come next. He knew her signs of nervousness well.

"They advised me to stay in the agency until the situation is under control. They can offer me more protection than if I'm out on my own." Tamara touched her fingertips to his cheek. "I know I said I was getting out, and I am, but I think they're right. I need to stay with them for now." With her heart in her throat, she waited for his response.

Grant studied her for a second, mulling over her words, not wanting to say something he'd regret. "You know I want what's best for you. Can they protect you?"

"God, I hope so. I feel they can if anyone can. They have good sources who feed them information," Tamara assured him.

"This is difficult for me, Tamara. I'd like to feel I could protect you. Maybe we should run off somewhere and just disappear."

Tamara laughed. "I wish we could run away from our problems, but it's not that easy. There's too much unfinished business to be taken care of, so we can have a life together. I want to tell my contact what happened to you tonight. I think he could be helpful. Let me check if he'll meet with us."

Grant glanced at his watch. "Tamara, I need to go to the police station, but let me order you some dinner first. I'll meet you back at your house when I'm through."

"I'm afraid I have to go back to my grandmother's. Gracie's coming home from the hospital in the morning. Don't worry about dinner. I'm not really hungry." Tamara continued, "Call me when you're through, and we can decide what to do."

"I'm sorry. I hate to run out on you." Grant walked Tamara out to her car.

Tamara immediately called Christopher and set up a meeting. She wasn't sure if Christopher would want to see Grant face to face, but when she told him the importance of the meeting, he agreed.

Later that evening, Grant called Tamara from his car when he finished filling out the report and filing charges at the station.

"I'm free," Grant said. "All the red tape is over. It looks as if Hani will be out on bail though. Unfortunately, he has a clean record."

"That's not good for you, Grant. Well, let's take one step at a time. I called my contact, and we're to meet him tonight at eleven. You want to come pick me up at Grandmother's? I'll tell her we're going out on a date."

Grant checked the time. "I'll be over in record time."

Tamara tapped on her grandmother's bedroom door. It was already ten o'clock, and she knew her grandmother would think it wasn't proper for a man to be calling so late.

"Come in," Grandmother called.

Tamara walked into the room and found her grandmother propped up in bed reading. She braced herself for the expected response.

"Sorry to bother you. I came in to tell you I'll be going out for a little while. Grant is coming by to pick me up."

Grandmother looked up from her book and frowned. "No proper lady would go out with a man at this time of night. Do you want him to think you're a floozie?"

"Grant is only up for the night, Grandmother, and he was detained at a meeting. It may not be proper, but I am going to see him. Please don't wait up. I'll be late." Tamara looked her grandmother directly in the eyes.

Her grandmother cast her eyes down at her book. "Do as you wish."

Tamara thought she detected a slight smile on her grandmother's face.

Tamara and Grant walked into the bar a little before eleven, and Tamara spotted Christopher at one of the tables in the back.

"Thanks for seeing us, Christopher. I'd like you to meet Grant Larson," Tamara said. The two men shook hands, and they all sat down around the small table.

"Tamara tells me that you had a run in with

Hani Alradi. Want to tell me about it?" Christopher asked Grant. Grant detailed what had occurred in the restaurant.

"We've been looking into Mr. Alradi's past, and although his record is clean, we've uncovered a few things. You need to watch your back, Mr. Larson. He's not what he seems to be. Thanks for telling us your story. We'll get back to you through Tamara, but you better be very careful. And remember, this meeting never took place." Christopher stood up and made his exit.

Grant turned to Tamara. "So, what'd you make of that? How much do you really know about Hani?"

"Not much. I thought he was very pro-American. He always seemed really happy to be in America. That was the impression he gave me. But, who knows. Maybe that was only a cover."

"I got a room for the night, and I'd love to take you there, but I think I'd better get you back to your grandmother's. I don't want to make a complete enemy of her. She already doesn't like me much." Grant laughed.

"I know, but she doesn't like anyone unless she's the one who picks him. Are you staying up here or going back home tomorrow?" Tamara asked.

"I'm leaving in the morning early, but I'll be back on the weekend if you think you'll be back home."

"Good, I should be home by then. Gracie's coming home tomorrow, so I'll probably stay there a couple of nights. I have someone coming in to help out for a week or so."

The next morning, Tamara picked up Gloria, the woman she had hired to assist with Gracie and her grandmother, and went to the hospital to bring Gracie home. Gracie was ready and waiting when they arrived.

"Tamara, you're a love to come and get me with your busy schedule. I'll call the nurse. I'm ready to go." Gracie rang the buzzer.

"Gracie, this is Gloria. She's going to be helping out until you're better."

"How nice. I'm glad to meet you, Gloria. I'll try and be a good patient," Gracie said, smiling.

"I'll be here to help you with whatever you need, Gracie. I don't want you worrying about Mrs. Lake. I'll take care of her needs too, so all you have to think about is getting better," Gloria said.

Gracie looked up at Gloria and gave her a grateful smile. "You sure know how to make a person feel better."

The days passed by quickly, and Gracie was

healing nicely with Gloria's excellent care. After two nights, Tamara felt it was time for her to go home. She packed her bag and had it ready to take with her in the morning. She told Gracie, Gloria, and her grandmother to call her if they needed her.

Tamara threw her bag in the trunk and left for work. She walked to her office, sat down at her desk, and for a long moment simply stared down at the surface. Many thoughts flooded her mind. A knock on the door broke her concentration. Lance walked in. "Hey girl, have I got news for you!" He strutted across the room and sank into the seat next to Tamara. "All due to you, mind you, I've found the girl of my dreams. I wanted to tell you first. I've bought a ring, and I'm planning to ask Kathleen to marry me this weekend."

Tamara stared at Lance in silence, observing the joy on his face. Suddenly, she burst into tears. Lance didn't know what to do, but he reached over and patted her back, trying to soothe her.

"Oh Lance, I feel like such a fool. I'm sorry. I'm spoiling your wonderful news. I'm so happy for both of you." Tamara gave a weak smile despite the tears.

"You weren't crying because you were happy

about us, Tamara. What's going on? What made you cry like that?" He lifted her chin to look her in the eye.

Tamara stood up, walked across the room and locked the door before returning to her desk. "I don't know what to do, Lance. I'm pregnant."

"God, Tamara. That's great. Are you happy about it?" Lance flashed a big smile.

"Yes...no...I don't know. I haven't told Grant yet." She ran her hands through her hair while her foot wagged up and down.

"Why not?" Lance frowned.

"I actually wanted to talk to you about this, Lance. I don't know how Grant will feel about me being pregnant. If it were you, would you feel I was pushing you into marriage if I told you I was pregnant? And then, I'm worried about what kind of mother I'd be. Would I be like my mother who ran out on her child? I'm so confused." Tamara shook her head, throwing her hands in the air.

"From just the little bit I know about Grant, I think he'll be delighted. He loves you, Tamara. I saw it in his eyes. As far as you not being a good mother, forget it. That just won't happen. Remember, you're not your mother. You're Tamara, and Tamara will be a great mom." Lance assured her.

"Thanks, Lance. Thanks for boosting my spirits. You almost make me feel like I can do it."

Tamara got up, walked over to Lance, put her arms around him and gave him a hug. “I’m so happy for you and Kathleen. You two deserve each other.”

“I’m happy too. I hope she says yes.” He managed a grin. “Want to see the ring?”

“You have it with you? Yes, I want to see it. You know Kathleen will say yes. She can’t hide her feelings for you. She wears her heart on her sleeve.” Tamara smiled.

Lance pulled the ring out of his pocket and held it up for Tamara to see.

“Oh Lance, it’s beautiful. She’s going to love it. You did a great job picking it out.”

“Thanks, I worked hard at choosing the right one.”

“Well, maybe I’ll tell Grant this weekend.” Tamara grinned.

”He’s supposed to come up.”

“Good, I don’t think you’ll be sorry.” Lance rubbed his chin.

“Sorry for the waterfall, but I guess the old hormones are turning somersaults right now,” she admitted.

“Think nothing of it. I’m happy you felt you could tell me. I’ll see you a little later.” Lance turned and walked out of the office, smiling.

Shortly after Lance left her office, Tamara received a call from Christopher telling her they needed her to make a quick trip to Egypt. She'd be working with Josh on the assignment. She was booked on Friday's plane and should be back for work on Monday. She remembered she'd have to make up a story to keep Grant from coming up on the weekend.

Tamara and Josh were to meet Christopher at the prearranged meeting spot in the park at five o'clock. Tamara arrived promptly at five to find that Josh had already arrived. The two men were deep in conversation.

"Hey there, Tamara. Come have a seat," Christopher said. He held out a bag to her. "Want some peanuts?"

"No, thank you." Tamara took a seat on the park bench.

Josh flashed her a smile. "Good to see you again."

Tamara nodded and turned to Christopher. "So, what's up?"

"Well, you know Egyptian officials have intensified security at all tourist destinations in their country. They've had their share of terrorist attacks and have been doing a good job of combating them. After the Sharm al-Sheikh attack, which was considered one of the most secure places in Egypt, they've really been shaken. In any event, we've had a tip that a terrorist attack is planned at Luxor led by one of the terrorists involved in the September 11 attack. His name is Kafele Ishi, and he's been on the FBI's most wanted list since 2001. Our goal is for you to capture him, and if that fails, eliminate him. I'll give you this folder with all the information we have on him, what the plan is, and a picture of him. You two can take it from there." Christopher handed the folder to Tamara, turned, and walked away.

Tamara looked at Josh. "It looks like we'll be working together on this one."

Josh looked her in the eye. "So it seems."

"I'm sorry we got off to a bad start, but Christopher should have filled me in about you."

"True. Let's put all that in the past and start out fresh... Hi, I'm Josh." He held his hand out. "It's nice to meet you, Tamara."

Tamara took his hand, laughing. "Hey there, Josh. Nice to have you on board. Let's take a look in the folder."

They sat back down on the bench and sifted through the papers.

Josh said, "It looks like there's explosives involved. This Ishi guy's a bad one. We need to put him out of commission."

A little later, Tamara and Josh boarded the

plane as if they were two tourists off to visit Egypt. When they were situated in their seats, they settled back and proceeded to get to know one another.

"So, are you married, Josh?" Tamara asked.

"No, not even close. How about you?"

"No, I'm sort of involved for the first time though."

"Is that a good thing?"

"Christopher doesn't think so."

They talked some more, and then they both took a nap, wanting to be sharp for the following day. They were told the incident would occur at the Valley of the Kings, a popular tourist destination. After arriving, they scoured the crowds of tourists, searching for Ishi. Buses arrived in droves, and as the tourists piled out of the buses, they continued to search. They covered all the souvenir vendor stands without success. The day wore on. Tamara wiped the perspiration from rolling in her eyes. The heat was unbearable. The Valley of the Kings was always hot, but today the temperature was at least one hundred and ten degrees. At last, they spotted Ishi in a group of tourists. Tamara singled him out and asked him for directions to one of the tombs. Meanwhile, Josh crept from behind, shoving a gun in his spine, taking him by surprise. He surrendered without incident, but admitted nothing. At that point, Tamara called in the Egyptian authorities and turned him over for interrogation, with the promise that he'd be sent back to the United States when they were finished with him. They informed the Egyptian authorities of their suspicions and suggested that they search the tombs for explosives. Ten explosives and a bomb were found in the tomb of Ramesses IV.

Arriving in San Francisco, Josh said, "Hey, we make a pretty hot team."

"You could say that," Tamara responded, flashing him a smile.

"Well, have fun with Mr. Sort of Involved. See you next time."

"Okay, Mr. Not Even Close. See ya."

CHAPTER FIFTEEN

THE SOUNDS OF SHANIA TWAIN FILLED THE CAR as Tamara drove from work toward her Seacliff home. Her mood was light and happy as her thoughts zeroed in on telling Grant the news about the baby. She tried several scenarios in her mind on how it would play out. All of them ended happily. She wouldn't allow herself any negatives. She unlocked the front door, switched on a light, and walked across the living room on her way to the kitchen. Suddenly, she froze. The hair on the back of her neck stood at attention. She thought she heard a rustling noise coming from the upstairs bedroom. She relaxed a little, thinking it was probably Christopher scaring her like so many times in the past. She called out, "Christopher, is that you playing your games again?" There was no response.

Maybe he didn't hear me. Where's Toby? He

usually comes running. I'm not going to let Christopher scare me like this.

She poured herself a glass of orange juice and walked across the room to the bottom of the stairs. "Christopher, stop playing games, and answer me. I'm tired of this crap. Is Toby with you?" She got to the top of the landing and stopped, listening. The sounds of soft music emerged from her bedroom. She stood in front of her bedroom door and slowly pushed it open. The aroma of roses filled her nostrils before she saw the petals strewn on the floor and bed.

Was Grant here? Was he creating this romantic scene?

The bathroom door opened, and there stood Hani in a silk smoking jacket with bare legs and feet. "Hello, Darling."

Tamara silently stared at him. He walked across the room, slowly poured two glasses of champagne and carried them over to Tamara, handing her one. "To us, at last. Drink up, my sweet. The night has just begun."

Regaining her senses, Tamara blurted, "What are you doing here, Hani? Where's my dog?"

"Why do you ask? You know what I'm doing here. We're meant to be together. You're mine. I don't know why people keep trying to keep us apart. As for your dog, he's fine. Now, come sit next to me on the bed." He patted the bed next to where he was sitting.

Tamara's mind was quickly analyzing her options. What was the best way to get out of this situation? She might get away if she ran. She was pretty fast. She didn't think she could out talk him. He was very set in his thinking. She could tell him she was pregnant, and maybe he wouldn't want her, but she didn't want him to know before Grant.

Hani interrupted her thoughts. "Drink up, my dear. Let me pour you another. I have some caviar here for our celebration."

She didn't want to drink the champagne because of the baby. After one sip, she said, "I'd really prefer my orange juice if that's okay."

"Anything you want, my dear," Hani said. "Let me take your glass and freshen it with some ice."

"Thank you," Tamara said, searching for time to make a plan. She thought if Hani believed she was going along with him, it would be easier to escape.

Hani brought out the caviar and handed back her juice, prepared with his special formula.

"Now, we'll have a feast. Drink up and enjoy."

Tamara suddenly felt very relaxed. Her thoughts seemed a little fuzzy. "I feel very tired, Hani. Perhaps you should go now, and come back tomorrow." She sat down on a chair.

"I plan to stay with you, Tamara. I want to

make love to you. We belong together," Hani assured her.

Tamara felt as if she couldn't move. What about her plans to run? She couldn't run. She couldn't move. Tamara panicked.

"Please help me, Hani. I don't know what's wrong with me."

"You'll be fine, Tamara. I'll take good care of you." Hani reached over and stroked her cheek. Tamara felt herself being lifted onto the bed. Her shoes dropped on the floor.

"Hani, please." Her words were slurring. She could feel her skirt sliding up.

Hani kept talking....words. "I'll make you more comfortable. First, I'll remove these stockings. I don't want anything between us." He carefully slid them down her legs. "Your legs are so long, muscular, and beautiful, Tamara." He kissed the inside of her thighs, running his tongue in little circles.

Oh God, what am I going to do? I can't stop him. What has he done to me? She tried to move, but couldn't.

He unbuttoned the buttons of her blouse and slipped it off. Then, he turned her on her side and unhooked her bra. It came free easily and set her large full breasts free. Hani feasted his eyes on her body before he leaned down and placed her nipples in his mouth, one at a time, gently sucking at first. He wasn't as gentle as his lust heightened.

"Oh God, where's Grant? Get this demented man off me," Tamara said in her mind. She could no longer make the words audible.

"I love you, Tamara, and I know you love me. You only need time. Don't worry about what's happening. We love each other, and I'm going to marry you. You're mine. God, that gorgeous chocolate brown hair drives me crazy. But, it's those golden highlights...it's like angel's hair. Let's see what it looks like under the panties." He couldn't wait. He grabbed them and tore them off quickly, gazing at the mound of chocolate brown hair. "I'll tell you everything I'm doing, Tamara. You won't miss a thing. I'm gently spreading your legs apart, so I can slide in you easily. But first, I'm removing my clothes now, so you can see and feel your lover's body."

Hani undressed quickly, leaving his clothes in a clump on the floor. "Now, I'm kissing the inside of your thighs. It feels good, doesn't it. You pretend you don't want me, but I know you do. Soon, my love, you won't have to wait any longer." Tamara's mind screamed, "No", but it did no good. Hani was already sliding into her, violating her body.

"I guess I don't have to tell you what I'm doing now. I know you feel me inside you. At last, I'm giving you what you wanted...needed."

When it was over, Hani stroked her gently. "Now, we're one, Tamara. You belong to me alone. I have to leave you now, but when you wake up, you'll know you're mine. I know you don't want me to go now, but don't worry. I'll be back. I love you, Tamara." He pulled the covers over her, kissed her sensually on the mouth, feathering his tongue over her lips, and turned out the light.

Tamara lay in the bed helpless, feeling sick to her stomach. Finally, sleep overcame her.

Tamara opened her eyes and looked at the clock. It was noon. The sunlight was streaming in on her bed.

What happened last night? Was it real? My God, Hani raped me!

She jumped out of bed and stood up, but felt unstable, needing to grab the chair to steady herself. Everything was in its place. There were no rose petals. Her clothes were folded neatly on the chair. There was no champagne, glasses, or caviar. There was a half glass of orange juice sitting on her night stand. Her pajamas were on.

I know Hani was here. I wasn't dreaming. Should I call the police? I don't understand. He's totally covered his tracks. When did he return? I only remember him turning out the lights.

Tamara dialed 911. Then, she went to look for Toby. After calling his name, she heard a bark at the side door. There he was sitting patiently at the door. She looked him over, and he seemed okay. Relief flooded her body. Hani must have sent him out to the beach.

Two police detectives came to her house. Tamara escorted them in.

"I'm Detective Branagan, and this is Detective Martin."

She looked at them a long minute before speaking. "I'd appreciate it if I could have Detective Martin examine me. I'd feel better with a female." Tamara paced back and forth.

"Certainly, Mam. Why don't you sit down and tell us exactly what happened as best you can remember."

Tamara sat on the edge of the couch. "I heard noises upstairs when I came home from work. He was upstairs in my bedroom."

"You knew the man?" Detective Branagan asked.

"Yes, his name is Hani Alradi, and he's a coworker of mine," Tamara explained.

"Are you involved with the man?" Detective Branagan asked.

"No, I told him I'm involved with someone else, and I'm not interested in him, only as a friend. His wife left him, and he said now that she's gone, he wants me." She went on to explain how Hani went after Grant and was put in jail, but got out on bail. "He must have come straight here when he got out." Tamara squeezed her hands together and tried to stop her foot from dancing, without much success.

"Okay, now, what exactly happened last night, Miss Mantz?" Detective Branagan asked.

"I think he drugged me. He offered me champagne, but I said I'd rather have orange juice. He took my glass to add some ice cubes, and–"

Detective Branagan interrupted, "So, you were having a drink with him?"

"I was trying to buy time to make an escape plan. I'm a good runner. I thought if I made him think I was going along with him, I could make my escape, but before I could put my plan in action, I was getting woozy," Tamara explained.

"I don't see any signs of a struggle," Detective Martin noted.

Tamara tried to hold her temper. "There wasn't a struggle. I told you. He rendered me helpless." She was shaking. "I can't help it. This man is crazy. Everything is gone that was here last night. The room was strewn with rose petals, champagne and caviar. They're all gone. My clothes are all folded, and I have pajamas on. He's covered everything up. He raped me," she cried, squeezing her eyes shut.

"Detective Martin will check you out, and we'll

go from there."

Detective Martin got out the rape kit, and Detective Branagan left the room. "You definitely had sex last night, but there's no signs of semen. He had to have used a condom. Did you wash yourself off, Miss Mantz?"

"No, I called you right after I woke up today."

"Well, you've obviously been scrubbed clean. And, did you know you're pregnant, Miss Mantz?" Detective Martin asked.

"Yes, I was planning on telling my boyfriend this weekend. Now, I don't know what to do. Could that monster have given me a disease?" Tamara asked.

"It's not as likely with a condom, but we're testing for that, and we'll let you know. Did he penetrate any other crevices?"

"I don't think so. He kissed me though." Tamara put her head in her hands.

"Everything else looks okay. He made no other penetrations. You're right, though. The man covered his tracks. It could end up with your word against his unless he left some evidence or someone saw him. Maybe he has a record of doing this to other women," Detective Martin said.

"I don't think so. He was let go on bail because he had a clean record," Tamara said.

Detective Martin walked over to the door and called Detective Branagan back in, handing him the report to read.

"I don't want to discourage you, but sexual assault cases are extremely difficult crimes to prosecute because there are rarely any witnesses, and it comes down to one person's word against the other. It's a tough thing," Detective Martin continued, "because so often it seems like the system puts the victim on trial, and the rapist gets off. The lawyers try to discredit the victim's character, particularly in acquaintance rape."

"What're you trying to do...discourage her from prosecuting the guy?" Detective Branagan asked with a frown.

"No, it's not that. I think she needs to know what she'll be put through and what the odds are," Detective Martin said. "Sometimes I feel like it's being raped all over again. I guess I see it from a woman's point of view."

"Well, you make up your own mind, Ms. Mantz, and let us know. I don't like to see the guy get away. He'll do it to some other woman," Detective Branagan said.

The orange juice was checked, the garbage and trash, but he was very thorough. Everything was clean.

"This man is a monster. He told me he loved me while he drugged and raped me. What am I going to do? I work with him." Tamara wrapped her arms around herself and shook her head. "I feel so vulnerable, and I'm pregnant."

"When a suspect thinks he's gotten away with a crime, he often comes back. We can keep a watch on your house. We can have a signal if he's in your house...like pulling your bedroom shade down," Detective Martin said.

Tamara extended her hand to the detectives. "I really appreciate all your kindness and help. Thank you."

"I know you feel violated. Just remember, it's not your fault, and we'll help you all we can," Detective Martin said.

Tamara wanted to stay home from work for the rest of the day, but she knew it would be better if she went in. She didn't want Hani to have the satisfaction that he had gotten the best of her. She turned on the shower, got in, and scrubbed herself clean, all the while thinking she could never get herself clean of Hani. She wasn't in good control of her thoughts, and fortunately, her car knew its way to work. As she pulled in the parking lot, she straightened her shoulders, flipped her head back, raised her chin up, and got out of the car. She walked through the door like a model on a runway without a care in the world, except winning. Her office phone was ringing when she entered the door. Walking across the room, she picked up the phone and answered, “Tamara Mantz speaking.”

“It’s Frederick, Tamara. Could you come up to my office for a minute?”

“Be right there, Frederick.”

Tamara walked out the door and down the hall when she saw Hani coming in her direction. Her stomach did flip flops. Perspiration appeared on her forehead. She tried desperately to keep her cool and ignore him.

When Hani was along side of her, he leaned over her shoulder and whispered in her ear, “How’s my girl this afternoon? You look ravishing, or should I say ravished?”

Tamara kept her eyes straight ahead as if he weren’t there. She stepped into the elevator. The door closed, and she unraveled. Her entire body shook.

I can’t let him do this to me. Pull yourself together, Tamara Mantz. Don’t let him win. This is what he wants.

Tamara’s eyes flashed, and she pulled her body erect. She exited the elevator and walked into Frederick’s office with a smile on her face.

“Hi Frederick. What can I do for you?” Tamara managed to maintain the smile.

“Come have a seat, Tamara. How’s your family coming along?”

“Gracie’s home now, and I hired a very

competent woman to take care of both my grandmother and Gracie for a week or so. I went home last night. Thanks for asking, Frederick."

"Well, I wanted to see if you were up to an assignment in Los Angeles. We need someone to attend a convention on Sunday and Monday. How about it? Would you be able to get away for a few days?"

"Sounds good to me. Why don't you fax me the particulars. I'm all yours," Tamara said.

"Great, I knew I could count on you. Thanks for stopping by," Frederick said.

"Anything else?" Tamara asked as she made her way to the door.

"Nope, I'll have my secretary fax you the info right away. Thanks." Frederick smiled.

Tamara walked back to her office and paced back and forth, unable to concentrate on her work. Hani's arrogant and smug attitude gnawed at her insides. She threw the papers she was holding on to her desk and flopped down in her chair. Her eyes fixated on the computer screen. A light knock sounded on the door, and Lance stepped in.

Seeing the distraught expression on Tamara's face, Lance said, "What's wrong? You look as if someone died."

"Oh God, Lance, shut the door. Come sit down a minute. I don't want anyone to hear us."

"What's going on?" Lance reached across the

desk and placed his hand on Tamara's. "You look terrible."

"I shouldn't be telling you this. Please don't say anything. Hani broke into my house and raped me last night."

Lance's face drained of color, and his jaw dropped. He sat up straight. His eyes became fiery dark. "That bastard! Did you call the police?"

"Yes, they came out to the house, but Lance, there were no witnesses, and he covered up everything. There was no trace of him even being there, so it's my word against his."

"Damn, Tamara, I'm so sorry. Shit! I wanna knock his block off. He can't just get away with it. What'd he do...take you off guard?"

"He drugged me with something. I couldn't move, but I was awake. It was horrible. He passed me in the hall this morning, and I got sick to my stomach. He made a smart-ass remark and acted smug like he knew there was nothing I could do."

"We're gonna have to figure out something to get that son of a bitch," Lance stormed.

While driving home after work, Tamara's cell phone rang.

"Oh, Christopher, you're just the person I want to see," Tamara answered.

"Oh?"

"Can you come by my house in about an hour?" she asked.

"What's the problem?"

"I'd rather talk to you in person."

"Okay, I can't make it until about eight. Is that all right?" Christopher asked.

"That's fine. I'll see you then." Tamara punched the phone off.

Promptly at eight, Christopher rang Tamara's bell.

"Come on in, Christopher," Tamara called.

"The traffic is still a bear." Christopher walked over to a chair across the room and sat down. "So what'd you want to see me about?" Toby immediately raced across the room and sat at his feet.

"I thought you said I'd be safe staying in the agency."

"Yeah, I said you'd be safer with us than without us. So what's happened?" Christopher asked with a frown.

"I was raped." Tamara's eyes flashed.

"You were raped? When? What happened?" Christopher bolted from his reclining position and sat up straight.

Tamara filled Christopher in on Hani's attack, including his remarks that day at the office.

"I'm sorry this happened, Tamara. We've been

investigating his background, but we should have watched him more closely. We did hear he was released yesterday afternoon."

Tamara glared at him. "You knew he was released, and you didn't do anything about it?"

He paused before he spoke again. "We really don't think Hani had anything to do with the leak. I think Hani's a totally separate issue."

Tamara's eyes went wide, and her mouth flew open. "But he threatened me with Armon Hadad."

"Yes," Christopher acknowledged. "But I think he was just guessing and wanted to see your reaction. I don't think he knows anything. He wants you, Tamara, and it sounds like he'll do anything to get you."

She shook her head. "So, I'm on my own on this?"

"No, I'm not saying that. We'll do our best to protect you now that we know what he did to you. You're one of us. We protect our own."

Tamara looked at Christopher closely before responding, "Good."

She walked Christopher to the door and locked it. Returning to the couch, she tucked her legs under her and picked up a magazine from the end table. Leafing through the pages mindlessly, her thoughts returned to Hani. Even with the reassurance from Christopher, she knew her safety was ultimately up to her. She needed to make certain it didn't happen again. She hadn't thought about how Hani got into her house in the first place. The police hadn't said anything. But, then again, she was so distraught that she probably didn't hear what they said if they did tell her how he gained entrance. She wondered if she'd left a door unlocked or a window open. She got up and meticulously went to every window and door in her house, checking them. After the thorough house check, she sank back on her couch, feeling a little safer. She knew she was well trained and could handle herself against most men. Hani had incapacitated her with drugs. He made her doubt herself. The difference was that now she knew what he was capable of. She was prepared for him.

After installing sensors on her windows, adding locks to the doors and rigging a cable at ankle height across her bedroom, Tamara was able to have a good night's sleep. The remainder of the week proved uneventful, and Saturday morning she was on her way to Los Angeles. Her flight arrived in LAX to an airport blanketed with fog. Hailing a taxi, she checked into the hotel room and made a call to Grant.

"Tamara," Grant responded to hearing her voice, "I was just going to call you again. I've been trying to reach you for days. Where've you been? You didn't answer your cell either."

"My cell phone's been screwed up, and I finally got in yesterday to replace it. Then, last night I charged it, so it's working now. But, what about the house phone? I didn't get any messages."

"No, the phone just rang and rang. The message machine never came on," Grant said.

"I can't figure that out," Tamara puzzled. "Anyway, what're you up to?"

"I had hoped to come up to see you, but I was sent out on an assignment and didn't get back until about an hour ago."

"Good thing you didn't come up," Tamara said.

"What d'ya mean, good thing I didn't come up?" Grant furrowed his eyebrows.

"I'm here in Los Angeles." Tamara gave a small laugh.

"You're in LA? That's great. You want me to come down?"

"I thought it might be nice. I'm here for a conference on Sunday and Monday. I don't have to speak. I only have to take copious notes, so I'm free tonight and tomorrow."

"That's great. Have you eaten? How about brunch?"

"Sounds good to me," Tamara said and told him where she was staying.

"Okay, I'll hang up and head out. See you soon."

Tamara heard the tap at her door and ran to open it. Grant scooped her into his arms, whispering, “God, I’ve missed you.”

Tamara drew slightly back to get a better look at Grant’s face and then pulled him snugly back to her, wrapping her arms tightly behind his neck. “You don’t know how much you were missed,” she murmured. She inhaled the subtle male scent of his after shave and felt stirrings of desire deep inside of her.

“The coffee shop is open, or we can have room service. What’s your pleasure?” Tamara asked.

“You know better than to ask that question. You’re my pleasure. Let’s have room service a little later,” Grant said and sat on the edge of the bed.

Tamara moved across the room and stood in front of Grant, looking down at him. He quickly gathered her into his arms, smothering her neck, face, and finally her lips with kisses. Thoughts of Hani’s assault continually invaded her mind. She knew this was Grant, not Hani, but Hani’s arrogant face kept appearing in her head. She tried to blot him out of her thoughts, but she could still hear his voice telling her everything he was doing to her.

She heard Grant’s voice breaking through,

"What's wrong, sweetheart? Did I hurt you?"

Suddenly, Tamara realized she was recoiled in the fetal position with her knees pulled up to her chin. She immediately sat up and put her arms around Grant. "No, I'm fine. I'm sorry. Grant, I have something to tell you." She took both of his hands into hers and looked into his eyes. "We're going to have a baby. I'm pregnant." Tamara watched the expression on Grant's face turn from surprise to joy.

"A baby! I can't believe it. We're going to have a baby? That's wonderful...Is it wonderful? Are you happy?" Grant beamed and hugged her.

She gave him a reassuring smile. "I'm very happy. I'm just scared."

He gave her an acknowledging nod. "I understand that. Of course you're scared, but it'll be fine. We're in this together. He'll have the best mom and dad a kid ever had. I'm using he in the generic sense. I'll be happy with a boy or a girl."

"Besides, I worry that I could follow in my mother's footsteps, and I haven't been working in the safest profession." Tamara dropped her head to her hands. "I could be a terrible mother."

Grant lifted her head up. "I understand your concern. As far as you being like your mother, that's just not in the mix. You aren't your mother or your grandmother. You're your own person and a very good person at that. Getting completely away from the agency is another thing. We'll have to figure that out together. Have you heard any more from Christopher?"

"I've heard from him, but nothing new," Tamara said. "I feel really vulnerable. I've always been such an independent person, but now I have to think about the baby."

Grant pulled her to him, wrapping his arms around her. "We'll get through this." He lifted her chin to meet his eyes. "I love you very much."

"I wish I could be as confident about it as you." Tamara looked at Grant with a weak smile.

The following morning Grant was getting ready to leave. "I wish your conference didn't start so early," he said. "What time is it over?"

"Around five, I think. You're coming back down, aren't you?"

"Of course I am. I'm meeting Lance and Kathleen for lunch in Santa Barbara. Lance came down to tell the folks the good news about their wedding plans. I'll be back by five."

When Grant walked into the restaurant, Kathleen and Lance were deep in conversation. Sliding into the bench across from them, Grant said, "Sure you two want me to join you? Remember, three's a crowd."

"Hey, Big Brother, sit your butt down right now." Kathleen frowned and then laughed.

"That's great language coming from a teacher. Okay, here I am. You've got me." He turned to Lance. "How you doin'?"

"Good, now that I have your sister by my side."

Kathleen reached across the table and grabbed Grant's hand. "Grant, I've got to tell you something, and it's not good. Tamara was raped–"

Lance interrupted, giving Kathleen a grim look, "I told you not to say anything."

"I know," Kathleen said, "but, I can't help it. He needs to know."

Grant sat frozen, absorbing the depth of Kathleen's words. Grant's silence was unnerving. Kathleen fidgeted in her seat. Lance looked from Grant to Kathleen.

At last, Grant spoke one word, "Who?"

"Hani came to her house and drugged her," Kathleen said.

The blood vessels on Grant's forehead stood out. His face flushed, and he stood up abruptly.

Lance jumped out of his seat and grabbed Grant's arm. "Don't do anything foolish. Sit down, and we'll work this out together. Anyway, you need to hear all the facts."

Grant stared at Lance with unfocused eyes. After a minute, his shoulders slumped, and he dropped back into his seat. He put his head between his arms on the table. Kathleen and Lance looked at each other with helpless glances.

Grant raised his anguished face and said, “She just told me last night she was pregnant.”

Kathleen reached over to Grant, taking his hand. “I’m so sorry, but the baby’s wonderful news.”

Lance filled Grant in on all the events of the attack, including Hani’s arrogant attitude toward Tamara at work.

“I can’t let Hani get away with this,” Grant said. “He thinks he can take what he wants, and no one can stop him.”

“I know. I’m with you, but we need a plan...a good one,” Lance said. “Listen Grant, you can’t tell Tamara Kathleen told you about this. Tamara told me in confidence, and she’d kill me for saying anything. Besides, I don’t think it’s a good thing if she knew we had any plans for Hani.”

“You’re right on that one. But I should be told. I need to know what’s going on with her. Why didn’t she tell me? I don’t understand.”

Chapter Sixteen

HE WAS A GOOD SPEAKER, BUT IT WAS DIFFICULT for Tamara to concentrate. Her stomach was cramping, and she had a sharp pain low in her back. She tried to take notes, but the notes weren't making much sense. Clutching her stomach, she squeezed her eyes shut and compressed her eyebrows. She felt a moistness between her thighs and knew she had to get up and attempt to find the bathroom. She carefully made her way out of the auditorium and into the foyer. Her eyes scoured the area and landed on the door worded "women's room." Once inside the stall, she pulled her skirt up and confirmed her fear. Blood was slowly oozing down her legs. She dabbed at it with toilet paper, cleaning it up as best she could. It seemed as if it took forever to flag down a taxi and get back to the hotel. Once inside her room, she sat on the edge of the bed, tears silently rolling down her cheeks. She knew instinctively she had lost the baby.

Grant arrived at the hotel a little before five. As soon as he entered the room and saw Tamara's face, he knew something was wrong. He quickly walked over to her, asking, "What's wrong? You look terrible."

Tamara sat down on the bed, looking up at Grant. "I'm okay," she said, "but I...I lost the baby."

Grant stood silently looking at Tamara for what seemed a very long time. Then, he turned and walked out the door without saying a word.

From her sitting position, Tamara jumped to her feet and called out, "Where are you going?" She ran to the door and called out again. She could see Grant walking down the hall away from her. She called out one last time.

He raised his arm in the air as if waving her away and said, "I need some time alone."

Tamara walked into the room and slumped down in the chair next to the bed, with his parting words echoing in her mind. She wondered what she had done wrong. Why was he upset with her? She thought he'd console her...not walk off to be alone. Tamara got up and started pacing back and forth. She stopped pacing, kicked the bed and stood still, staring out the window. *Well, that did a lot of good. Now, I'm acting like a child.*

About twenty minutes later, Grant returned to the room and said, "I needed time to get my thoughts together. I shouldn't have left you alone. I went down to the bar and had a drink. Did you see a doctor?"

Tamara was upset over Grant's reaction and couldn't understand him walking off, but she didn't say a word. She kept it to herself. Instead, she calmly said, "No, I think I'll see my doctor when I get home."

"I don't think you should wait. How about I make an appointment with my doctor? Are you sure you lost the baby?"

"I must have. I'm bleeding heavily, and I've had some blood clots," Tamara said, "and I've been having bad cramps. I think I'd rather wait. I'm going home tomorrow after the conference is over. I'll call my doctor then and tell him what happened."

"I guess you know best."

Tamara returned home at the end of the conference to find Christopher waiting, sitting in his car outside of her house.

"I'm glad I didn't leave. I was getting ready to pull away. Well, Tamara, the heat's off. I've been trying to reach you to let you know."

"What's happened?" Tamara pulled out her keys and opened the front door. "Let me know what?"

"It seems they found their assassin, and you're no longer a suspect. You can relax on that end."

They both walked into the house, and Tamara dropped her bag near the front door. "How'd that happen. Who?" she asked.

"That's not your problem. You know all you need to know for now. You're out of the picture as far as they're concerned."

"I guess you're right. I'm not feeling too good." She walked to the easy chair and sat down. "I'm pretty sure I lost the baby."

"Oh? Well, now you won't have that worry. A baby's a big responsibility."

"Christopher, you are so damn insensitive." Tamara glared at him. "You know, I'm feeling lower than a skunk. I feel as if I have an empty hole in me right now. You obviously don't understand how I feel."

"I'm sorry," Christopher said, "but it's not like you'd be mother of the year. Anyway, you're better off not having the worry of a baby."

"You may be right, but that's not what I'm feeling right now. You sure aren't the one to call when someone needs a friend."

"That's probably true. So, you're telling me I need to work on my people skills? Changing the subject, as for that low life at work, Hani Alradi, he hasn't come near your house." Christopher stood up. "Well, I've gotta get going. I hope you're feeling better."

"Thanks for letting me know. At least that makes me feel better."

Tamara picked up the phone and left a message with her doctor's answering service. It was a long day, and Tamara felt the strain of the last two day's events. She sat down on the couch, rested her head back, kicked off her shoes, and soon drifted off to sleep. The ringing of the telephone startled her. She shook her head and stretched her eyes wide before answering it.

"Hello."

"This is Dr. Mason returning your call."

"Oh, thanks for calling back, Doctor. I was at a conference in Los Angeles, and I started bleeding. I think I miscarried."

"Is it like your normal periods?" he asked.

"I had cramping and some blood clots. There was some tissue I couldn't really identify as anything."

"It sounds like you did miscarry, but maybe I should take a look at you. Why don't you come by my office in the morning. Call my receptionist, and tell her I said to work you in."

"Okay, thanks Doctor Mason."

Grant didn't waste any time. Immediately after Tamara left, he called Lance on his cell phone.

"Hey Lance, I don't think we can wait. We need to act right away. Are you still in Santa Barbara, or have you gone home?"

"Nah, I just got in," Lance said. "You're right, Bud. Why don't you come on up Friday and bunk at my place. We'll put our heads together and go from there."

"Sounds good. I have a few ideas, but need to work some of the kinks out. That'll give me time. I'm afraid Tamara lost the baby. She thinks she miscarried."

"Damn, I'm sorry to hear that. Is she holding up okay?" Lance asked.

"I guess, as good as expected. I better run. I have to fly to Chicago for a conference in the morning. See you Friday night."

In the meantime, Tamara had her own plans. When she arrived at work in the morning, her first item of business was to knock on Hani's office door. Hani called out for her to come in. Tamara pushed the door open, walked across the room, and stood in front of his desk. Hani came to his feet and looked at Tamara, giving her a broad smile.

"So nice to see you, Tamara. I've missed you."

"Hani, we have some things we need to discuss. Can you come to my house this evening...say eight o'clock?"

"I hope this means you've had a change of heart. I can't get you out of my mind. I'll be there. You can count on it."

"Good, I'll see you at eight." Tamara turned around and walked out of the office.

Moments after she returned to her office, Lance appeared. He walked over to her, wrapping his arms around her and said, "Grant told me about the baby. I'm sorry. Are you sure?"

Lance was a good friend. It felt good having him comfort her. She pulled back from Lance and dropped into the chair. "Yes, I'm sure. I stopped by my doctor's this morning on the way to work, and he confirmed it."

She saw Lance shaking his head. He noticed she was on the verge of tears. "I'm sorry," she continued. "The baby's probably better off without me for a mother anyway. Maybe it's for the best." Her voice trailed off.

"That's not true. You'd be a great mother. You'll have another. Give it time."

"I'm sorry, Lance. I'm just depressed."

Lance patted her hand. "I know you are. You have a right to be. I'll be in my office if you want to talk."

On Tamara's way home from work, she placed a call to Grant. It was time to inform him of Christopher's visit. Plus, she had promised to let him know what the doctor had to say.

"Hey, Grant. It's me."

"Did you see the doctor?"

"Yes, I miscarried just as I thought."

"I'm really sorry, Tamara."

"I know."

"You all right?" Grant asked.

"Yes," she lied. "I wanted to tell you Christopher came by, and I guess I'm off the hook. I'm no longer a suspect. They've found the assassin."

"That's wonderful news. That means I won't have to worry about you any more."

"I guess you could say that."

"Well, you know what I mean. At least, I won't have to worry about you getting shot."

The blazing orange sun sank into the sea with an explosion of colors matching Tamara's anticipation of Hani's arrival. Toby watched Tamara pacing back and forth across the living room floor. She could almost hear him telling her to stop and sit down next to him on the rug. "It's okay, Toby. It helps me sort my thoughts."

The sound of the doorbell pierced the air. Tamara stopped dead in her tracks. She turned and calmly walked to the door with Toby close in pursuit. She looked down at Toby and frowned. "Why are you wagging your tail? Don't you know this is our enemy?"

After opening the door, Tamara led Hani into the living room. Giving Tamara his brightest smile, Hani reached for her hand and said, "I knew you'd finally come to your senses and realize I'm the man for you."

Tamara instinctively drew back. "What's wrong?" Hani scowled. "I thought you wanted me. Why're you pulling away from me?"

"I'm sorry. I need to take it slow, Hani." She turned and smiled at him. "Why don't you sit here on the couch, and I'll make us a drink. Would you like bourbon, scotch or vodka?" She felt Hani's eyes piercing her back.

After a few moments of silence, Hani responded. "I'll have a scotch and water, thank you."

With her glass in hand, she handed Hani the drink and sat on the couch next to him. Looking Hani directly in the eyes with a small smile on her lips, she held her glass up to his. "To a new understanding between us."

She first noticed the bewilderment in his eyes

before the fright appeared. He clawed at her as realization of what she had done hit him. She jumped back and wrestled free from his grasp. "Are you wondering what's happening to you, Hani? Well, stop your wondering. You'll find out first hand exactly how I felt when you gave me your little cocktail. You know what they say, 'Tit for Tat,' Old Boy. Isn't that right? I'm surprised you didn't suspect I might do the same to you. But, of course, I forgot you don't give women any credit."

Hani's body had collapsed into the cushions of the couch, but his eyes were open wide, staring at her.

"Oh, poor Hani...what? You can't say anything? Well, don't worry. I'll tell you everything that's happening so you won't be left out. First, I'll remove your shirt and then your pants. You'll like that, won't you, Hani? Then, I'll wrap you in a sheet and drag you bare ass to the car. That won't be quite as nice. Good thing I'm in shape. The best part we'll save for a little bit. I don't want to spoil your surprise. And guess what? Maybe you'll find out you can't screw around with me, or any other woman and get off scot-free."

Tamara waited patiently until dawn was breaking as she pulled up to the park in downtown San Jose, opened the back door of the car, and dragged Hani out by the sheet. She got her black indelible marking pen and said, "Here's the good part, Hani." She wrote, 'I'M A RAPIST!' in bold black letters across Hani's abdomen. "Just remember," she said, "You're lucky. I could have had you raped."

No one was in the park at this early hour...not even the usual drunk sleeping on a park bench. Tamara looked at her handiwork and gave Hani a satisfied smile. Soon, the park would be bustling with life. "Well, Hani, You'll be back to normal in about an hour. I'll see you at work. Bye." Tamara looked back and saw a couple of drunks entering the park. She turned away and disappeared.

Tamara felt good. She felt terrific, in fact. At last Hani got a little of what he deserved. He didn't realize how easy he got off. He was fortunate she was in a good mood. She all but pranced into her office after stopping at a nearby Starbucks to purchase a mocha coffee. Rounding the bend in the hallway, she ran directly into Lance.

"Oh, sorry, Lance. I wasn't paying attention." She glanced at the floor, observing she had knocked several papers out of his hand. "Let me help you," she said, bending down and picking up the papers.

"No big deal. How you doin'? You seem in

better spirits."

Tamara reached out and pulled Lance by his arm into her office. She shut the door, lowering her voice, and said, "Hani's been taken care of."

"What'd ya mean...taken care of?"

Tamara laughed. "Well, I think about now he's wandering around San Jose bare ass naked, trying to regain some sense of well being. I only wish I had stayed to enjoy the show."

"What'd you do?"

Tamara filled him in on the details.

"Wow! Scary. I'd be afraid he'd come after you, Tamara. He's the kind of guy who'd want revenge." Lance shook his head back and forth, rubbing his hands together.

"Don't worry, I think with Hani's Arabic background, he'd die of embarrassment if any one knew. I honestly believe he'll disappear. And if not, I'll make sure he doesn't come near any woman again."

"I'd hate to be on your bad side." Lance laughed. "Well, good for you, Tamara. Keep me posted on Hani."

Later in the day, the office was buzzing with the news that Hani had quit his job. No one seemed to know why.

Also, later in the day, Christopher gave Tamara a call and informed her he had an assignment for her in Boston. He said Josh would also be on the assignment. She needed to leave immediately. Tamara called Grant and told him she had to make a quick trip to Boston to give a speech.

When she got on the plane, she searched the seats, but didn't see Josh. After arriving at Logan Airport, she rented a car and called for instructions. Her mark was a major drug trafficker and money launderer from Brazil by the name of Caesar Henrique. Every time the prosecution thought they had him nailed, he always managed to wiggle off. Christopher's sources received word that Henrique would be in Boston and was making an exchange with several major distributors. One of the distributors was selling him out in exchange for immunity. Henrique would be meeting their distributor outside at Faneuil Hall Marketplace.

That evening Lance called Grant. "Hey Bud, it looks like we don't have to formulate our plan for Hani. At least, I think we should wait a few days and see what happens. Tamara has taken care of the situation herself." He proceeded to relate what had occurred.

Grant's jaw dropped open. "She did what? I can't believe it. Is she crazy? Hani could have killed her."

"I'll tell ya what. I'm gonna see if I can get an address on him and see what he's up to. I can always take a few things he's left at work over to his place...you know, be a good citizen and all. That'd give me an excuse to stop by. It'd be worth a look-see."

"Good idea. He's not the pussy cat Tamara seems to think he is. I think I'll still plan to come up this weekend. I'll see you Friday night as planned, if that's okay. We can check things out. Tamara won't be around since she's off to Boston, so she won't know what we're doing."

"Sounds good to me," Lance said. "Why'd she go to Boston?"

"She said she had to give a speech at a conference for work."

"Funny I didn't hear about it," Lance said.

Grant put the phone down and walked over to the bar, making himself a martini. With the drink in hand, he walked outside on his deck and sat down. The magnificent Santa Barbara sunset was exploding over the ocean. His eyes caught a Golden Eagle and reeled it in, not letting it escape. But it did escape. It soared upward and then tucked its wings and swooped to apprehend its victim, making a sound like that of a small airplane. It was almost faster than Grant's eyes could track. Grant's martini was still in his hand...untouched.

Lance entered Hani's office, carrying a paper bag. His eyes roamed the room, landing on a picture of an older woman holding a young boy by the hand. He thought perhaps it was Hani's grandmother. That should score some points. He placed the picture in the bag. He continued to place everything he knew wasn't company issue into the bag as well. After manipulating his way into the personnel file, Lance had Hani's address in hand. The following day, he left work at the end of the day and proceeded to the address shown in the file. He drove into an old neighborhood, on a tree lined street, and pulled up in front of an apartment complex. Cutting the engine, he got out of the car and walked up two flights until he stood in front of the number matching his sheet of paper. He knocked on the door and waited. He knocked again.

The door next door opened and a man stuck his head out. "You lookin' for the guy who lived here? He's not there. He moved out this morning. Real noisy, he was."

"You know where he went? I have some things of his I'm returning."

"Nope, have no idea. He kept pretty much to

himself. Guess you have yourself some stuff." The man chuckled as if he'd just told a funny joke, and then he closed the door.

CHAPTER SEVENTEEN

IN THE MEANTIME, FOLLOWING HIS PHONE conversation with Lance and becoming suspicious, Grant flew to Boston. He thought he'd track Tamara and see what she was up to. He gave her a call from the airport.

"Hi Tamara, it's me."

"Hey Grant, what's up?"

"I was missing you and needed to hear your voice. Where are you staying?" Grant asked.

"I'm at the Omni Parker House. I miss you too."

"I know you're busy getting ready for your speech. I won't keep you. Like I said, I just needed to hear your voice."

"Okay," Tamara said, "I'm glad you called. I'll call you when I get back."

Holding a newspaper in his hand, Grant positioned himself in the lobby of the Omni

Parker, adorned in a gray wig, mustache, and a pair of glasses. He saw Tamara exit the elevator and immediately placed the newspaper in front of his face until she passed him. He then arose and proceeded to follow her. After several blocks, he noticed she walked like a woman on a mission. He didn't know what the mission was, but he hoped to find out. Grant was absorbed watching Tamara and didn't see the man following him. He could see Faneiul Hall in the distance as he turned the corner. Suddenly, he felt a searing pain in his left shoulder. Grabbing his shoulder, the blood oozed onto his hand, and he realized he'd been shot. He dropped to the ground. The sound of a bullet whizzed over him, barely missing his head.

Tamara walked around the square, searching faces for a likeness to the picture. After several minutes, she spotted Henrique with the distributor. It looked as if they were making the exchange. The square was crowded with sightseers. Tamara took her camera out of her bag and held it up to her eye, making certain there were no pedestrians inadvertently getting between her and Henrique. She snapped the button, and he dropped to the ground. Her dart camera did the job. The fright was evident on the distributor's face as he ran from the scene. Several people scrambled to assist the fallen victim, but it was too late. Tamara turned and walked away. About a block away, on her way back to the hotel, she passed an ambulance pulling away from the curb. Tamara returned to the hotel, threw her things in her bag, and left for the airport.

Meanwhile, a surgeon at Massachusetts General Hospital was excising a bullet from Grant's shoulder.

"You're a lucky man. If the bullet was a little lower, we might not be having this conversation right now. We'll keep you over night and let you go home tomorrow. The police are here and need to talk with you when my job is completed."

A detective pushed the door open and walked into the room. "How you doin'? I'm Detective Ahn. Looks like they have you all patched up." She pulled a notepad and pen out of her pocket.

"Hello, Detective. I'm Grant Larson. I don't have much to tell you. I sure didn't see this coming."

"Is there anyone you've had trouble with who could be out to get you?"

Grant thought of Hani, but didn't really think

Hani was connected to this. Plus, he didn't want to get Tamara involved in any way. "No, I don't even live in Boston. I'm from California. I have no idea why someone would shoot me."

The detective asked, "You didn't see a car, or any one following you?"

"No, I didn't see anything. The bullet came out of the blue."

"It seems strange to me that we had two incidents a block from each other within a five minute time span."

"Someone else got shot?" Grant asked.

"Well, no, the second incident was with a dart gun," Detective Ahn said. "But, he wasn't as fortunate as you. He's dead."

Grant choked on his own breath.

Detective Ahn said, "You all right? You want me to get the nurse?"

"No, I'm okay, I was just choking. I must have swallowed the wrong way. My mouth's really dry."

"Don't think there's anything else we need from you right now, Mr. Larson. I'll get your address and phone number, and we'll be in touch if we need something else or find the suspect." The detective walked out of the room.

Grant's suspicions were almost confirmed. He knew Tamara must be back in business, but he couldn't figure out who shot him and why. What the hell was he doing with a woman like that?

What did he really want? Grant shook his head. He needed to find out if she was involved and if she was lying to him when she said she was getting out.

Grant picked up the phone on the night stand and called Lance.

"Hey Lance, it's Grant."

"Hey there. What's up? How's that sister of yours...the love of my life?"

"She's good. Listen, could you do me a favor and find out if Tamara was sent to Boston to speak for your company?"

"Well, sure, I could ask, but what's up?"

"I just want to clear some things up in my mind. I'll let you know later."

"I found Hani's address and went by his place. He moved out. No one seems to have any idea where he went."

Grant said, "That's interesting. Oh, by the way, I'm in the hospital. I was shot. I won't be making it to your house tomorrow."

"You what? You were shot? Are you okay? Where are you? I'll come over."

"I'm at a hospital in Boston. It's only a shoulder wound. I'm okay."

"What were you doing in Boston?"

"I was on a field trip. I'll tell you more when I get home."

Lance was left staring at the phone. He

wondered if Grant thought Tamara was meeting someone else. He went to the office secretary and asked, “Is Tamara at a conference?”

“No, she’s out on sick leave.”

Lance mulled it over in his mind and wondered if she went to Boston to see a doctor. He knew there were great hospitals in Boston. He hoped she didn’t have something wrong and wasn’t telling anyone. He called Grant back and informed him.

A few minutes later, Grant called Tamara and said, “Oh, you’re home. I wasn’t sure you’d be back yet.”

“Yes, of course I’m home. I told you I’d be back by now. Where are you?”

“I’m in the hospital. I’m okay, but I’ve been shot.”

“What? I don’t understand. What happened?” Tamara asked.

“I was lucky. They only got me in the shoulder. Another bullet went right over my head after I dropped to the sidewalk.”

“My God. Where were you? Do you know who did it?”

“I have no idea who did it...and I was in Boston,” Grant said sheepishly.

“Boston? What were you doing in Boston?” she asked skeptically.

“I came to surprise you.”

"Sure, tell me the truth, Grant. Why were you there?"

"Okay, I was following you. I needed to know if you were going to a conference, or if you had gone back to your old job."

"Did you find me?"

"Yes, I followed you from the Omni Parker."

"I guess I should have told you, but you didn't want me to do it, and I knew you'd only worry. I'm sorry."

"So, you were there with the agency," Grant said.

"I thought you said you followed me."

"I did, but I got shot right when I saw you walking over to Faneuil Hall."

"What do we do now? I'm sorry I had to lie to you, and I'm really sorry you got shot. Who could have done it?" Tamara asked.

"You tell me. You were the one I was following. Could it have been someone from the agency?"

"I can't imagine why they'd do that." But, she thought to herself that she knew Josh was supposed to be there, even if she hadn't seen him. If they thought one of their own was being threatened, it was a definite possibility. "Sure you're okay? Should I fly up?" Tamara asked.

"No, I'm not that bad. I'm leaving in the morning. I'll be in touch."

Tamara's emotions were in turmoil. She couldn't get over Grant being shot...and the fact that he followed her to Boston. She went to the kitchen and pulled a frozen dinner from the freezer and stuck it in the microwave. When the doorbell rang, Toby ran to the door, barking. Tamara called out, "Who's there?"

"It's Josh, your cohort, sidekick, whatever..."

Tamara opened the door to Josh's smiling face. She could tell immediately he'd had more than a few drinks. "What are you doing here? How'd you know where I live?"

"Josh flashed her a grin. "You forget who I am. I've learned something in the agency."

Tamara stood back and made way for Josh to enter. "What's up?"

"I needed someone to talk to. Mind if I sit down before I fall down?" He laughed, thinking himself very funny.

She eyed him for a moment and then motioned for him to sit. "Of course, my manners aren't very good tonight. This is my dog, Toby. I can see he likes you. But, tell me, were you in Boston?" Tamara asked.

He hesitated and then spoke slowly. "Why do you ask?"

"I was on a job, and my boyfriend got shot. He followed me." She gritted her teeth.

Josh's eyebrow arched. "That was your boyfriend?"

Tamara's mouth flew open, and she groaned. "So, it was you. Oh my God, I knew it."

Josh placed his hand on her arm. "Tamara, this isn't the first time I've watched your back. I thought this guy was after you. I only fired a shot to wing him. I wanted to scare him off. If I'd aimed to kill, he'd be dead. I guess I shouldn't have told you, but partners cover each other's asses, right?"

She narrowed her eyes at him. "What do you mean, it wasn't the first time?"

"I've been on other assignments." He shrugged his shoulders. "You just didn't know I was there. How's your boyfriend? He's okay, isn't he?" He placed his head against the back of the chair and rubbed his forehead.

"Yes, he said it was only a shoulder wound. But he also said another shot went over his head."

"Aw, that was just to scare him."

"He followed me because he didn't trust me. He wanted to see if I came to give a speech or if I was on another assignment. I told him I was quitting." She looked away, suddenly embarrassed. "I'm going to get you a cup of coffee." Tamara stood up and moved into the kitchen.

Josh got up and followed.

"This is exactly what I came to talk to you about. I'm thirty six years old, and I have no one. I've always been afraid to get involved, but it gets damn lonely."

Tamara groaned, "Tell me about it."

"You said you were sort of involved, and I wondered how you managed it, but I see it's not that easy for you."

She mulled over his words. "No, it's not. I'm still trying to work it out, but I've done a good job of botching it up."

"I met a woman I like a lot, but I've been afraid to see her again. I'm afraid of getting involved. I thought maybe you'd have the answer."

Tamara swept her hair off her face. "Well, you can see, I'm the worst one to ask. When I have it figured out, I'll let you know."

Josh nodded without smiling, acknowledging an observation that was self evident. "Sorry about your boyfriend."

Tamara handed Josh the coffee as they walked back to the living room and sat down on the couch. "Drink up. You need it. How much have you had to drink?"

"Not much...maybe three or four whiskeys, but I've got a God awful headache."

"You shouldn't be driving. Why don't you sleep on the couch and leave in the morning."

"Well, I'm not that bad, but I suppose you're right." Josh put his head against the back of the couch and was asleep almost before he got the words out.

There was nothing about the way Tamara's Monday began to indicate it would be an Earth-shattering day in her life, but the day had probably been in the making for some time. Seeing that Josh had folded up the blanket neatly and made his departure, she went to the office as usual. She did routine work, but couldn't shake what happened to Grant out of her head. He had been shot. He could have been killed...all because of her. What did she really want? Why couldn't Grant accept her for who she was? Was she ready to give up her life's work? Besides, she didn't know if she could have a relationship with any man. When the work day ended, she got in her car and headed home, the Monday traffic appearing more like Friday. It seemed everyone was either heading for the beach or out of town. Tamara resigned herself to the wait, turned up the stereo, and settled back in her seat. Finally arriving home, Toby greeted her at the door, ever forgiving her for being late for dinner.

"Hey boy, I'm glad to see you. That's enough sloppy kisses. I love you too."

Tamara flipped on the light. “I almost left you in the dark.” She dropped her purse on the chair and hung her jacket on the coat rack. After slipping a DVD in the slot, the voice of Norah Jones followed her into the kitchen as she searched the refrigerator for leftovers. Finding nothing that captured her interest, she opened the freezer and took out a frozen chicken pot pie. She fed Toby and settled back on the couch with the newspaper, waiting for her pie to bake. After eating, she rinsed her plate and placed it in the dishwasher. As she was returning to the living room, the doorbell rang. ”Who is it?” she called.

She heard a muffled voice from behind the door answer, “It’s me, Grant.”

Tamara pulled the door open and stared at Grant. A strained silence cut a void between them. After a full minute Tamara said, “You surprised me. I didn’t expect to see you. Come on in. How’s your shoulder?”

“It’s okay, I guess,” Grant lied. The pain pills are keeping it under control. If I told you I was in the area and thought I’d drop by, it wouldn’t cut it, right?” “Why didn’t you tell me you were coming here before going to Santa Barbara?”

He shrugged his shoulders and quickly grabbed his wounded shoulder, grimacing. “I don’t know. I didn’t know I was coming here myself until I did. I’ve had a hard time dealing with it all."

"You what? You've had a hard time?" She folded her arms across her chest. "What about me? I lost a baby! I could have used a little support. I told you, and you left and went to the bar. You didn't even bother to call and see what the doctor said. I had to call you. But, the worst thing...you didn't trust me. You followed me to Boston."

"You told me you'd call me. If you hadn't called, I would have called you that night. I made a mistake with the support thing. I got scared. I didn't know what to do, so I left the room to get my head together. I was wrong...dead wrong. I had just found out you were raped...not told by you, mind you. I had to find out from someone else. And you didn't bother to tell me about the baby right away either. Apparently, you keep a lot of things from me." He raked his hand across the stubble on his chin. "Tamara, I'm having a hard time understanding. You were raped, and you didn't tell me. My God, didn't you trust me? You say I don't trust you, but I think it works both ways." He tried to force himself to relax, taking a few deep breaths. The more he tightened up, the more his shoulder hurt.

"I was trying to protect you. I knew if you knew about it, you'd try and do something." Her eyes sought his for confirmation.

"I'm sure you're right, but that's not something you keep from the person you love."

Grant walked over to the couch and flopped down, stretching his legs out in front of him. Toby nuzzled him, but Grant paid no attention. "I want to be honest with you, Tamara. Lance and I were planning to do something to take Hani down. We didn't know you were going to get into the act. Now, it looks like it's a mute point. Hani's disappeared. I'm sure you knew he quit his job, but he also moved out of his apartment."

She sighed, staring at him through narrowed eyes. "That doesn't surprise me. I expected him to disappear."

"Now, about this Boston episode, you lied to me."

"I had to. You wouldn't let me go if you knew." Tamara stopped and silently gazed at Grant. "Grant, you're not going to like what I have to say, but I have to say it." She paused, looked down, and then raised her eyes to his. "I really don't think I can be with any man. I'm meant to be alone. I'll always love you, but I can't be with you."

"That's a crock of bull shit." Grant jumped to his feet, glaring at her. "You can't be with me...or you don't want to be with me?"

"I guess I don't want to. I'd always be worried I'd be placing you in danger. Look what happened to you now. I like the life I lead. Maybe ten years down the road I'll be ready to settle down, but right now, I think I'd make us both miserable."

"So this is it? You're telling me it's over?"

"Yes, that's what I'm saying. I'm sorry, Grant. I guess what I only just now discovered is that I have a passion for serving my country in the way I know I can. I'm not ready to give it up, and you aren't accepting me for who I am."

"Hold on a minute. Let me get this right. You're telling me you've decided to break it off? I thought we had something together...something we could build on. You're choosing your job over me." He paused to catch his breath. "Let's get a few more things straight before you say any more. I love you, but it's hard because you won't let me in. You keep things from me, and that's not what people who are in love do. If you believe there's still some love between us, can't we roll the clock back and start over? We need to tell each other everything...no holding back...no secrets."

"Roll back, is that what you want to do? How can you roll back what's already happened? There's no trust between us, and it was probably because of me that you were shot. How will rolling back change anything? No, Grant, I can't see you changing the way you think. I can't do this. I told you. I'm not ready to give this up, and I know that's what you want. It's over."

"Wait a minute," Grant said. "You really want

to give up what we had?"

"The key word is 'had.' Grant, you let me down when I needed you. I don't know. Everything is so screwed. I don't want to quit my job, and you got shot!"

"You let me down too, Tamara, besides lying to me. Everyone makes mistakes. Come on...you gonna hold that against me forever? I'm sorry. I made a mistake, but I came back. Damn it, Tamara, I love you. I don't want to be without you. I don't care if you walk tight ropes upside down. You can keep your job. But, tell me you haven't stopped loving me."

Tamara stared at him for a full minute before answering, "I didn't say I don't love you anymore. I do. No, Grant, I could forgive everything else, but I couldn't live with myself if something happened to you because of me."

"Yeah, and I could get struck by lightening. I'm not gonna say something macho like I can take care of myself, but hell, life's a risk. I can't promise you I'll always be safe, and neither can you make that promise. Playing it safe and never sharing your life with someone you love, makes life worthless. The only time you really live is when you have someone to share life's moments with."

"You may be right, but I need to be on my own for now. I need time to know what I want...what I need."

"You're making a big mistake, Tamara...huge. I'll leave if that's what you want, but I hope you'll mull over what I said. Think about what makes life worth the ride." Grant searched Tamara's eyes, turned and walked out the door.

Chapter Eighteen

Several months passed and Tamara found she was unable to shake Grant from her thoughts. He crept into the deepest crevices of her mind. She received some satisfaction from the assignments she had accomplished in the last few months, most of them with Josh, but a nagging feeling of unfullfillment and discontent consumed her.

Why? Why does he have this hold on me?

She lost her appetite. Nothing gave her pleasure, even chocolate.

The phone rang. It was Christopher. "Pack your bag. You're off to Amsterdam. You'll get further instructions when you arrive."

"Will Josh be there?" Tamara asked.

"I don't know if this is a one or two man assignment. You'll find out when you arrive. Your flight is on Delta at six tonight. Go straight to the hotel, and I'll be in touch."

Tamara hoped to have a relaxing weekend, but it wasn't going to happen. She made arrangements for Toby, threw a few things in a bag and left for the airport.

Fortunately, Tamara was able to catch a few hours sleep on the plane and arrived at Amsterdam's Schiphol Airport feeling only partially like she had been crammed in a box for almost twelve hours. She gathered her belongings and disembarked the plane. Being Tamara's first time in Amsterdam, she looked forward to seeing the city. It was pouring down rain, making it difficult to see. She rolled down the taxi's window, but the rain splattered the side of the cab, soaking Tamara's jacket.

She entered the hotel's lobby, situated at Dam Square in the heart of the city, and there sat Josh in a big easy chair, playing a game on his laptop. Spotting Tamara, he saluted.

"About time you got here. I'm starving. I can't tolerate airplane food. Let's get a bite to eat."

"You're gonna have to wait a minute. I need to at least get checked in and stash my bag. As a matter of fact, I really want to take a quick run. I feel stiff after the long plane ride. You go ahead and eat, and I'll meet you later. You could always join me." Tamara laughed, already knowing his answer.

"I guess I can let you do that. I'll wait, but hurry up."

Tamara looked at him and shook her head as she walked over to the reception desk. From her room, she admired the view of the palace and the Uitmarkt statue in the square in front of the hotel. After changing clothes, she stepped out of the hotel and set off running. Suddenly, there was a downpour. People, running for cover, scattered in all directions. Tamara threw her head back and let the rain wash over her face, using her long lashes for wipers. After about thirty minutes of running past Amsterdam's lovely canals, admiring the narrow distinctive gabled houses, as well as checking out the colorful houseboats along the canal walls, she took a minute to sit on a wooden bench on a canal street leading back to the hotel. She could hear the clanging of trolley cars passing by and the street singers hoping for donations. During a break in the rain, she saw a mother and child skipping and dancing along the sidewalk, and a woman pushing a baby in a stroller with an unleashed dog trailing behind. To her left a man was breaking up pieces of bread and throwing them to the pigeons. The city was teaming with life. On the bench to her right, a young man placed a piece of apple in his girl friend's mouth and reached over and kissed her. Tamara felt an ache in the pit of her stomach, her eyes fixed on the tender scene. Remembering Josh was waiting, she continued her run back to the hotel. As she got closer to Dam Square, she heard a band concert and saw people sitting in the stands, ignoring the showers.

Later, during dinner, Tamara asked Josh, "So, what's with your girlfriend? You still seeing her?"

"We've decided to cool it for now." Josh turned to the waiter, signaling him to return to their table.

"We'd like another bottle of cabernet, please." Turning back to Tamara, Josh crossed his arms over his chest and asked, "So, have you seen Christopher lately?"

Tamara narrowed her eyes at him. She couldn't help but see Josh was trying to divert the conversation away from him. "What's going on, Josh? You don't want to talk about your girlfriend, or what?"

"Shit, Tamara, she doesn't know if she can handle what I do. She broke it off cold turkey. Doesn't want to see me. You're right...no, I don't want to talk about it."

"I'm sorry, Josh. Sounds like we're both in the same boat. Grant wanted me out of this work. I had to break it off. Well, he's a thing of the past. I'm over him."

He studied her for a moment. "How long has it been since you've seen him?"

"I don't know...maybe three months. Long enough to know he was nothing but trouble. I'm better off having no one to worry about but me. It makes life easier." Tamara took a sip of wine.

"You're right. No ties...no one to mess your head up...a free agent." Josh managed half a grin and held his glass up for a toast. "Here's to no involvement, just great sex."

They drained their glasses. After a third bottle of wine, Josh said, "I'll walk you to your room."

"No need unless you're afraid I'll get lost."

"Come on now. Let me be the gentleman my mama trained me to be."

Tamara rolled her eyes and laughed. "I wouldn't want to cross your mama."

When they arrived at her door, Tamara placed her key in the lock. She turned to say goodnight and Josh's lips captured hers. She felt warm and relaxed from the wine. She didn't push him away. Instead, she opened the door and led him in.

The following morning as Tamara was sipping her coffee at breakfast, she spotted Josh making his way to the table.

"When'd you come down? I reached for you and you weren't there." Josh rubbed his head.

"I needed my coffee. Plus, look at these great rolls they put out for us."

Josh reached across the table and lifted Tamara's chin. "You okay about last night? About us?"

"Of course. You said something about great sex and no involvement, right?" She looked him straight in the eye.

"Was that all it was to you?"

"Let's keep it at that. We don't need to complicate matters worse than they are. We work together," Tamara said, taking a sip of coffee.

Josh drank his coffee, picked up a roll, and told himself he'd hold to her wish for no involvement, keeping his feelings in check. He knew his desire for a meaningful relationship with Tamara wasn't in the cards."

The maitre d' came to the table and summoned Tamara. "A call for you at reception, Ms. Mantz."

Tamara got up, excused herself and walked to reception. Christopher's voice was at the other end of the line. "Scratch the assignment. The mole has gone back in his hole."

Tamara continued her noninvolved relationship with Josh for the next month, but as each day passed she knew she needed to bring it to an end. She really liked Josh, but she sensed he felt something more, and she had nothing more to give. After mulling it over for days, she called him to meet her for a drink. She didn't want to hurt him. And besides, they still had to work together. With trepidation, she entered the bar and saw Josh already sitting at a table.

"Hey Josh, thanks for coming."

"I've missed you. I haven't seen you for a whole week. What's up?" He looked at her with a question in his eyes.

"This is really hard for me, Josh. I like you a lot, but we need to break this off. We can't see each other any more except for–."

Josh interrupted, "Wait a minute. What's happening here? I haven't asked you for a commitment. Why can't we keep seeing each other? We've had great sex...haven't we? And we have fun together."

"Yes, we have. But, it's not fair for either of us. You should be out finding someone who wants to be with you forever. That's what you want, isn't it?"

"Well–"

"Be honest." Her eyes sought out his for a confirmation.

"Yes, that's what I want."

"Okay then. Friends?" Tamara asked with watchful eyes.

He heaved a sigh. "Friends."

Tamara worked with Josh on assignments, and nothing was mentioned about their month long relationship. In fact, they became good friends. One day at lunch about a month later, Tamara asked Josh if he was seeing anyone.

Josh responded, “Well, if you must know. I’m back with Bonnie, the one I told you about.”

“That’s so good. What happened?”

“She just came to my place one day and said she’d rather be worried about me than to not have me in her life at all.”

“That’s great. I’m so happy for you.”

Josh smiled. “Oh yeah. Actually, things are going great. She’s the best thing that’s happened to me since I discovered sex.”

Tamara wrinkled her nose and said, “I could have done without that analogy, thank you very much. Sounds serious.”

“It is. I’m thinking about popping the big question.”

“When do I get to meet her?” Tamara took a sip of soup and wiped her mouth with her napkin.

“I’m trying to keep it low key so Christopher doesn’t get on my case. I don’t think he knows about her, although he seems to know everything. He hasn’t said anything yet.”

Tamara shook her head. “That’s not going to be easy, Josh. How do you keep her under wraps when she's that important to you?"

"I didn't say it would be easy, but I'm sick to death of this lonely life." Josh looked down at his food, picked up his knife and fork and cut a piece of pork. "You should know how I feel since you dumped Grant. Anyone can see you're still in love with him. And I thought you were smart. Don't think I'll be taking advice from you any time soon."

Tamara kept quiet, but silently agreed. She missed Grant more than she thought possible. It was as if a chunk of her was missing...a chunk that only Grant filled. She picked at her food, but nothing entered her mouth.

Meanwhile, Grant was feeling sorry for himself. He thought that Tamara, after thinking it over, might come running back to him. He even visualized the scene in his head where she begged him to take her back, crying that she couldn't live without him. It didn't happen. Months had gone by with no word.

On one of his few weekends off, he went on a bird watching retreat to Mono Basin, home to millions of birds. He felt he needed the peacefulness and solitude of getting away to a place that was wild and natural. Grant believed

Mono Lake was the place to do just that. The absence of noise was a refreshing change, with only the sounds of the wild to intrude on his thoughts. Many of the field trips were already closed. He joined a group of fifteen birders touring the June Lake Loop, which covers a variety of habitats.

A woman approached him asking, "So, what do you think we might see today?"

Grant responded, "Possibly a Western Tanager or a Mountain Chickadee. You never know for sure."

He observed she was an attractive woman, even with her hair pulled up in a baseball cap.

"Have you been doing this long...birding, I mean?" she asked.

"I guess you could say that. I don't know how many years. You?"

"No, I'm pretty new at it. Actually, this is my first time."

"It's good you came." Grant smiled and walked to catch up to question the leader.

Later in the afternoon, Grant walked into a workshop that had already commenced and noticed the same woman was sitting in one of the seats. He took a seat next to her. She turned and smiled, showing him her notes. They walked out of the room together.

"Are you going to the buffet dinner?" she

asked.

"I wouldn't miss it...a great chef, I understand." Grant grinned. "You?"

Stacy gave him a broad smile. "Yes, I thought I would. Maybe we could go together," she suggested.

"Sure, I'd love to. You know, I don't even know your name. I'm Grant Larson."

"Stacy Peters. Nice to meet you, Grant."

During dinner Grant questioned Stacy, "So, what got you interested in bird watching?"

She picked up her glass and swirled the wine. "I needed something to get me completely away from everything. I needed peace and quiet...no complications."

"Sounds like you chose the right activity. It gives you a better perspective on things."

"My life has been so hectic lately with everything from work to my private life."

"Then it's good you got away," Grant assured her.

Stacy ran her fingers through her hair as she spoke. "What about you? What are you doing here?"

"Probably the same thing as you. I needed some attitude adjustments."

Grant walked her to her cabin after dinner. When they approached the door, he said, "Good night, Stacy. I'll see you in the morning."

She turned to him, making eye contact, and said, “Want to come in? I have some great wine I brought with me.”

There was a few seconds of silence. “Why not. Can’t turn down a glass of good wine from a beautiful lady.”

“Good. Thank you. Have a seat.” She motioned to the chair, picked up the bottle of wine and handed it to Grant along with the opener. Grant shrugged out of his jacket and threw it on the bed. The room was warm and cozy as his eyes roamed the room. It was a one room cabin with only a bed, two chairs and a small table. Grant looked at the label as he sat in one of the chairs, and opened the bottle with ease.

“I’ll enjoy trying this. I’m not familiar with the Corison Kronos Estate Vineyard. I do like a good cabernet though.”

Stacy replied, “Unfortunately, you can only get it at the winery. It has a hint of cherry and blackberry. I’m anxious to see how you like it.”

Grant poured the wine in their glasses and after the first sip said, “It’s good...very good. I like the subtle oak presence.”

“I’m glad you like it.”

After another bottle was opened and a few glasses consumed, Grant said, “So, are you getting away from a man? What’s the deal here? What are you really escaping from?”

"Is it so obvious? Yes, I am. I'm sick to death of being pressured." Her hands went up in the air. "I'm either supposed to marry him right now or he wants out. I don't know what I want."

"Why are so many women afraid of commitment?" Grant asked. "It used to be men. Now, I'm seeing it all the time with women. I'm facing a similar problem, Stacy. My woman needs time to know what she wants. I gave her plenty of time. I haven't seen her in months now."

"That's really funny. Maybe it's karma. I was supposed to meet you and see what it's like for the other person." She looked him up and down. "Anyway, let's forget about them and have another glass of wine. I like you, Grant. You seem like a really good guy. You want to spend the night?" Stacy gave him a sensual look as she touched her fingers to his arm.

"I appreciate the offer, Stacy, but I think I better get going. Thanks for the wine and the great company." Grant turned to walk out and Stacy shrugged and said, "Your loss."

The following morning, Grant joined a bird watching group before heading home. He was relieved Stacy wasn't among the group. Much to his delight, he sighted a Golden Eagle. As he stood watching the graceful bird for several minutes, he wondered why his thoughts always turned to Tamara whenever he saw one. He realized

Tamara wasn't a thing of the past. She was very much a part of him, and he needed to get her back. He was glad he didn't succumb to Stacy's charms.

A few months later, Tamara received a summons for an assignment in London. Although the majority of terrorists were captured in an unsuccessful terrorist attack of U.S. planes out of Heathrow to America, a new plot was uncovered disabling all transportation simultaneously in the United States and England by blowing up trains, the tube, and subways in New York and London. It was disclosed that the main terrorist behind the plan was holed up in the Arab district of London. He was released because of insufficient evidence. Tamara's agency discovered he was involved in a prior terrorist incident that killed several Americans. Her assignment was to eliminate him before he left London or was picked up again by the British government.

She looked at the photograph of Asad Alhamzi. He appeared young. She couldn't imagine this innocent looking young man could commit such ghastly crimes against humanity. But then again, she knew looks could be deceiving.

Tamara picked up her purse and left the hotel

to scout out the area. As she left, although she saw no one, she had the uneasy feeling someone was watching her. Knowing her inner feelings or intuition, whatever one calls it, was usually right, all systems kicked into red alert. She continued to walk the streets of the area, familiarizing herself with the surroundings. She glanced in a store window and caught Grant's reflection. Her head swung around, but there was no one in sight. He was driving her crazy. Now, she was seeing him in store windows. As she walked the neighborhood, she saw it was highly populated with Arabic women dressed in black with scarves covering their heads. Some women had only their eyes exposed. She stopped in a small grocery store and bought an orange from the assorted fresh fruit on display. The red double decker buses, so typical of London, charmed her, making her wish she were a tourist. But, hearing the many people speaking Arabic, she surmised she was chosen for this particular assignment because she understood the language. Tamara jolted back to reality, stopped at a phone booth, and called Christopher.

"It's about time you called. A successful attack on a section of the New York subway occurred today with hundreds of civilian casualties. The plot was foiled in London and the rest of New York's subway system. We were fortunate. It could have been much more devastating."

"Oh, no. Was it Asad?"

"We don't know for certain yet. He could have been involved. Three terrorists were caught, but their names are being withheld at this time. Continue with your assignment, and I'll get back to you with more information on his exact location."

It was leaked that Asad was spotted leaving a flat only a few blocks from Tamara's hotel. Christopher called Tamara. "You must act quickly. The British will be picking him up today." He continued to relay the necessary information, also informing her Asad was seen eating lunch at the same cafe for the last two days. Tamara made the decision to go to lunch. She walked a block and entered the Lebanese cafe. Luck was on her side. Seated at the counter was Asad Alhamzi. She recognized him instantly. Sliding into the seat next to him, she picked up a menu and studied it. She felt his eyes studying her. She turned, glanced up and smiled.

"Do you know what's good on the menu?"

He looked at her. "I come here for Kafta Meshwi." He turned away.

"What's that?"

He gave her another hard stare. "It's charcoal grilled skewers of seasoned minced lamb with onions, parsley and garlic."

"That sounds good to me." Tamara closed her

menu and signaled the waiter. She flashed a smile to Asad.

A twinge of suspicion crossed Asad's mind. He knew he wasn't a particularly good looking man. He was obviously ten years younger than this amazingly beautiful woman sitting next to him. She appeared to be flirting with him...or was she only being friendly? He turned away and continued eating.

Tamara asked, "Do you live in London or are you just visiting?"

Asad turned and gave Tamara another hard stare. Grabbing her wrist, he pulled her from the seat and shoved her out of the restaurant. She was backed against the wall. His hand was unyielding around her neck. She could feel the point of something sharp against her ribs. The smell of garlic and onions emanated from his breath as he uttered, "What do you want from me? What are you after?"

Tamara hid any sign of fear and glared at him. "I'm not used to being manhandled just for being friendly. What's wrong with you?"

He dug his fingers deeper into her throat. "Don't play innocent with me. Who are you?"

The innocent looking young man wasn't looking so guiltless any longer. He looked vicious and threatening. His body pressed against her. There was no way she could raise a knee or elbow to him.

She tried to talk, but no words could escape through his rigid fingers. She felt a sharp pain before losing consciousness, realizing the object was a knife.

From somewhere in a far corner of her mind Tamara heard Grant's soothing voice, felt his fingers stroking her forehead.

I love you, Tamara. Hold on, and come back to me. Don't give up. Fight, Baby, I need you.

She wanted to. She really did. She didn't like the dark place where she was living. Every time she thought she could see Grant's face, pain gripped her, and he disappeared.

Then, one day, Tamara opened her eyes and was awake. She saw Grant sleeping beside her in a chair. She didn't want to awaken him, but she needed to reach out and touch him to see if he was real. At first contact, Grant jerked himself into an upright position and grabbed both of Tamara's hands. "You're awake. You've come back to me."

Tamara stared at him. "Where have I been? What happened to me?"

Grant said gently, "You were stabbed, Tamara, but you're going to be okay."

"Oh God, I remember the pain. Asad...what

happened to him?"

"Don't worry about him now. He's taken care of. You just need to heal and get better."

"Don't treat me like a child, Grant. I remember what happened now. But, I don't remember anything after that monster had me gripped by the throat."

"I have something more important to talk to you about. I can't lose you. I don't know if you're ready to hear this, Tamara. I love you. I love you so much I can't get you out of my mind. I know you said it's over, but it'll never be over for me. I know now more than ever that I want us to be together for a lifetime. I want us to grow old together. I–"

"Don't say any more, Darling." Tamara stared at him for a full minute before continuing. "No matter how I try to get you out of my system, I can't." Tamara's smile turned to a frown. "I'll still always be worried you could be put in harm's way because of me, but I feel as if my heart is withering up and dying when I think about not having you as part of my life. I've been so stupid...wasting precious time when we could be together. You were right. Having you in my life is what makes life worth the ride."

Grant squeezed her hand and smiled.

Tamara continued, "I only need to stay active for five more years, and then I can retire. How about we compromise? When I get pregnant again, I quit. I don't think my kind of work and motherhood make a good match."

"I couldn't agree with you more. We could start working on that now." Grant winked.

"Yeah, right, in about four years."

"What'd you say about compromising? I remember Gerald Ford saying 'Truth is the glue that holds government together. Compromise is the oil that makes governments go.' Well, I say love is the glue that holds marriages together, and compromise is the oil that keeps it going."

Tamara folded her arms with a smirk on her face. "What should we start working on first...babies, marriage or my job?"

"What do you say to marriage first, and the compromise is right now or as soon as you're out of the hospital."

Tamara wrapped her arms around Grant's neck. "Next week would be nice."

"In the meantime, I've come to a decision, Tamara. It's not a bad idea to make this a family affair." He paused to let it sink in. "I have something to tell you. I had a little chat with Christopher. He was a little skeptical at first, but after thinking it over, he agreed you and I might work well as a team."

Tamara threw her head back and laughed softly. "You've got to be kidding. Are you putting me on?”

“I’m dead serious. I guess Josh’ll have to find himself a new partner. He was pretty good at watching your back when he shot me.”

“He feels bad about that. He didn’t know you were my boyfriend.”

”Well, I guess I need to tell it all. After you left me, Tamara, I convinced Christopher I’d make a great agent and went into training for several months. I was on this assignment with you as your backup, but I didn’t do a very good job. You almost lost your life before I got him.”

“You got Asad?”

“Yes, but you got stabbed before I got him.”

“I can’t believe this. I thought I was crazy. I saw your reflection. I wasn’t seeing things.”

“I guess I have to get better at that too. You weren’t supposed to see me.”

“Oh, Grant, that’s so good you got him.” Tamara stopped and gave him a quizzical look. “You are serious, aren’t you. I don’t know what to think about us being a team.”

Grant brushed Tamara’s lips with a light kiss, hesitated, and then spoke, “You’ll get used to the idea. Give it time. You might like it.”

THE END

Printed in the United States
86615LV00002B/106-120/A

9 781602 640382